DISCAR

LAND OF THE SILVER DRAGON

Recent Titles by Alys Clare

The Hawkenlye Series

FORTUNE LIKE THE MOON
ASHES OF THE ELEMENTS
THE TAVERN IN THE MORNING
THE ENCHANTER'S FOREST
THE PATHS OF THE AIR *
THE JOYS OF MY LIFE *
THE ROSE OF THE WORLD *
THE SONG OF THE NIGHTINGALE *

The Norman Aelf Fen Series

OUT OF THE DAWN LIGHT *
MIST OVER THE WATER *
MUSIC OF THE DISTANT STARS *
THE WAY BETWEEN THE WORLDS *
LAND OF THE SILVER DRAGON *

* *available from Severn House*

LAND OF THE SILVER DRAGON

An Aelf Fen Mystery

Alys Clare

severn
House

This first world edition published 2013
in Great Britain and the USA by
SEVERN HOUSE PUBLISHERS LTD of
19 Cedar Road, Sutton, Surrey, England, SM2 5DA.
Trade paperback edition first published
in Great Britain and the USA 2013 by
SEVERN HOUSE PUBLISHERS LTD

British Library Cataloguing in Publication Data

Clare, Alys.
  Land of the silver dragon. – (An Aelf Fen mystery ; 5)
  1. Lassair (Fictitious character)–Fiction. 2. Fens, The
  (England)–Fiction. 3. Great Britain–History–Norman
  period, 1066-1154–Fiction. 4. Detective and mystery
  stories.
  I. Title II. Series
  823.9'14-dc23

ISBN-13: 978-0-7278-8276-9 (cased)
ISBN-13: 978-1-84751-482-0 (trade paper)

All Severn House titles are printed on acid-free paper.

Severn House Publishers support The Forest Stewardship Council [FSC],the leading
international forest certification organisation. All our titles that are printed on
Greenpeace-approved FSC-certified paper carry the FSC logo.

MIX
Paper from
responsible sources
FSC® C018575

Typeset by Palimpsest Book Production Ltd.,
Falkirk, Stirlingshire, Scotland.
Printed and bound in Great Britain by
MPG Books Ltd., Bodmin, Cornwall.

For Mr and Mrs David Skinner,
8.ix.2012
my lovely son and daughter-in-law,
with very much love

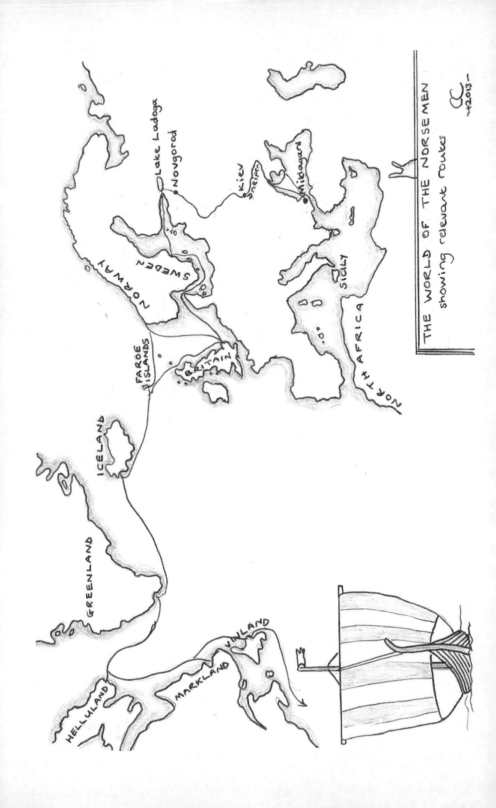

THE WORLD OF THE NORSEMEN
showing relevant routes

GREENLAND

HELLULAND

MARKLAND

VINLAND

ICELAND

FAROE ISLANDS

NORWAY

SWEDEN

Lake Ladoga

Novgorod

Kiev

Dnieper

Miklagard

BRITAIN

SICILY

NORTH AFRICA

CC 2013

The Descendants of Thorkel Jorundson

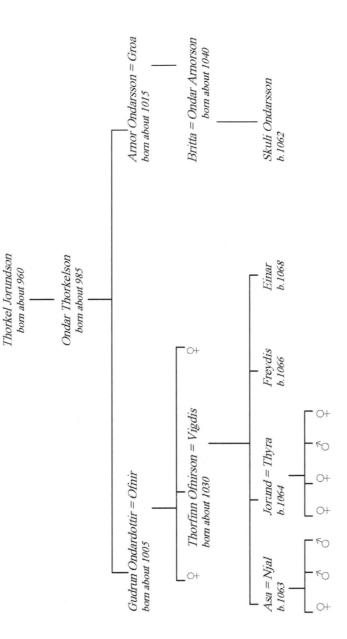

ONE

A murder seems a hundred times more shocking when you know the victim. It seems to make the danger personal.

It is an exaggeration to say I *knew* Utta of Icklingham: more accurately, I knew who she was. She was my sister Goda's mother-in-law, and, although one should not speak ill of the dead, by common consent she was a shrew of a woman and no great loss.

Word of the drama first reached us in Aelf Fen via the peddler who regularly wheels his barrow from village to village. Icklingham is about six miles away, and by the time he reached us, the peddler had already told his tale to several groups of wide-eyed people in the hamlets and settlements dotted along his route.

'They say a great, fair, red-bearded giant of a feller burst into the house,' the peddler announced, gazing round at his audience with a face twisted into a rictus of horror. 'And, lacking a single drop of Christian charity in his stone of a heart, he set about breaking every pot and every stool, chair, bed and board in the place!' Peddlers, I have observed, tend towards the dramatic when they tell a tale. 'Not that they had much,' this particular peddler added prosaically. 'It was a poor sort of a household.'

'What about the murder?' a voice yelled from the back of the crowd, which had grown sizeable by now. I wasn't the only one to spin round and glare at the speaker – it was the old washerwoman, Berta – since her remark had been singularly heartless and spoken with detectable relish.

'I'm coming to that!' the peddler yelled back. 'Seems like the poor, pitiful victim came home unexpected-like and surprised him, and he hit her on the head with whatever he had in his hand. Must have been something big, hard and heavy,' he added thoughtfully, 'given the mess it made of the poor old girl. Skull driven in like an eggshell, blood and brains all over the place, and—'

'Enough,' came a quiet, firm and very authoritative voice. It was my aunt Edild's, and she, as a very fine healer, is held in respect by almost all in the village.

The peddler subsided, although not entirely. He went on muttering to those crowding most closely around him, and suddenly we heard the name of the victim, hissed and whispered from person to person like the wind in the rushes: *Utta, Utta of Icklingham, it's old Utta who's been killed!*

My mother, who had quietly come to stand beside me, paled visibly. What on earth was wrong? I put out my hands to her, for I thought she might be about to faint, but she threw me off. Shouldering her way into the knot of people (my mother is a big woman, and there were several muttered curses and cries of *ouch!* as she trod on toes and dug her elbows into tender ribs) she thrust a path through to the peddler.

'Is anyone else hurt?' she demanded. She gave him a shake – he's a runt of a fellow, certainly no match for my mother – and even from where I stood I heard his teeth rattle. *'Tell me!'* my mother yelled.

It was then that I remembered who Utta of Icklingham was. With the horrible feeling that someone had put ice down my back, I understood why my mother was so distressed.

'There *was* another person hurt, yes,' the peddler said, trying to wrestle himself out of my mother's grip and regain some semblance of virility in the face of this fury of a woman towering over him. 'Big, fat, bad-tempered lass as is married to Utta's lad Cerdic. She—'

My mother did not wait to hear the details. She didn't even pause to reprimand the peddler for his description of Goda (which I reckoned was in fact pretty accurate). She spun round, strode back through the crowd and grabbed me.

'Where's Edild?' she demanded, looking round wildly. 'She must go, straight away, and she's got to—'

'I'm here, Essa,' my aunt said calmly. She took my mother's hand, gently stroking it. Edild is very fond of her sister-in-law.

'Edild, Goda's hurt, she's been attacked, and you must go to her straight away. You—'

'Lassair will go,' my aunt announced. 'I am in the middle of a very busy day attending to our own sick and wounded, and I cannot leave them. Lassair is fully competent,' she added. Turning to me, she said, 'You have your satchel with you, I see.' Indeed I did; when the peddler arrived, I'd been about to set out to visit an outlying dwelling where I was to dress the infected toenail of an elderly man. 'Have you everything you might need?'

I ran through a mental list. Bandages, ointments to stop blood flow and to knit bones, lavender wash to remove dirt; gut and fine needles for stitching large wounds.

Oh, but this was my sister I was preparing to treat! The realization brought me up short. I was not, admittedly, very fond of Goda, and it had been an enormous relief when she'd left home to wed Cerdic, but nevertheless she was my own flesh and blood. I might not like her, but I recognized that I loved her.

I would not, however, be the efficient healer that she needed just then if I allowed my emotions to undermine me. I straightened my back, raised my head and, fixing my aunt with a firm stare, said, 'Yes, I have. I will leave immediately.'

I made the best speed I could to Icklingham. The weather was fine – we were all hoping we had seen the last of winter – and the tracks were dry, and, with the fen waters low, I was able to leap over the few meandering streams and ditches I encountered without having to hang around waiting for someone to ferry me across.

I did not allow myself to speculate on my sister's possible injuries. I knew I must stay calm, so that I would arrive in the best frame of mind to treat her. When I walked into her village, I had almost persuaded myself that this was just another patient.

There was a large gaggle of interested onlookers milling around outside the little house that Cerdic built for his wife, all craning their necks and trying to see round one another. I heard snatches of fascinated, avid gossip. *They say there's blood all over the floor! Smashed her head, he did, and her brains flew everywhere! Huge, he was, like some giant out of the old legends!*

I did not yet know who was within: my sister, presumably,

but what of her husband – the dead woman's son, after all –
and the couple's two little children? This lurid talk of blood,
brains and a giant of supernatural size was hardly going to
calm them and help them cope with sudden, violent death.
My instinct was to wade in and give the thoughtless gossips
a good ticking-off, but my years of study with my aunt Edild
– the epitome of calm in a crisis – had taught me that there
was another, better way.

Approaching the stocky, tough-looking man at the back of
the crowd who had just made the remark about spattered brains,
I touched him on the arm and said quietly, 'I wonder if you
might let me through, please? I'm a healer and I've come to
see what I can do to help the injured woman.'

The man turned, a slightly guilty look on his face, and I
gave him my best meek smile. Perhaps pretending to be helpless brought out some latent chivalry in him; anyway, he
changed instantly from leader of the gossips to my champion,
pushing his fellow villagers roughly out of the way and
shouting, 'Make way, make way, you feckless lot, the healer
lass is here!'

The interior of the cottage was dark and smelled of blood and
something else: somebody – perhaps the dead woman, in her
terror – had lost control of their bladder. I set my satchel down
on top of a stool and, as my eyes adjusted to the gloom, looked
around.

There was no sign of the body. To my enormous relief, they
had already taken poor Utta away.

My sister was lying on the bed against the far wall; the bed
she shared with Cerdic. I knew her house and its contents
well, for, in addition to my occasional subsequent visits, six
years ago I had been summoned by my newly married sister
to look after her through her first pregnancy. An arduous,
painful and all but unendurable pregnancy, according to the
disgruntled Goda; in my view, she had suffered no more than
any other woman, and most of her problems had come about
because she'd been bone idle and far too fat.

I pushed my unpleasant memories of that earlier time right
to the back of my mind.

Suddenly I noticed Cerdic, who was hovering around behind the door and looking like a man who has just endured slightly more than he can stand. His mother had been brutally murdered and, knowing my sister, I would have been surprised if she had been the consoling, loving helpmeet that he needed at that moment. I had a very quick look at Goda – she was pale, there was blood on her face and neck, but I judged by the way she was opening her mouth to shout at Cerdic, or me, or both of us, that she was in no immediate danger – and then crossed swiftly over to Cerdic.

I reached out and took hold of his icy hands. He looked vaguely at me for a moment, then managed a feeble smile and said, 'Hello, Lassair.'

Good, he knew who I was. I did not think this was the time for commiserations, and instead I said softly, 'Cerdic, where are Gelges and little Cerdic?' My niece and nephew are five and three; far too small to be coping with this by themselves, and they were not in the house with their parents.

Cerdic made a helpless gesture. 'Oh, someone took them.' Even he seemed to appreciate that this was hardly adequate and, frowning, added, 'My cousin. She lives along the track.' He waved a hand.

His cousin. Yes, I recalled that Cerdic had many kinsfolk in Icklingham. The first time he'd set eyes on Goda, he'd been accompanied by his father and his uncle, and I remember lots of aunts, uncles and cousins attending the wedding. Cerdic's father had died a couple of years ago, and that was why his mother had moved in with her son and my sister.

No doubt I was going to hear a lot more about that over the next few hours.

'Go along to your cousin's house and reassure your children,' I said quietly to him. 'I'll look after Goda.'

For the first time I saw a sign of life and light in his face. 'Am I allowed?' he asked.

I realized that being with his little daughter and son was exactly what he wanted most, and guessed that only my sister's imperious command that he must stay there with her had prevented him from doing what he surely knew he should.

'Of course you are,' I said. 'They need you, Cerdic. Go and take them out to play.'

He looked aghast, as if I'd suggested something sacrilegious or downright criminal. Then his expression cleared, and he squared his shoulders and stood up straight. 'Yes,' he murmured, 'yes, that's exactly what I'll do.'

Without so much as a glance at Goda, he wriggled out through the door like an eel escaping the jaws of the trap and ran off up the track.

I turned to face my sister.

The deluge of words started even before I'd had the chance to roll up my sleeves and begin my examination of her wounds. Without even bothering with *hello*, never mind *thank you for coming so quickly*, at the top of her voice she screeched, 'Fool of a girl, what do you think you're doing? Go and get him back – I need him, I've been viciously attacked and he ought to be here to protect me!' She shoved me roughly aside so that she could peer out through the doorway, her eyes wide. 'That great brute's probably lurking outside, just waiting for me to be alone so that he can come and have another go, and he won't rest till I'm as dead as Utta!'

There were so many things with which to argue in her outburst that I didn't know where to begin. I opened my mouth to start with the obvious – that there was half a village loitering about outside the house, and no assailant in his right mind would risk an attack with so many witnesses – and planned to go on to tell her, in no uncertain terms, that her little children needed their father much more desperately than she did.

But then I seemed to hear my aunt's soft voice inside my head, issuing a timely reminder that people who have just had a bad shock are not themselves, and must be treated with a tender kindness that makes allowances for temporary unreason.

I ignored the part of me protesting that this demanding, selfish behaviour wasn't in the least out of character for my sister. I also ignored her hands batting out at me as I crouched over her; admittedly, this was a little more tricky. Then, in my most reassuring healer's voice, I said, 'Lie back now, Goda, and let me look at you.'

*   *   *

Her injuries were not too bad, although I did put a stitch in the cut on the side of her head, mainly because I was finding it hard to stop the bleeding. Otherwise it was mainly a bit of bruising, incurred as she fell over after the assailant hit her.

As I helped her into a clean gown, promising I'd put the bloodstained one in to soak, my sister's angry resentment came galloping back. It had hurt her when I'd put in the stitch, although I'd done it as gently and swiftly as I knew how, and the pain had temporarily shut her up. It soon became clear that she was intent on making up for lost time. I had been trying to ignore her loud rantings, hoping she might stop, but presently I realized it was a vain hope.

'—and when you've got the blood out of my gown, you can finish laundering it, and there's a bag of the children's clothes waiting so you'd better do them too. Then you can clean the floor, because I can't be expected to put up with lying here and staring at all those muddy boot prints all over the place.' The men who had come for Utta's body evidently hadn't paused to wipe their feet. 'That pool of piss needs mopping up, it stinks,' my sister's dictatorial tones went on, 'and then you'll have to see about getting a meal ready, although, God help us, if you still cook as badly as you did last time you were here then I don't suppose anyone'll have much appetite for it, and then you can—'

'Stop,' I heard myself say.

For a moment, I was dumbstruck, amazed at my own daring. Then I knew exactly what to say.

I went to sit on my sister's bed and stared right into her eyes. Taking a steadying breath, I said, 'Goda dear, I will not be staying.' Her deep, furious frown and gaping mouth suggested she was about to protest, so I plunged on. 'I have my work to do and I cannot abandon it. I will come to see you again in a week or so and remove that stitch, unless someone here can do it, and, in the meantime, you should keep the wound clean and try not to get it wet. I'll leave you some lavender oil and you must put a drop or two on to the cut each day.'

I stood up, packing the tools of my trade into my leather satchel and preparing to leave. I took a step towards the door. Two steps; three. I thought I'd got away with it.

I should have known better.

'How *dare* you speak to me like that!' my sister yowled. 'That's quite enough of your cheek, Lassair. You'll remain here as long as I need you, and I just hope you know a bit more about how to run a home than you did the last time you made your feeble attempt to look after me! You—'

I watched all my fine resolutions about being calm, digni- fied, firm and a credit to my profession grow little wings and fly out through the door. As if I were a child again, and Goda my horrible, bossy, selfish, demanding and cruel tormentor, I raced back to her bed and shouted, 'I did my best! I was thirteen years old and you were nothing better than a bully! You were such a fat, lazy cow that it was no wonder you had a rotten time – it was all your own fault, and yet you made absolutely sure that I was the one to suffer for it!'

For the first time in my life, I saw my sister shocked into silence. It occurred to me that I should have tried shouting at her before.

There was a long pause – I fought to bring my ragged breathing under control – and then Goda said in a very small voice, 'But, Lassair, I really do need you. Who else will be strong enough to drive away the horrors when I see it all happening over and over again?'

Remorse flooded through me. My sister had witnessed murder today, and she had come close to being killed herself, yet the best I could do was yell at her.

I knelt down in front of her. 'I'm sorry,' I said humbly. 'You've had a very frightening experience, and I shouldn't have shouted at you.' But some devil in me made me add, 'I'm still not staying.'

The ghost of a smile crossed Goda's plump face. 'You've grown up, little sister,' she said, and I detected grudging admiration.

The silence extended, but it was a more companionable one now. Presently I said, 'Why don't you tell me all about it?' It might help her get over it, I thought, to relive the dreadful events while they were still fresh in her mind.

She lay back on her pillow, and the hand in mine relaxed. 'Not much to tell, really,' she said. 'Utta and I were out with

the children, setting off to the place where the peddler usually
stops, since he was due this morning. I bought a few bits, and
Utta moaned because he was out of fine thread.' A look of
intense irritation crossed her face and she added angrily,
'Lassair, you have no idea what it's like living with that cranky
old bat! She's self-centred, lazy, she thinks the sun shines out
of Cerdic's arse and, according to her, the woman's not been
born who's good enough for him!' I thought Goda had temporarily forgotten Utta was dead. The tirade ended as quickly as
it had begun, and Goda said, 'Where was I? Oh, yes. The old
cow went on moaning all the way home and, in desperation,
I told her that if she was going to be such a misery, she could
go on ahead, and I'd stop and sit with the children in the sun
for a while.'

I knew exactly what Goda was about to say, and I felt deep
sympathy for my sister. I wondered if I should prevent her
continuing, but, for one thing, it would probably do her good
to express what was troubling her, and, for another, preventing
my sister from doing virtually anything has always been a
challenge.

'If I hadn't been so impatient, we'd all have got home
together,' she said on a sob, her face crumpling into an expression of remorse, 'and then Utta would still be alive.'

'But you and your children might not be,' I said softly. 'And
Utta had already had a long life. If any of you had to die,
better that it was the eldest.'

Perhaps not my most compassionate piece of reasoning, but
I know my sister.

After a while she sniffed, wiped her nose and her eyes on
her sleeve and said, 'I suppose you're right.'

To encourage her away from her guilty thoughts, I said,
'What happened when you got home?'

'There was this great hulking brute of a man smashing up
my house, *that's* what happened!' Goda cried. 'Utta was lying
on the floor, and she wasn't moving. The children were behind
me, so I pushed them back outside and slammed the door. The
giant was crashing round the room, picking things up, hurling
them about, poking under the beds and into all the corners
– honestly, Lassair, you'd have thought he was looking for

something, only we've got nothing anyone would want!' Bitter resentment filled her face, as if, in the middle of this new trouble, her perpetual, underlying anger at being married to a hard-working but poor man, who could not afford to buy her the luxuries she craved, had surfaced once more. 'He looked up and saw me standing inside the door, and he gave a great yell, and came across and took a swing at me. Then he wrested the door open and fled.'

Her eyes wandered away in the direction of the shelf where she stores her cooking utensils and her few bits of good pottery. The utensils were bent and dented, and the pots were smashed to pieces.

'I *liked* those pots,' my sister said. Then, softly and quietly, she began to weep.

TWO

I hurried back to Aelf Fen, eager to find my mother and reassure her that Goda wasn't about to die. I found all my family at home – it was evening by now – and so was able to give them the news together.

'She's all right,' I panted as I burst in – I'd run the last half mile. 'A cut and some bruises, but not badly hurt.'

My mother, my father, my brother Haward and his wife Zarina, with her ten-month-old son in her lap, and my two younger brothers all breathed a sigh of relief.

'Sit down here by the fire and have a drink,' my father said solicitously, elbowing my little brother Squeak out of the way. 'Yes, Squeak, I know you've had a hard day,' he said in answer to my brother's mutinous look, 'but Lassair's just walked to Icklingham and back, *and* she's had to deal with Goda. She truly is all right?' he added, a big, firm hand on my shoulder as gratefully I sat down.

'Yes. But Utta . . .' I paused, glancing at my brother Leir. He was not yet seven.

'They all know Utta's been killed,' my father said quietly. 'We'd like to know what happened, Lassair.' Then, just for me, he muttered, 'No gory details, mind.'

I nodded my understanding, then briefly repeated what Goda had told me.

My mother's face was creased in perplexity. 'It was a robbery, then?'

'Apparently so,' I replied. 'Goda thought the intruder was looking for something specific, but, as she said, she and Cerdic haven't really got much that's worth taking.'

'What about Utta?' my brother Haward asked. 'Might she not have some savings, or something, that she'd brought with her when she moved in with Goda and Cerdic?' He looked at my mother. 'Isn't she . . . er, wasn't she a skilled weaver or something?'

'She was a wool worker,' my mother said, nodding. 'She made cloth of a very smooth, soft quality.'

Suddenly I remembered something: an image from six years ago, when I'd gone to look after Goda. 'She made Goda and Cerdic two beautiful blankets for a wedding gift,' I said.

'Well, then!' Haward exclaimed.

My father gave a deep, rumbling laugh. 'Well then, what?' he said with a smile. Please don't think my father callous; it's the last thing he is. But none of us had anything more than a bare acquaintance with Utta, and to put on long-faced grief at her death would have been dishonest.

'Oh.' Haward frowned, putting his thoughts in order. 'Er, she probably made lots of money making and selling her nice blankets, and that's what the thief was after,' he said. 'Her bag of coins!' he added, as if to make sure we all understood.

'It's possible,' I said, smiling at Haward. I love my brother very much, but I didn't really think his theory was very likely. 'Although I don't think Utta was by any means rich.'

My mother got to her feet and, picking up a ladle, began to stir the stew that was bubbling aromatically over the hearth. 'Supper's ready,' she announced. 'Going to stay and eat with us, Haward, Zarina?'

Haward glanced at his wife, and she gave a little nod. 'Thank you, Mother, yes please,' he said. He and Zarina haven't long moved into their own little dwelling, built on to one end of my family home, and I know Zarina tends to be sensitive over any implication that she doesn't keep house as well as my mother. Haward, bless him, often appears torn between accepting our mother's food whenever it's offered (she is an excellent cook) and not offending his wife (she isn't).

We settled down to eat, and for a while were too busy with our food to talk. Then, as the platters gradually emptied and the sounds of knives and fingers scraping against wood ceased, my father said, 'Let's hope there are no more such incidents in Icklingham, or anywhere else for that matter. The intruder must have realized Goda saw him, and could describe him, so maybe that will have persuaded him that it's in his best interests to get as far away as he can.'

There were several murmurs of agreement.

'Has any action begun to find the killer and bring him to justice?' my father went on, turning to me.

'I don't know,' I answered. 'I was busy tending Goda, and did not think to enquire.'

My father smiled understandingly. 'You probably had your hands full,' he observed. 'Still, I bet they'll have organized some sort of a search by now. They'll find him and deal with him, and that'll be that.'

If only we'd known.

Next morning, I woke up in my usual place in my aunt Edild's house, my father having walked me back there after supper. Despite his confident words, he must have been less sure than he made out that the vicious intruder was now far away.

Since Edild and I work together, the decision was made some years back for me to live with her. At the time when I moved in, it relieved some of the pressure on the family house, then accommodating my parents, my three brothers and me, not to mention my beloved Granny Cordeilla, although she was tiny and didn't really take up much room. She died, two years ago, and we all miss her very much. Often I see her, sitting in the corner of the room where her little cot used to stand. Invariably she gives me a smile, her deep, dark eyes crinkling up. Her smile could always light up even the dullest day.

As Edild and I ate breakfast, I told her in more detail what had happened in Icklingham, having only provided the briefest outline the previous evening and concentrating on the news that Goda was not badly hurt. Not one to gossip or speculate, now Edild listened in silence, nodded, then suggested we ate up and got on with our day's work.

We dealt with the usual crop of minor hurts and seasonal ailments – for some reason, half the village seems to develop sore throats and runny noses as soon as the weather warms up – and I found that having my hands and my mind fully occupied drove yesterday's disturbing incident out of my thoughts. It was thus something of a rude shock when, as dusk was falling and we were tidying up after the last of our patients, Hrype arrived on the doorstep and said quietly, 'There's been another attack.'

Edild took one look at him, then grabbed his arm and drew him inside, closing and barring the door. Clearly, she did not want to be disturbed by some latecomer demanding the services of the healer. She sat Hrype down beside the hearth, took his hands in hers and, turning to me, told me curtly to prepare one of her restorative drinks. Torn between handing him the remedy as quickly as I could and giving the two of them a few private moments to mutter together (they have long been lovers, a secret known to only the three of us) I opted for speed.

If ever a man needed a restorative drink, it was Hrype. He looked exhausted, and the deep frown line between his brows suggested some serious anxiety. Edild waited till he had finished his drink, then she said, 'Tell us what has happened.'

She sat down on the bench beside him, once more holding his hand. I crouched on the floor at his feet. Looking from one to the other of us, he drew a breath and said, 'I was over on the western side of the fens, and I heard a rumour that there has been violence at Chatteris.'

Chatteris is the abbey where my sister Elfritha is a nun. The previous year, there had been trouble there; a nun had died, and my beloved sister had also come close to losing her life.

And now this!

Hrype was leaning down towards me, his silvery eyes intent on mine. 'No harm has come to Elfritha,' he said. He must have seen doubt in my expression, for he took hold of my shoulders and said firmly, 'Lassair, hear me! Elfritha is quite all right.'

Slowly I nodded, and he let me go.

'Is anyone else hurt?' Edild asked. I admired the control in her voice.

'Two nuns were thrown to the ground. One has a broken arm and the other has slight concussion,' he said. 'It appears that someone broke into the abbey very early this morning, when the nuns were at prayer, and ransacked the dormitory. The two who were hurt had returned to their cells after prayer, where they disturbed the intruder in the middle of his search, and they had the courage to challenge him. He was a huge man, tall and brawny, and very fair-skinned.'

'You said the nuns interrupted his search,' I said, a chill of fear making me shiver.

Hrype looked at me. 'Yes. The sisters said he seemed to be hunting for something, for he had turned over the nuns' cots, ripped open the straw mattresses, and strewn their bedding and their few personal possessions all over the floor.'

'It's the same,' I whispered. 'It's like at Goda's house, yesterday.'

A glance passed between Hrype and my aunt, and I heard her muttering to him. I remembered that he hadn't been in the village yesterday, or, if he had, he'd kept well out of sight. He did not know about Utta's death.

My mind seemed to be behaving oddly. Instead of facing up to this new worry, I found myself puzzling over how it was that Hrype can come and go pretty much at will. None of us are meant to leave the village without Lord Gilbert's permission, but somehow this rule does not apply to Hrype. When he's in the village, he looks just like the rest of us, performing his work alongside the other villagers with nothing to distinguish him. He has a talent for blending in with his surroundings, and with the people around him, that is truly exceptional. I suppose that it's the very ordinariness of his appearance that aids him, for if he seems exactly like everyone else, nobody looking on would be able to tell if he's here or not. It would be like the addition or removal of one tree in a forest.

I don't know why Hrype absents himself so frequently. I have my own ideas on the subject, but they are only vague. He is far too fearsome a man for anyone to dare to ask him. When he stops being a lowly peasant and stands straight and proud in his true skin, he appears tall and lordly; you could almost believe him to be the descendant of kings. As if all this were not enough, he is also a very powerful magician.

My aunt's voice brought me out of my reverie. '. . . better ask Lassair, since it was she who went to care for Goda,' she was saying.

I looked up at Hrype. His eyebrows went up in a silent question.

'Goda said it looked as if the intruder there was looking for something,' I said. 'She reckoned that her mother-in-law got killed, and she herself injured, simply because they were in the way.'

Hrype nodded. 'Whatever this man wants, he wants it very badly,' he observed.

Edild's face creased in a frown. 'You are assuming the two intruders are one and the same,' she said.

Hrype turned to her, his expression kind. 'I think they must be,' he said gently.

'But . . .' My aunt's protest stopped before she could utter it. 'Of course,' she whispered, her horrified eyes turning to me.

'Yes. It was the area of the dormitory where Elfritha sleeps,' Hrype murmured.

And then I, too, understood. I also understood why they were both looking at me with such anxiety.

The intruder had just broken into the places where two of my sisters lived. One person was dead, three injured. Unless this fearsome man had already found what he was after – which didn't seem likely, since proceeding to Elfritha meant he obviously hadn't got whatever it was at Goda's, and Elfritha surely didn't have anything anyone could want – then he would go on with his violent attacks.

'Haward is second in age after Goda, followed by Elfritha,' Edild said. 'Yet no intrusion has occurred at his home.'

And I came after Elfritha, followed by Squeak and little Leir . . .

Hrype stood up. 'I shall go to Wymond and Essa's house immediately to warn them, and Lassair shall come with me,' he announced. Turning to me with a smile, he went on, 'Your father is a big, tough man, Lassair. He is also fiercely protective of his children, and you and your two younger brothers will be safe under his roof. I'll suggest that Haward and his family move back into the family home, for the time being anyway. There's safety in numbers, and it would take a desperate man to force his way into a house where there were two grown men and a pair of fierce boys.' My little brothers would have been delighted at the description.

Hrype swung his heavy cloak around him and headed for the door, raising an eyebrow at me. Reluctantly I got to my feet. The prospect of a night – or, more likely, several nights – crowded in with all my family back at home was not very appealing. Much as I love them, I had become used to the peace and calm of Edild's little house. Hrype was looking quite determined, however, and it did not seem that I had any choice.

Later, trying to get to sleep, I wondered suddenly if this giant's interest in my family was restricted to my generation, or if Edild too was in danger. She was all alone, and –

Then I understood, as if I had just been told, that she wasn't alone. Nobody outside my family knew that Hrype was back in the village, and we would keep it to ourselves. For this night at least, Hrype could sleep not where his conscience dictated – in the home of his late brother's frail and dependent widow – but where his heart lay. With Edild.

We were lucky, in a way, for our house was ransacked while there was nobody within to get in the giant intruder's way. It must have happened some time in the late afternoon. I was working with Edild; my father and Squeak were out on the water studying the movements of the eels; Haward had taken Leir out to the higher ground, where Haward was working that day; and my mother had gone to help Zarina with the washing.

I was the last to return home, and by then my capable mother had dried her tears and was already rearranging all her precious domestic possessions while my father set about repairing the broken leg of Leir's little stool. Haward and Zarina were looking on helplessly.

'I've offered to help,' Zarina whispered as I went to stand beside her, 'but your mother says it's best if she does it all herself as she'll never be able to find anything if anyone else tidies up.'

I suppressed a smile. My mother defended her right to be solely in charge of her own hearth like a she-wolf protecting her den full of helpless young.

My mother had stopped in the middle of rearranging the straw-stuffed mattress and bedding on Squeak's cot. She was holding up a woollen blanket, displaying a large hole in one corner. 'Why did he have to do *that*?' she demanded furiously, poking her finger through the hole. 'It's nothing more than spiteful, wanton destruction!'

I agreed with her. Whatever the intruder had been hunting for, it would hardly be hiding within the weave of a blanket. I was suddenly very glad that the precious shawl that Elfritha made for me hadn't been lying around waiting for similar treatment. I went over to my mother, gave her a hug and took the blanket out of her hands. 'I'll darn it,' I offered. She eyed me dubiously. 'Yes, I *know* you'd do a better job, but you have enough to do.'

She gave me a swift smile, then returned to restoring order to her wrecked home.

When we finally sat down to eat, the house looked much as it had done before. That was the advantage of everything you possessed being old, worn and mended; one more repair didn't really make much difference.

My father had asked all of us to check through our own small sum of belongings, to see if anything was missing. As one by one we all reported that nothing had gone, his expression went from puzzlement to fury.

'Then he's caused us all this work and distress for no reason,' he muttered. His light eyes narrowed, and, as his right hand closed into a huge fist, I reflected that I wouldn't want to be in the intruder's boots if my father ever caught up with him. This phantom stranger might well be the giant that he was claimed to be, but then my father was scarcely small.

I studied him as, still muttering under his breath, he returned to his food. My father is the middle child of the five who were born to my Granny Cordeilla and her husband. I never knew my grandfather, for he died before I was born, but apparently he was a quiet, mild man, hard-working and steady. My granny, or so they say, had been a sparkling, enchanting girl, full of magic and mystery, lively as a tree-full of starlings, and everyone fervently hoped that early marriage to a steady but dull fenland fisherman would calm her down and keep her out of mischief. Knowing my granny, I doubt very much that it did.

She bore her husband two sons, Ordic and Alwyn, both of whom were made in their parents' exact mould: slender, dark, and not very tall. In their temperament, however, the little boys were faithful copies of their father. A few years passed, and Granny's third child was born: my father, Wymond, in whose blood ran the echo of his three huge uncles, Granny Cordeilla's brothers. To complete her family, Granny bore twin girls, my aunts Edild and Alvela.

Everyone always says parents don't have favourites, and I dare say that's true. You would have had to be blind, however, not to see the truth: Granny Cordeilla might well have loved all five of her sons and daughters equally, but there were without doubt two with whom she preferred to spend her time. Edild was one, for she and Granny were so attuned that they rarely had need of words. My father – my big, strong father with his sea-coloured eyes – was the other. When Granny became too old and frail to manage on her own, nobody even thought to ask which of her children she would go to live with. We all knew.

My father's voice broke into my reverie. We'd all been virtually silent as we ate, even Squeak's usually high spirits squashed by the prevailing mood of depression. As one, we turned to look at my father.

'I can't for the life of me think what we've got that he'd want!' he said, echoing Goda's sentiments of two days ago. 'We've got no treasures, no store of coins, no valuable possessions, no mighty sword or shield handed down from father to son from the glory days!' He glanced around, looking slightly sheepish. It was as if only now, as the echo of his words faded away, did he realize how loudly he had spoken. 'We've only got what everyone else like us has, and yet two of my daughters' dwellings, and now our own family home, have been searched as roughly and as thoroughly as if we possessed the riches of King William himself.'

Nobody spoke for a moment. Then Zarina, newest member of our family, cleared her throat. Quietly and, I thought, tentatively, she said, 'You do have treasure, Father.' I love the way she calls her father-in-law *father*. She once told me her story, and it was very sad; her own father had been a terrible man, and I'm glad she has found a better one. Her eyes going from my father to my mother and back, she whispered, 'You've got a house full of love. That's the best treasure of all, believe me.'

My father looked embarrassed for a moment, then reached for Zarina's hand, giving it a quick squeeze.

Squeak gave a noise that sounded like someone trying not to be sick. Haward leaned over and lightly cuffed him.

Then, of all people, little Leir spoke up. 'We've got Lassair's stories,' he said. 'I like Lassair's stories.' He grinned up at me, his sweet face still round and babyish. He's growing tall, and sometimes I forget he's only six.

My mother grabbed her baby boy and settled him on her lap. 'Lassair's tales, eh, Leir?' He nodded solemnly. 'You reckon they're a treasure?'

Leir nodded again. 'They're our family treasure,' he said.

It was a lovely thing to say. Had he not looked so comfortable on our mother's capacious lap, I'd have grabbed him and given him a hug.

Squeak, further disgusted by all the sentiment flying around, made another being-sick noise and muttered, 'I'd rather have a sword.'

Squeak is thirteen. From both his own and everyone else's viewpoint, it's a ghastly age for a boy.

I had hoped that, since our house had now received the attentions of the giant intruder and presumably he'd finished with us, I might be allowed to return to Edild's. I remarked in an offhand way, over breakfast in the morning, that I'd probably stay with my aunt that night, hoping my father would just say *all right, then*.

He didn't. He stopped eating, fixed me with a penetrating stare and said, 'One more night with us, Lassair.'

I was about to protest, but then his expression softened and he added, 'Please?'

I've always found it very hard to disobey my father, especially when I know that to do so would mean hurting or disappointing him. Meekly I nodded. 'Very well.'

* * *

Edild and I had a hectic morning. Spring might be on its way, but nobody had told the elements, and the raw day was one of misty rain blown on a spiteful easterly wind. By midday we had treated so many people for the usual phlegmy cough that afflicts fenland people – it's the perpetual damp that causes it – that we had run out of Edild's expectorant medicine. I knew then how I would be spending the remainder of the day: in assembling all the ingredients and preparing them so that Edild could work her magic on them and turn them into a healing elixir.

On the shelves where we store our ingredients I found most of what I needed. We were having to rely on dried herbs, which in the main lack the potency of fresh-picked plants. Nothing much was growing yet; another reason why we were all longing for spring.

One element was missing. Recently Edild had passed on to me an unlikely piece of medicinal lore, which she herself had been taught by a very old woman who claimed she was from Viking stock. In the far north, the old woman said, the people used a special lichen to treat chest ailments; a lichen that was the food of a deer that lived in the snowy wastes where little else grew. This lichen did not grow in the fens, but Edild had discovered a similar moss-like substance thriving in the thin soil beneath the line of pine trees away over on the fen edge. After experimenting on herself, she found that it was very good at bringing up catarrh from the lungs and throat, and she had taken to including it in her remedy.

The jar in which we kept it was empty.

With a sigh – for the misty rain had grown heavier – I collected my shawl, put on my boots and, wrapping myself up tightly, set out on the mile-long trudge to the water.

THREE

The weather was so foul that I didn't concentrate on anything much beyond staying on my feet against the force of the rising easterly wind. I was soaked to the skin within a few paces of leaving the house, and my attention was focused on images of how good it would be to get back to the fireside and start drying out.

All of which explains why it was not until I'd gathered my lichens and was well on the way back that I realized what I ought to have spotted straight away: somebody was watching me.

I did as I've been taught, and gave no indication that I knew of the unseen watcher's presence. I carried on without breaking stride, thinking all the time what I must do to keep myself safe.

I should never have gone out alone! It was so easy to be wise after the event, and, indeed, who could I have asked to come with me? Everyone was out working, either on their own behalf or on Lord Gilbert's land. People like us didn't sit around in our houses all day waiting for someone to invite us out for a walk.

My mind was racing, going through possibilities. I didn't dare stop and look around; it still seemed best to go on pretending I didn't know anyone was there.

But he was there, all right. And I was afraid.

Given what had so recently been happening within my family, fear was quickly turning to terror.

With a huge effort, I brought myself under control. I had decided what to do.

I'd gone out to the south of the village, down beneath where the bulge that is Aelf Fen sticks out into the watery marshland. Between the road and the shore there's a line of pine trees, their roots in the band of sandy soil that meanders along for half a mile or so before petering out. The lichen grows in the shadow of the trees.

Lord Gilbert's manor, Lakehall, was some way off up to my right, and between it and the village was the church. I would pretend that, on my way home, I was stopping to kneel by a relative's grave and pay my respects. With any luck, my pursuer would be deterred by the proximity of the church, and the possibility of goodly, decent people within, and slip away. As soon as I sensed he had gone, I could leave the graveyard by the side gate and hurry across the higher ground to Edild's house.

That was the plan.

I reached the graveyard and, choosing a random mound, knelt on the wet grass and pretended to pray. Peeping between my hands, pressed against my face, I looked all around.

There was nobody there.

I made myself go on kneeling, keeping very still, and with all my senses I tested to see if I still felt I was being watched. After a long, cold, shivery moment, I realized I was alone. He'd gone.

Slowly I got up, picking up my small sack of lichen.

It was then that I noticed.

Somebody had disturbed the graves over beneath the stumpy trees on the far side of the churchyard. They were the most recent graves, of those villagers who had died within the last couple of years or so. Aghast at such desecration, all thoughts of my unseen pursuer flew out of my head and I raced across the sodden ground as if it was my job to grab a spade and instantly start repairing the damage.

I slid, panting, to a halt beside the first of the ruined grave mounds. Staring down into the muddy hole – the incessant rain had already made large puddles in the earth – I was horrified to see the yellow-white of human bone. Leg bones, ribs arching up like a cage, a domed skull and blank, unseeing eye sockets. I stumbled on to the next grave. This one was worse, for it was more recent and, in places where the shroud had torn or been chewed by rodents, I could make out putrefying flesh. As if in a ghastly daze, I moved on to look at the rest.

In all, seven graves had been violated. Seven of my fellow villagers lay exposed in death, and I had known every one. In age, they ranged from the very old to the newborn, and that grave – of a tiny boy who had come into the world too soon and survived only for three days – was the most poignant of all.

I could not leave them like that. Wiping my hands over my face, wet with both rain and tears, I silently promised the dead that they would soon be decently buried once more and, at last tearing my eyes away and turning my back, I hurried off to find the priest.

Father Augustine was in his little house, adjacent to the church. He was alone. The house smelled of onions and cabbage, and I guessed he had just eaten. I blurted out my news, and the expression in his face suggested he was as horrified as I was.

'How many graves?' he demanded, grasping my arm in a tight grip.

'Seven, all quite recent.'

'The ones beneath the trees?'

'Yes.'

Slowly he shook his head. '*Why?*' he breathed.

I had no answer. Belatedly he realized he was still clutching my arm and, abruptly letting go, he muttered an apology and stepped away.

For a moment we both stood there, not moving, not speaking. It was as if we were frozen with shock. I studied his face, which had gone quite white. He's always pale; he is tall and thin, and has one of those aesthetic faces that seem made for suffering. He is an intelligent man, learned and devoted to the minutiae of the Bible; there's no doubting his faith or his devotion to his saviour. However, I think if Father Augustine's heavenly lord were to be asked to judge the man's performance, he might be inclined to say that our priest lacks the human touch. No matter how hard I try, I can't really imagine Father Augustine consorting with and comforting beggars, cripples and lepers. He just doesn't have the compassion.

Father Augustine gave a deep sigh, as if coming out of a reverie, and said briskly, 'I shall go straight to the graves. Fetch the sacristan, if you would, and bring him to me there.'

I nodded. Hurrying out of the house, I ran down the track to the sacristan's house and, dragging Old Will away from his hearth, took him to where the priest crouched by the spoiled graves

Father Augustine was beside the grave of the newborn baby. He had one long arm stretching down into the earth and he was stroking the tiny skull. He had tears in his eyes.

I stepped away, embarrassed at having witnessed such emotion. I realized, as I stood there, that my assumptions on the nature of our priest were going to need urgent and fairly drastic revision.

Presently Father Augustine stood up, brushing the dirt from his black robe. He nodded to Old Will, who spat on his hands, picked up his spade and began to repair the damage.

Back at Edild's house, I got straight down to helping her prepare the expectorant remedy, so relieved to be out of the rain and back in the warmth that I didn't mind the minor inconvenience of my clothes steaming as they began to dry. I had told her as soon as I got in about the despoiled graves, and of my suspicion that somebody had been watching me. As we worked, we speculated on what could possibly be going on, and tried to decide whether my hidden watcher, and whoever had tampered with the graves, were somehow linked to Utta's murder and the searching of Goda's, Edild's and our family's dwellings. Was the same person responsible for everything that had happened? Had it been the red-bearded giant who'd been spying on me, and was it also he who had dug down into the graves in search of heaven knew what?

Our musings were interrupted by a tentative tap on the door, and Edild left me chopping and crushing while she went off to see to her patient. Something was nagging at me, demanding my attention, and, as my aunt has taught me, I stilled my mind to let the inner voice speak.

After a few moments, I knew what it was. My kin had been the object of all three searches; as far as we knew, we alone had been targeted. Now, someone had disturbed the peace of the recently dead, and now I realized why: it was an extension of the same search. One member of my family had died within the last couple of years – my Granny Cordeilla – and whoever had ransacked the homes of the living had also attempted to discover what he sought within her grave.

He had failed. Having somehow discovered that Granny had died recently, he had gone to the graveyard thinking to find her there. He had investigated the newest burials, ruthlessly breaking into the eternal peace of the dead, but it had all been in vain. My Granny Cordeilla, of course, did not lie in the graveyard, for we had buried her out on the secret island, in the company of her ancestors.

Edild was busy with her patient, and, out in the still room, I was not visible to her. There was no let-up in the rain – I could hear it beating on the ground outside – but, since I was still almost as wet as when I'd just returned, that didn't really matter.

I knew I wouldn't be able to rest until I knew.

I draped my sodden shawl around me and slipped outside, emerging at the rear of Edild's house. It was getting dark. The sky was thick with cloud, and twilight was fast approaching. Good. I would be that much harder to see. I circled round to the track that ran in front of the house, keeping my distance so that no one would hear my footfalls. Swiftly I crossed the track and set out across the marsh. When I had gone perhaps a quarter of a mile, I stopped and made myself stand quite still. I strained my ears for any sound other than the driving rain and the rising wind, and then set my other senses to work, trying to detect if anyone had followed me or was watching me.

Nobody was there. The certainty I'd experienced earlier that I was not alone had gone, as if it had never been. Whoever he was, he'd obviously had enough of the foul weather and, very wisely, had sloped away to find shelter.

I smiled in grim satisfaction and continued my quest.

The island where our ancestors lie buried is only a short distance from the fen edge, rising like the humped back of some sleeping animal out of the black water. Some time in the distant past, my kinsmen drove stakes of alder wood down into the mud and, when access is required, struts and timbers are fitted to them to make a temporary walkway to the island. The timbers were not now in place, for it was months since anybody had visited the island.

I stood on the bank looking out over the water. Although it was raining now and the levels were visibly rising, the past few weeks had been dry. I could wade out to the island, and the water would only come up to my thighs.

Probably.

There was no point standing there thinking about it. The sooner I went, the sooner it would be over. I lifted up the skirts of my robe and under gown and secured them around my waist. I took off my boots and tied them round my neck. Then I went down the steep, slippery bank and walked into the water.

It was *so cold*. I'd thought I was wet and uncomfortable before, but it was nothing compared to this. The mud beneath my feet was slimy, thick and very slippery, and I had to lurch from one stake to the next to avoid falling. As it was, the water quickly rose up to my knees, thighs and my belly. I hitched my clothes higher, although they were so wet already that I didn't really know why I was bothering.

After an eternity, the claggy marsh bed began to rise again and I clambered out on to the island. I shook the water off my legs, let my robe fall to the ground and strode off to where Granny Cordeilla lay buried.

The low bump of her grave lay nearest to me as I approached. Beyond her were our honoured ancestors, and I liked to think they had given the newest arrival a warm welcome. The kin who Granny would most have liked beside her, however, were not there; of her three beloved brothers, two had died at Hastings, their bodies lost for ever, and the third, Harald, had left England after the Conquest, never to be heard of, or from, since.

Hardly daring to look, I crept up to Granny's grave. I realized I was holding my breath.

With a rush of relief, I let out a sob. Granny's last resting place lay undisturbed, the turf over it green and smooth. I knelt down and, as if I were kissing her dear face, pressed my lips to the springy grass. I closed my eyes, visualizing her, and instantly images burst into my mind.

At first they were all of Granny Cordeilla, as she had been in life. I saw her seated beside the hearth, telling a story to an enthralled audience. I saw her face creased in wicked laughter as she played a trick on Goda; she never had much time for my eldest sibling. I saw her watching my father, her expression so soft, so piercingly loving, that it moved me to tears.

After a time – I don't know how long – I became aware that the visions had changed. Now I no longer saw things from my own memory. I knew, without knowing *how* I knew, that I was seeing into the past . . .

I saw a long shore, the sea grey and shot with silver where a ray of sun pierced the heavy clouds. Through the mist I saw a ship, its square sail filled with a powerful wind, racing towards land. The ship had a high prow, and the prow terminated in the startling, frightening figurehead of a dragon. Its long neck curved gracefully, its snout ended in a curling swirl that suggested fire and smoke, and its elongated eyes stared out with furious determination. Inside my head someone said, *Malice-striker*.

The ship was running before the wind, its long, graceful lines appearing to fly over the waves as if the dragon had spread its wings. It was stunningly beautiful, and, at the same time, deeply frightening. Had the ship come for me? Was it headed for this shore, where its fierce crew would disembark and fall on my own village?

No, said the voice in my head, *for this is not now, but a window into the past.*

I felt an instant of sweet relief.

Then abruptly the ship disappeared into the mist and the vision faded. Coming back to myself, I shook off the trance and struggled to sit up. Staggering slightly, I stood up and made my way back to the end of the island nearest to the shore, gathering up my garments once more and bracing myself to plunge back into the dark water.

I scrambled ashore and set off for the village, telling myself over and over again, *It's over, it's done, Granny's safe*. It helped, a little.

I was almost back at the track when it happened. I hadn't

seen a soul; my fellow villagers apparently had far more sense than I, and, once the day's toil was done, had headed for home and shut themselves firmly inside. Smoke rose from many rooftops, and imagining the warmth of the hearth fires was making me feel even colder.

I saw a huge figure: a giant of a man, broad-shouldered, his pale-coloured hair hanging in braids either side of his heavily bearded face. His light eyes seemed to shine in the deepening dusk, as if lit from inside. He stood on the edge of the track, looking up at the village.

He was half-turned away from me, and I did not think he had seen me. I dropped to my knees, then to my belly, wriggling through the tufty grass and the low knolls that dotted the sodden ground of the fen edge. I made my way to the meagre shelter of a clump of scrawny hazel bushes, then lay still. I could feel the water soaking into my clothes, from my neck to my knees, but I ignored its chilly embrace. Better to be wet than visible to that monster of a man . . .

After a moment, I made myself look up.

He had gone. He was nowhere to be seen.

I shook my head, puzzled, for surely my eyes were playing me false. In the short time that I hadn't been watching him, it was inconceivable that he'd managed to get out of sight; there was simply no place of concealment he could have reached so quickly.

Had I imagined him, then? Was he a vestige of that strange vision I'd had out on the secret island?

I did not know.

I was shivering, my teeth chattering. I was so cold that I couldn't feel my feet, and my hands were blue-white and clumsy. If I didn't get into the warmth soon, I'd make myself ill.

I checked once more, very carefully, to see if the giant had reappeared. There was no sign of him. Then I got to my feet and, stumbling, tripping over my own feet, I hurried home to Edild.

She was alone, sitting cross-legged by the hearth, hands folded in her lap. I wasn't taken in for a moment by her air of serenity.

I could feel her ire crackling and fizzing just beneath the surface.

She looked up at me, raising one eyebrow.

I flopped down beside her, drips from my hair and garments hissing into the fire. 'I've been out to the island to check on Granny,' I said. There was no point in dissimulating.

She did not speak. Shooting a quick glance at her, I noticed that she had gone very white, and her instant concern for the danger I'd just put myself in touched me. It also made me feel very guilty.

'I worked out that the giant who's been searching for whatever he's after in all our dwellings has turned his attention to trying to find Granny's grave,' I hurried on. 'He seems to know a lot about us, such as where all of us live, and apparently he's also aware that Granny died only a couple of years ago, since it was only the most recent graves that he disturbed. We know she's not there, of course, and I suddenly had the most awful fear that maybe he had found that out too.' I hesitated. 'I'm sorry I worried you. I just had to go and make sure.'

'And?' The single syllable was barely even a whisper.

'It's quite clear that nobody's been on the island for ages,' I replied. 'All the graves, Granny's included, are just as they ought to be.'

I felt my aunt's relief coming off her in waves.

After a short silence, she said, 'How can you be sure your rash action didn't lead this giant straight to the one place we don't want him to find?' She quickly corrected herself. 'I mean, one of the places. We don't really want him near any of us!'

I wondered at her suddenly light tone. It was unconvincing, and I thought perhaps she was trying to take my mind off the dark threat that seemed to swirl around us.

'Don't worry, I was very careful,' I assured her. I told her briefly how I'd checked for any malicious presence, and detected nothing. 'But I . . .' I was on the point of telling her how I'd thought I'd seen the figure of a huge, bearded man just as I returned to the village, but I decided to keep it to myself. Now that I was back in the warmth and safety of Edild's house, I was even more convinced that it had been merely some sort of after-image from my strange vision.

My aunt was looking at me oddly It felt almost as if she was trying to see inside my head. Deliberately I put up a barrier, and after a moment she turned away.

Presently she said, 'Your father will be here to collect you soon.'

I had quite forgotten my promise to my father that I would sleep under his roof again that night. Getting up and going out into the rain again was the last thing I wanted to do, but a promise is a promise. I stretched out my hands to the flames and waited for his knock on the door.

FOUR

After a restless night, I got up early and set about helping my mother prepare the first meal for all of us. I had barely slept, and I was grumpily – but silently – asking myself how on earth I'd managed to get a decent night's rest in the days when I'd lived permanently at home, in the midst of my large family. You can, I suppose, get used to anything. The trouble was that I'd become accustomed to the luxury of peaceful nights, either just with Edild for company or, when living in Cambridge with my teacher, Gurdyman, alone in my little loft.

My mother looked exhausted. My heart went out to her and, putting aside my self-pity, I took the large stone vessel out of her hands and went outside to fetch water.

My father was looking thoughtful as he ate his porridge. I had told the family the previous evening about the disturbed graves and about my hasty (and highly foolhardy, according to my father) dash across the marsh to check on Granny out on the island. I guessed this was what was occupying him and, when at length he spoke, I was proved right.

'It's no longer common practice to bury grave goods with the dead,' he mused. 'Hasn't been for many a long year. Not something the Church approves of, telling us as they do that we go to meet our maker mother-naked, just as we entered the world.'

My mother gave him a swift, impatient look. She is a woman who always keeps both feet firmly on the ground. If anyone had the temerity to ask her opinion on some question broadly to do with the realm of gods and spirits, she would brush the question aside with some sort of dismissive comment, such as, 'I know what I believe and that's good enough for me.' She does not waste her time pondering unanswerable questions, and has little patience with those who do.

I thought I knew what my father was thinking. I often do. 'The giant intruder has exhausted the places where the living members of our family could have hidden whatever it is he's searching for,' I said quietly, just to my father. 'You're thinking, too, that he's been driven to looking in the graves of our dead?' It was just what I'd concluded the previous day.

'I am,' he agreed softly. He smiled grimly. 'Just as well he doesn't know about the island, isn't it?'

I nodded. It was, of course, because it would have been dreadful if, like the relatives of the disturbed dead in the churchyard, we'd been faced with the desecration of a loved one's grave. Had it happened, it would in any case have been all for nothing.

I saw my granny in her grave and I knew there was nothing buried with her except for some of her most treasured possessions and a scattering of flowers. By now the flowers would be turned to dust, and the few simple personal objects had already been worn down by a lifetime's hard use when they went into the ground. A bone comb, beautifully carved but with half its teeth missing. A prettily crafted drinking cup, mended at least twice. A soft woolly shawl, much darned. There was surely nothing in the grave with Granny that anyone else would take such extreme steps to retrieve.

I reached out and took my father's hand. He had loved his mother dearly. I was so glad, for all of us but especially for him, that her eternal sleep had not been interrupted.

I worked hard all day with Edild, my thoughts fully occupied so that there was little time for wondering whether my father would relent and let me return to sleeping at my aunt's house. When I did briefly dwell on it, it occurred to me that perhaps he wasn't only thinking of me. If, as it seemed, it was my father's children who were the objects of the giant intruder's search, then my presence in Edild's house might also put her in danger. Edild, I knew, was under Hrype's protection, but I very much doubted that anyone else was aware of it.

Spring was getting into its stride. The worst of the various weather-related sicknesses was over, and soon I should start thinking about returning to my studies with Gurdyman. A part of me longed to be back with him in the twisty-turny house in Cambridge, engrossed in the fascinating things he was

teaching me and with the lively, vibrant town all around me.
But such thoughts seemed disloyal to my family, especially
under the current circumstances, so I tried to suppress them.

We were just clearing up for the day when there came the
sound of running footsteps on the path leading up to the door.
There was a perfunctory knock, then the door was flung open
and my cousin Morcar burst into the house.

There was no need for even the swiftest glance at his poor,
haggard face to know that something terrible had happened.
Distress radiated out of him, reaching me with such force that
I staggered back. Edild ran to him, took his hands in hers and,
on a huge sob, he cried, 'My mother's dead!'

Instinctively, Morcar had come first to Edild, his mother
Alvela's twin. But Alvela had had other siblings, and one of
them was my father. Even as Edild led Morcar over to the
bench beside the hearth and gently persuaded him to sit, I
gathered up my shawl and ran across the village to my family
home. By the time Morcar was ready to tell us what had
happened, he had the meagre comfort of his uncle's, his aunt's
and his cousin's presence while he related his tale.

'I'd been working on a job some way from home,' he began.
Morcar is a flint knapper. His and Alvela's neat little house is
up in the Breckland. 'I finished off this morning, sooner than
I'd reckoned, and I headed home with coins in my purse,
hoping to surprise Mother.' Tears filled his eyes. 'She was
lying there, amid the wreck of all the bits and bobs she'd cared
for so well. They didn't amount to much, but she loved them.'
He buried his face in his hands, his shoulders shaking with
sobs. He is by nature a reserved, taciturn man, and to see him
torn apart by his grief was hard to bear. Alvela had doted on
him, and I had always assumed he'd found her fussing something of a trial. Watching him now it was clear that, even were
that true, he'd loved her deeply.

He raised his wet face and looked at my father, then at
Edild. 'Whoever broke in beat her, very badly,' he said, his
voice breaking. 'Her poor face was . . .' But he couldn't bring
himself to tell us. He waved a hand vaguely in my father's
direction, shaking his head in anguish.

'Never mind that now,' Edild said gently. 'Do not distress yourself further by making yourself think of it.'

'But why did they hurt her?' Morcar asked, his brow creased in a perplexed frown. 'She was a small woman, and not strong. Once he'd broken in, he could have taken all he wanted and she wouldn't have been able to stop him.'

'*He?*' my father asked.

Morcar glanced at him. 'Yes. Great big fellow, bearded, built like an ox.'

'Somebody saw him? Edild demanded.

'Yes, yes, a couple of our neighbours had heard the commotion and gone to see what was up. The man ran off just as they arrived.' He paused. 'They found Mother lying there, but it was too late to help her. She was already dead.' He dropped his face into his hands again.

I saw my father and my aunt exchange a glance. Then my father looked at me. I understood. 'It's as if her killer had been trying to make her tell him something,' I whispered, the words barely more than a breath.

My father heard. His expression grim, he nodded.

Morcar must have heard, too. Perhaps – probably – he had already arrived at the same conclusion. 'I don't know what he thought she could tell him!' he cried, tears running down his face. 'If he was after some treasure, some object of value, that he believed we had hidden away in our house, he had been wrongly informed. And now she's dead.'

We fell silent. In Edild's warm, fragrant little house, the heart-rending sound of a grown man's weeping was the only thing to break the silence.

My poor father was quite clearly torn between staying with Edild and me while we tended Morcar – well, it was Edild who patiently went on trying to calm and comfort him, while I set about making a remedy to dull the agony of his shock and grief – and returning to protect his family home. In the end, perhaps frustrated by his indecision, Edild said firmly, 'Go home to your wife and your sons, Wymond. You should send word to Ordic and Alwyn, who must be informed of our sister's death.'

My father looked at her uncertainly for a moment. Then, his face working, he said, 'Goda wounded, old Utta dead, Elfritha's dormitory searched and two nuns hurt, my family's home – where Lassair is temporarily living – ransacked, and now this – poor Alvela. It's the *women*,' he added in a low, furious voice. 'My daughters, and now my sister.' He took a deep breath. 'What sort of a man attacks women? What is worth finding, for which he'll kill so casually and thought-lessly?' His eyes, normally warm with affection and humour, were suddenly cold as ice. There was, I realized, another side to my father; one that an enemy would do well to fear.

I think it was Edild's remark about informing Ordic and Alwyn that finally persuaded my father to leave. Although the third-born son, he is the acknowledged head of the siblings, probably because he's both the wisest and the biggest of the brothers. He got up to go, leaning over Edild and muttering something I did not catch. She looked up at him with a smile, made a soft reply and nodded towards the door. She murmured some-thing that sounded like a reassurance. Whatever she said seemed to convince him.

As he stood in the doorway, he turned back to me and beckoned. 'A word, Lassair.'

I wondered what he wanted to say. I got up and followed him outside.

My father turned to face me. 'You should go back to Cambridge,' he said. 'You're due back with your teacher round about now, aren't you?'

'Yes,' I agreed. My father's suggestion was making me feel very guilty over my thoughts of that morning, when I'd been longingly imagining being back with Gurdyman. 'But what about poor Morcar?' my conscience made me ask. 'He's grieving, and there'll be the funeral to endure, and—'

'Edild and I will look after Morcar,' my father said, quietly but with the sort of tone that informed me it was not my place to take the discussion further. 'You will return to your studies in Cambridge tomorrow. We'll go to Lord Gilbert first thing in the morning, and I'll ask his permission to take you.' He fixed me with a stare. 'I will not let you go unprotected, Lassair.'

Part of me sang with joy, despite the dreadful circumstances. The prospect of a day alone with my beloved father was a rare treat. But then I wondered why he was suddenly so eager for me to return to Gurdyman.

Anticipating the question, my father looked down at me, his eyes full of love and concern. 'My daughters and my sisters,' he said, repeating his earlier words. 'Of them all, the most precious is you, child.' It was, I well knew, an admission he had never made before and would never make again; torn from him, I'm sure, by the emotion of the moment. 'How can I keep you safe here?' he demanded, his voice raw and angry. 'I work all the hours the good Lord sends, and so do you, and I am not close enough to protect you if he . . . if danger comes. Yet in Cambridge, according to Hrype, you live in a house so well-hidden that even he occasionally has trouble finding it.'

'It's a wizard's house,' I said softly. 'I expect concealing it comes easily to someone like Gurdyman.' I didn't think my father heard; if he did, he did not acknowledge the remark. It was, I expect, implicit of things he didn't really want to think about.

'You'll be safe in Cambridge,' my father reiterated.

He was right. Without being aware of the details of how it was achieved – I wasn't sure I wanted to know – I was quite certain, beyond any doubt, that no bearded stranger, even a giant one, would be able to harm me once I was under Gurdyman's roof.

The fact that my father was apparently aware of this, too, suggested that perhaps he thought about arcane and magical matters rather more than I'd imagined.

Early the next morning, my father and I presented ourselves up at Lakehall. Lord Gilbert's reeve, Bermund, greeted us – if opening the big door the merest crack and peering out with a look of deep suspicion qualifies as a greeting. Bermund may be secretive and withdrawn, unsmiling and a bit rat-like in his appearance, but he's reasonable. Once my father had explained our presence, Bermund had a think, sniffed, then nodded curtly and opened the door a little wider. 'You'd better come in,' he said with obvious reluctance. 'I will enquire whether Lord Gilbert is willing to receive you.'

I did not dare meet my father's eyes, and I'm sure he felt the same. After a moment, Bermund returned and, without a word, jerked his head in the direction of the big hall. Lord Gilbert sat at a large table by the hearth, alone, a muddle of tattered and much-handled pieces of vellum spread out in front of him, a quill in his hand and ink all over his fingers. He looked up at us with a smile, as if any distraction from his task was welcome.

'Good morning, Wymond!' he exclaimed. 'Eels thriving?'

'They are, my lord,' my father replied gravely.

Lord Gilbert turned to me. 'And, er . . .?'

'Lassair,' I prompted.

'Lassair, Lassair, yes, Lassair,' Lord Gilbert said enthusiastically, perhaps hoping that repetition would at last commit my name to his memory. 'Our apprentice healer!'

At least he recalled my profession. 'It is time for me to return to my studies in Cambridge, my lord,' I said quickly, capitalizing on the moment. 'With your permission,' I added respectfully.

'Of course, of course,' Lord Gilbert responded. 'The more you know, the more use you are to your own community. Eh, Wymond?' He turned to my father.

'Indeed, Lord Gilbert,' my father said. Then, his face intent, he went on, 'My lord, I have come to ask your leave to escort my daughter to Cambridge. There have been certain attacks on members of my family, and I am concerned—'

'Yes, yes, so I hear,' Lord Gilbert interrupted. 'Bermund has kept me informed, and I had half-expected you to come before now, Wymond. I am always here, when my village faces a threat!'

It was true, I reflected. Up to a point.

'There is nothing I would ask for, my lord, except this one concession,' my father said. 'I would not risk my daughter's safety by making her travel unprotected from here to Cambridge.'

'And nor shall you,' Lord Gilbert said grandly. 'You have my permission to escort her, Wymond.' Turning to me, he wagged an inky finger. 'Take care that you work hard, child, so that you repay our faith in you!'

I bowed my head, pretending meekness, and muttered, 'Yes, my lord.' I kept my head down; I didn't want Lord Gilbert to see my expression. I did not need a bumbling fool like *him* to tell me to work hard. Gurdyman would not give me the option of doing anything but my best, and the most vital stimulus of all was my own hunger to learn.

My father dug me in the ribs, and I managed a sincere-sounding, 'Thank you, Lord Gilbert,' as we turned and hurried out of the hall. Once we were out of the courtyard and on the track leading back to the village, my father leaned down and said quietly, 'No need to antagonize him, Lassair. You and I both know you are a great deal cleverer than him, but there's no need to tell him.' I heard a smile in his voice, and glanced up to verify it. 'Our masters hold the ordering of our days in their hands, be they worthy of the responsibility or not,' he continued, 'and there is nothing we can do about it. Be thankful, child, that Lord Gilbert has a wise wife, and enough sense to listen to her.'

My father was right, as he usually is. Lord Gilbert's wife is Lady Emma, and I'm sure I'm not the only resident of Aelf Fen who appreciates that it is she who is responsible for the good things that happen to us. She agreed with my aunt when Edild suggested I should be trained as a healer; I've never known if Lady Emma spotted some latent talent in me, or if, knowing and trusting Edild, she was prepared to take her word for it. The latter, I suspect. Then, when the chance arose for me to study with my Cambridge wizard – not that anyone except Hrype, me and Gurdyman himself would refer to him as such – I'm all but certain it was Lady Emma who pointed out to Lord Gilbert the advantages that my new knowledge would provide for their family and the village.

It's just as well, I suppose, that in addition to hinting at magic so potent that it makes me shake with fear, Gurdyman also instructs me on more practical matters. I like and admire Lady Emma, and it would not feel right to deceive her.

My father and I were back in the village. I ran inside our house to bid farewell to my mother, then I picked up the bag containing my few possessions. My father took it from me, swinging it up over his shoulder as if it contained no more than a handful of feathers. He gave me a smile. 'Ready?'

Excitement bubbled up in me. 'Ready!'

The day was fine, the going was easy, and we made good time. We picked up a ride for the long stretch that runs south-east of the Wicken peninsular, and, by the time we stopped at midday to eat our bread and cheese, there were only a few miles to go.

It was a rare delight to have my father to myself. Walking along side by side, we talked incessantly. He works so hard, and makes such strenuous efforts to care for and protect his family, that the deep, thoughtful side to his character is easily missed. A man like Lord Gilbert, for example, would doubtless think that his favourite eel catcher's head is as empty of anything other than the basics of day-to-day life as his own. Not many people know of my father's true nature, and I'm only thankful that I am one of them.

My father spoke of Alvela. I had assumed, since he had rarely seen his late sister and did not appear to have much to say to her when he did, that they had not been close; not in the way that he and Edild are. Alvela, I had always thought, was of the same level of importance as my father's two elder brothers: all three kin, and therefore always linked to him through the blood, but not necessarily people with whom he chose to spend his small, precious amount of free time. To hear him speak of his youngest sibling – Alvela was margin-ally the younger of the twins – made me appreciate that love takes many forms. Through his eyes, I saw the nervous, tense woman I knew as my aunt as she'd been when a girl, worrying because she could not grasp things as quickly as her sister. I saw her as a young adult, secretly in love with the flint knapper who would become her husband, and desperate because she believed he hadn't even noticed the self-effacing girl who adored him from afar.

I think that sharing his memories with me was my father's way of grieving for her. My mother hadn't liked Alvela – they just didn't get on – and I imagine that my father's tender reflections would have received short shrift at home. When finally he fell silent, I saw him wipe tears from his face. I gave him a moment to recover, then quietly reached out and took his hand.

Once or twice, as we walked and talked, I felt as if part of me was trying to catch my attention. Trying, perhaps, to warn me. I ignored it. I was with my big, strong father. No harm could possibly come to me when he was there to protect me.

Gurdyman did not seem surprised to see me. After a short pause, he opened the door in answer to my knock, his round face smiling, his eyes bright. I detected a faint aroma about him: musk, I thought. We had clearly disturbed him in the middle of some preparation or experiment down in his crypt. He ushered us along to his sunny little courtyard, and bade us both sit down on the bench while he fetched refreshments.

'You are welcome to stay with us overnight and journey back in the morning,' he said to my father as he poured out a mug of frothy, fragrant ale.

'Thank you, but I must return before nightfall,' my father replied. He paused to take a long draught of the ale. 'That's *good*,' he murmured. He glanced at me, then at Gurdyman. 'There has been some trouble,' he said briefly. 'Lassair will explain, but, in short, I'd not rest happily tonight away from my family and my home.'

Gurdyman nodded. 'As you wish. We will not detain you, then.'

My father wolfed down the meat pie that Gurdyman had set out, drained his ale, then stood up. Face to face with Gurdyman, who is not even my height, he looked taller than ever. 'Look after her,' he said, his expression intent. 'Your house is well-hidden, here in this maze of alleyways, and I am reassured by that, but . . .' His voice trailed off and he shrugged, as if not sure how to go on.

'Do not worry,' Gurdyman said calmly. 'The old stones of my house have protected those within from many foes and evils over the years, and they will do so again.' He met my father's eyes, and I had the sense that something more than words passed between them. 'Do not worry,' he said again. 'While Lassair remains under my roof, she is safe.'

My father went on staring down at him for a moment. Then, nodding, he turned to me. He wrapped me in a bear hug, kissed the top of my head and murmured, 'May the good Lord above look after you.' Without another word – he was, I guessed, finding this as painful as I was – he let me go, and hurried away up the passage towards the door.

Gurdyman went after him. I stood alone in the open court, surreptitiously wiping my eyes. By the time Gurdyman returned, I was ready. With a smile, I said, 'I'll take my satchel and my bag up to my room, then I'll come down to the crypt to help you with whatever you're doing.'

He looked at me kindly, his eyes crinkled up with affection. 'It is good to have you back, Lassair,' he said. 'Already your enthusiasm fills this house like a stream of light. I appreciate your willingness to get straight down to work, but I think we shall take the rest of the afternoon off.' I began to protest, but he held up a hand. 'We shall sit here together in the sunshine, finishing the food and this jug of rather fine ale, and you shall tell me what has so alarmed your father. I judge,' he added, seating himself in his big chair with a wince and a creak of bones, 'that he is a man not easily thrown off his stride, and yet here he is, escorting you on a journey you have done many times by yourself.' He reached for his mug, took a drink and fixed his eyes on me. 'Proceed,' he said, with a wave of the hand holding the mug. 'I am listening.'

I obeyed, concentrating on doing as he had taught me: telling the tale in the right order, succinctly, yet leaving out none of the important facts. When I had finished, he studied me for a few moments. As I looked into his eyes, I had the strange yet certain sense that none of this was news to him.

Before I could put the suspicion into words, he was already responding to it.

'Quite right!' He gave a delighted chuckle. 'Indeed, I have been informed of these events. Well *done*, Lassair!' He chuckled again. 'You are learning to trust your instincts. As I have so often told you, the more you do so, the more reliable your instincts will become.'

'Who told you?' I demanded. One look at his smiling face informed me that he wasn't going to reveal his source, so I puzzled it out for myself. When I was sure, I said, 'Hrype,' managing not to make it sound like a question.

'Hrype,' Gurdyman agreed.

My self-congratulatory smugness was rudely interrupted by a frightening thought: if Hrype had been here in Cambridge telling Gurdyman about the deaths of Utta and Alvela, and the alarming attacks on the dwellings of my family, who had been back in Aelf Fen looking after Edild? Oh, and I'd been so sure; so happy, to think of Hrype slipping unnoticed into Edild's little house, protecting her with his strength and his strange powers!

Gurdyman waited patiently while these panicky thoughts ran their course. Then he said, 'Child, do not underestimate Hrype. His presence is not necessarily required in order for a shield created by him to maintain its efficacy.'

My mind filled with questions. How could my aunt be kept safe, even by some magic shield of Hrype's, if she was left all alone? And what of my father, so desperate to protect those he loved, and who had been reassured – untruthfully, it now appeared – by his dear Edild that somehow she was being guarded? That question led straight to the next: did my father know about Hrype? *No, no, and you must not tell him!* came the instant reply, although I had no idea from where.

As I tried to frame the words to demand some answers, I sensed Gurdyman's resistance. I stared at him, and saw in his face that it was no good.

I could ask as many questions about Hrype as I liked. I wasn't going to get any response. With a resigned sigh, I got up and emptied the last of the ale into our mugs.

Gurdyman was watching me. He said, very softly, 'Magical protection or not, Hrype would take no chances where your aunt is concerned. It is perfectly safe for him to leave her, for her nephew is still staying with her.'

Morcar! So he hadn't yet left Aelf Fen.

Despite the fact that I was already prepared to believe in Hrype's shielding powers – Gurdyman had a very persuasive way with him – all the same, it was good to know that Edild had a flesh-and-blood protector too.

FIVE

In the morning, I woke refreshed and ready to work. Gurdyman had retired to his crypt the previous evening, and I knew he would be down there all night. He tells me he does sleep – he has a cot and blankets always set ready – but I have my doubts. He has a capacity for concentration that astounds me, and is able to keep going, without a break for food, drink or rest, for a length of time that one would have thought unendurable.

He had instructed me to come and find him when I was up, dressed and fed, and accordingly, once I had tidied away the remains of my breakfast, I trotted off through the house, heading towards the door that opens on to the alley, and, just before it on the left, the twisting passage leading to the steps down to the crypt.

The passage wasn't there. Where the arched entrance normally was, I found myself face to face with a blank wall. I stopped in amazement, totally confounded. Stupidly I put my hands up, feeling along the stonework, as if my fingers could find what my eyes could not see. What had happened? Where was the passage? Oh, dear Lord, where was Gurdyman? Had he somehow walled himself up in his crypt, destined to remain in that dark, deep, windowless place till he slowly starved to death?

I banged against the wall, fighting panic, listening for the hollow sound that would indicate an empty space on the far side. Nothing. I banged again, feeling a frantic sob rise in my throat. I drew a deep breath, preparing to shout, to scream.

There was a sharp click, and as if by magic the outline of a door appeared in the stones. The door opened, and Gurdyman's smiling face came into view. He swung the door fully open, pinning it back somehow so that it was no longer visible. He had put it, I guessed, in its usual position. Observant as I pride myself on being, I had never noticed it before.

He must have seen that I'd been alarmed, which is putting it mildly. He said, his face straightening, 'I'm sorry, child. I did not mean to frighten you.' His smile crept back. 'Did you think I had performed some powerful magic, Lassair? Some spell that made a door, doorway and passage vanish as if they had never been?'

Since it was exactly what I had thought, I made no reply.

He took pity on me, emerging from the arch of the doorway and coming to stand beside me. 'Magic spells can achieve many things, child,' he said gently. 'Making doorways disappear as if they had never been is not one of them, or, if it is, it's magic beyond anything I have ever heard of.' He patted me on the shoulder. 'You're quite pale,' he observed. 'You really were frightened, weren't you?'

I wondered if I should tell him the truth, and decided there was no reason not to. 'I thought you'd somehow shut yourself in down there, with no means of escape,' I muttered. 'I was terrified because I thought it was up to me to get you out, and I had no idea how to do it.'

There was dead silence. Then he said, 'It would have distressed you, then, if old Gurdyman had carelessly managed to bring about his own demise?'

He was trying not to smile, but I saw no humour whatsoever in the situation. Rounding on him, tears pricking behind my eyelids, I cried, '*Of course* it would have distressed me! I really, really like you!'

It was a silly thing to say; the sort of thing a child would blurt out. I was already framing an apology, but then I caught the fleeting expression in his blue eyes.

He was touched. Very touched.

I wondered how long it was since anyone had told him they cared for him.

We were both embarrassed now. He was the first to recover. Taking my arm, he stepped back into the entrance to the passage and said briskly, 'See, child, how the door is fastened, flat against the wall? You don't notice it unless you know it's there.' He undid the restraint, closing the door again, with us on the crypt side. 'Now, from the other side it is as you just saw it: invisible. It is made of stout, thick oak, as you can see, and its outer side is covered with a thin facing of the same stones that form the wall. It *blends in*, do you see? And it can only be opened from this side.' He demonstrated.

'Why?' I asked. 'I can see how very effective it is, but why is it necessary?'

He frowned in concentration, as if the answer to my question needed thought. Then he said, 'Do you remember, Lassair, that I once told you this old house of mine holds many secrets?' I nodded; it's something not easy to forget, if you're actually living in the house in question. 'You will, I am sure, have noticed the peculiar layout.'

'You mean the way the crypt isn't actually beneath the house?'

'Exactly,' he said, beaming. 'I *thought* you'd have spotted that,' he muttered. 'I cannot claim to have designed that feature myself,' he went on, 'for the house and its neighbours had stood here for many lifetimes before I took up residence. However, there came a moment when the opportunity arose for me to – ah – acquire the crypt beneath the house to our right –' he waved his arm to indicate – 'and I did not hesitate. That dwelling was then temporarily vacant, and I was able to ensure it remained so while the modifications were carried out. My house, as you no doubt realize, fits in between its neighbours like a serpent weaving its way between rocks.'

It was not a description I liked – not for this house I'd come to love – and, besides, I was not primarily concerned with the *how*; what I was still burning to know was *why*. 'So, you created access to a secret crypt that can be totally hidden from within your house,' I summarized. 'For what purpose?'

He looked slightly impatient. 'Why do you think, Lassair? You have been with me down there in the crypt; you have observed me working. Can you not see why it might be necessary to hide both the crypt and the work?'

I could; of course I could. 'And also the wi— the person doing the work,' I added quietly. I'd almost said *wizard*, but I wasn't at all sure he'd like the epithet. Not on my lips, anyway, although I had heard him refer to himself thus, usually with a self-mocking smile.

'Quite so,' he murmured. He glanced at me, looked away

and then met my eyes again. I guessed he was unsure about whether to say what was on his mind. Eventually he did. 'There have been times when I have offended people,' he said, with obvious reluctance. 'On occasions, men of power have resented my . . . er, things I have done.' I opened my mouth to ask what sort of things, but he hurried on, not allowing me to speak. 'It has proved useful, on more than one occasion, to have a safe place in which to hide while the storm wore itself out above me.' Suddenly he grabbed my arm, turned me round, hurried me back along the passage and said, 'But we have spent quite long enough on the secrets of my house, Lassair. It is time to get to work!'

Gurdyman never acts without a reason. It was only later that I wondered why he had chosen that particular morning to show me his house's hiding place.

We settled in the little courtyard, sitting either side of a trestle table on which Gurdyman proceeded to spread a huge sheet of parchment. Fairly soon I recognized what was inscribed on it, although the work was a great deal more advanced than when I had seen it before. Now, the surface was covered in blocks of small, neat lettering and tiny, vivid pictures, illustrating dwellings, palaces, churches, trees, flowers, rivers, and even, on a big expanse covered with ripples that I assumed to be the sea, a ship with a square sail and an imaginative sea monster blowing a huge spout of water from its mouth.

Hrype had been there, that day when I first saw the parchment; it was the day he first introduced me to Gurdyman. He had explained to me what Gurdyman had been trying to do, which was no more and no less than making a visual representation of the voyages of his ancient Norse ancestors. I hadn't really understood then, when the manuscript was in its early stages. Now that it was nearing completion – if the fact that almost the entire surface of the parchment was covered in pictures, writing or both was any guide – I knew I was going to need some help.

Side by side, Gurdyman and I sat staring down at the manuscript. I remembered how, on that first visit, he'd asked me to try to draw the journey I'd just made from Aelf Fen to

Cambridge, and all I'd managed was some rudimentary
sketches of trees and barns and a feeble, wandering line that
ran off the edge of the parchment long before it got to my
village. Now I said, 'I think I understand what you're trying
to do, but I'm afraid this –' I waved a hand over the entire
parchment – 'doesn't really mean anything to me.'

'No reason why it should,' he replied. He drew a breath,
held it and then said, 'I am not the only man attempting to
map the world, Lassair.' *Map*. I memorized the word. 'Men
of the Church are working on it, although from what I have
seen and heard of their travail, their faith is the driving force,
and Jerusalem is always presented as the world's centre: its
navel, if you like, for the Greeks used the word *omphalos*,
meaning the same thing. Not that their world's navel was the
Christians' Jerusalem, of course, but Delphi,' he added, half
to himself. 'But I digress. This map –' he put his fingertips
delicately on to his own beautiful work – 'represents a different
aspect of the world; or, more accurately, the world viewed
without the bias of faith. Here is the land, and here are the
surrounding seas.' He indicated first a large, amorphous shape
covered with pictures and writing, and then the rippled area
I'd already identified as water. 'See these ships?' Once more
he pointed, and, now that I was looking more closely, I saw
that the same little images of square-sailed ships were dotted
all over the manuscript.

'Yes,' I breathed.

'Behold the voyages of the Norsemen,' he said eagerly,
excitement thrumming in his voice. 'Into the north and the
west they went, heading out on the wide ocean that has no
end.' The left-hand edge of the map, indeed, ended in a mass
of ripples, gradually decreasing in size. 'Down into the great
land mass that lies to the south and the east, those long, narrow
boats edging ever onwards down the great rivers until finally
emerging into seas very different from those that we know in
the north. One such voyage led to Miklagard, their Great City,'
he said, his voice dropping to a whisper. I thought for a moment
he was going to elucidate; explain, perhaps, that strange name.
Miklagard, I repeated silently. But, with a shake of his shoulders, he went on in a different direction. 'So many miles they

travelled, pushing on, on, into strange lands where unknown trees and flowers flourished, where unlikely animals thrived, where a man's very skin was of a different hue.'

'What drove them on?' I whispered. It was all but unimaginable, to think of those men in their frail boats, so far from home, voyaging into the unknown.

'Trade, for the most part,' Gurdyman said, grinning as my face fell in disappointment. 'Trade, or the need to find new lands to live in. I am sorry to give you so prosaic an answer, child, but we must always face the truth, even when it is not what we had hoped it would be.'

A memory surfaced. 'Hrype's rune stones!' I exclaimed, remembering.

Gurdyman looked at me approvingly. '*Yes*,' he agreed. 'They were fashioned from the translucent green stone that is brought out of the east.' He grabbed a fold of the glorious, heavy silk shawl that he always wore and thrust it at me. 'This, too, reached my hands only after a very long journey. The fabric is precious, Lassair, and silk of this quality is reserved for great kings and emperors.' He smoothed the shawl delicately, his fingers hovering over the image of a magnificent and surely imaginary bird, with a brilliant blue head and a great fan of tail feathers that seemed to be dotted with eyes. Elsewhere, set against the same dark red background, flowers, leaves and lithe little creatures like weasels flowed together in an intricate pattern. 'One of my own forebears brought home this shawl. It cost him dear, for in exchange he had to part with a lot more of his skins than he would have liked. But, you see, he fell in love with it, and from the instant he set eyes on it, he knew he had to have it.' He looked down fondly at the shawl. 'He brought it for his sister, my mother, whom he dearly loved,' he added softly, 'because she was barren and he wished to bring the smile back to her face.'

'But she can't have been barren because . . .' I began. Then I stopped, because I recalled what he had once told me: *My mother was advanced in years, and my birth was treated as a miracle.*

Gurdyman acted as if he hadn't heard. 'There is a great road that stretches for thousands of miles,' he began, his face dreamy, 'and along it pass caravans of merchants, their pack animals laden with the treasures of the east. They travel westwards, and the traders of the west journey eastwards to meet them, and where the two converge there is a great city on the water. It is a city of graceful towers and warm, honey-coloured stonework, and it is riven by a stretch of water where the tides rip through as fast as a galloping horse. There, where men go to trade the greatest treasures of East and West, there are markets so vibrant, so thrilling, that all are reluctant to waste their time in sleep.'

I tried to imagine such a place. I failed. The biggest town I knew was Cambridge, and, although we undoubtedly had our share of merchants from near and far, I hadn't noticed anyone here being all that reluctant to retire at nightfall.

With a start, Gurdyman came out of his reverie. 'Enough,' he said. 'It is time to begin our lesson.'

Having aroused my curiosity by showing me his map, Gurdyman seized the moment and leapt straight into explaining how the Norsemen had succeeded not only in discovering the routes to the far-flung places they visited but, perhaps even more importantly, had managed to find their way home again.

'They had faith in their ships,' he said, 'those light, sure-footed vessels that were sufficiently shallow-drafted that they did not run aground as they traversed the great river routes. Under sail, the ships were so fast that they seemed to skim over the waves. When the wind failed, the mariners removed the mast to prevent wind resistance and set to at the oars.'

It seemed to me, listening, that Gurdyman must surely have been speaking from personal experience. At what point in his long and eventful life, I wondered, had he sailed with the Norsemen? And how had he come by all this knowledge? He had told me once that he studied with the Moors of Spain when he was a youth, but today's lesson concerned the wisdom of a very different sort of people . . .

What he told me next sounded like magic.

He had been describing the ways by which the Norsemen navigated, and much of it was based on sound common sense. Sailing close in to shore, a mariner would look out for familiar landmarks, noting them in sequence, much as I had tried to illustrate my pathetic little attempt at indicating the way home to Aelf Fen by drawing a particular tree, stream or cottage. The mariners also used the Pole Star to steer by; that, too, was familiar, for one of my earliest childhood lessons was how to locate the bright star that lies where the Pointers indicate. *If you know where North lies*, my father had explained, *you can find your way*. It's very easy to become lost in the fens, where it's often misty and where the land and the water are constantly changing. All fen children learn young how to find the Pole Star. If you're lost out on the fens overnight and nobody finds you, you'll likely be dead by morning.

Gurdyman told me of other ways in which the Norse mariners had used the world around them to navigate. Over many generations of observation, they built up a knowledge of the winds: if it was warm and wet, it blew from the south-west; if it was cold and wet, from the north-east. They learned to utilize the length of daylight as an indicator of how far north they were. They observed bird behaviour. They studied the tides. There was more, much more, and it was all based on sound common sense.

Then Gurdyman's voice changed – I *know* it did, I heard it – and he moved on to tell me of things that were nothing to do with common sense at all.

'The Norse ships frequently carried a dragon's head,' he said. Fleetingly an image formed in my mind – something I had seen, in a dream, perhaps? Then it was gone. 'But the dragon was a creature of the sea,' Gurdyman went on, 'and drew his power from the water element. Approaching land, the figurehead had to be removed, for the people on the shore feared that the mighty dragon would offend the good spirits of the earth.' He leaned closer. 'The mariners believed a ship found her own way home,' he said, very softly. 'Their skills helped, of course, but ultimately it was up to the craft herself, and a powerful dragon's head on the prow would cleave a way through the mists, the storms, the flooding tide and the howling winds and bring the ship safe to port.'

Then the fleeting image clarified.

I saw a ship. It was a long, sleek craft, flying through the

spray and the wave-tops like an arrow shot from a bow. Her
square sail was stretched taught with the wind that drove
her, and the dragon on her prow breathed flame and smoke from
its flared nostrils. The dragon – or perhaps it was the ship –
spoke a name: *Malice-striker*.

I became aware of Gurdyman's voice. It seemed he spoke
more loudly, as if calling me back from wherever it was I had
strayed. It seemed that now he was quoting the words of
someone else; perhaps from one of the sagas of long ago.

'. . . and the heavens were heavy with snow-bearing cloud,'
he intoned. 'The king sent his men to search the skies for a
clear patch, so that they might see the Sun and note his position, but no break in the clouds was to be found. Then the
king summoned his steersman, and commanded him to tell
him where the Sun was, and the steersman took his stone,
and, putting it to his eye, stared up at the angry skies. Then,
lo!, through the power of the sunstone he could see wherefrom
came the Sun's light. Bowing to the king, he said, *Behold,
Lord, the invisible Sun is no longer hidden*, and he indicated
to the king where the Sun rode, high above the snow clouds.'

I was there. I was standing beside the king – a tall, broad,
burly figure; bearded, a gold circlet on his long hair, wrapped
in heavy furs – and I felt his power and his majesty coming
off him like the heat from a fire. I saw his steersman, kneeling
before him; in his hands he held a square-cut crystal, translucent, softly shining. A deep voice said, *solstenen*.

'Sunstone,' I whispered.

I felt strange. My head was light, as if I hadn't eaten for a
long time. I stared around the familiar little courtyard, but it
seemed to be obscured by a wet, cold mist that swirled up out
of some unknown, dread source.

Through the mist I thought I heard Gurdyman's voice; at
least, I believed it was his. The voice spoke of a talisman; an
object so sacred, so secret, that few even suspected its existence. It came from far away and its powers were legion.

Its powers were *terrifying*.

It sharpened inner sight; it both permitted entry to the
unknown realms and provided protection from their perils. It
gave access to . . .

Abruptly the voice ceased, as if a thick, heavy door had been closed on the speaker. My head spun and, although I tried to cry out, I was dumb. Then I fell forward on to the table, my head cushioned by my arms, and everything went dark.

Gurdyman sent me to bed early. It was, I suppose, a way of acknowledging that he might have pushed me a bit too far in the day's instruction. While I'm delighted that he treats me not as a fragile female but as someone desperate to learn and ready for any challenge, at times I feel it would be nice if he remembered that we aren't all as tough and experienced as he is. In fact, I doubt if *anyone* is, with the exception of Hrype.

I hadn't wanted to eat, but Gurdyman insisted I cleared my bowl of stew before I went up the ladder to my room. When, at last, I took off my boots and my over gown and lay beneath the covers, I was so exhausted that I fell asleep almost immediately.

I am dreaming. I see a tall, broad, burly figure, no more than a dark outline, on the edge of vision. When I turn to face it – *him* – there's nothing there.

I'm in a long, narrow passage. Outside? Within a building? There is no way of knowing. I look up, searching for a ceiling or the night sky, but all I can see is darkness. Whatever is hunting for me is right behind me. I spin round to look *and I can't make it out.* I sense hands, long-fingered, reaching out for me. The flesh of my back chills and contracts, as if in terrified anticipation of the touch that must surely come. Suddenly I hear a noise . . . it's a thin, whistling sound, almost like a signal . . . one predator calling to another?

I stifle a moan. They must not know I am there. But then I hear a series of slow thumps, very near.

They have found me.

Then I am thrust abruptly into wakefulness.

Gurdyman was bending over me, his laboured, whistling breathing loud in my ear. He said, very softly, 'Get out of bed, Lassair, and come with me. We must hide.'

I did as he commanded, grabbing my shawl off the bed and wrapping it tightly round me. Gurdyman preceded me down the ladder, puffing hard, his feet making the thump I had heard in my dream. In a moment of perception, I realized then why it is he was happy to let me sleep in the room that was once his: it was becoming just too much of a struggle for him to climb up there.

I knew where we were going. Keeping very close behind him, I followed him along the passage and through the arched entrance to the corridor that leads down to the crypt. I helped him close and bar the door. Suddenly in total darkness, I was glad of his hand, reaching for mine, leading me on down the steps, left, left again, down more steps, and into the crypt.

He guided me to the left of the entrance, turning me. I felt the softness of his cot behind my legs and sank down on to it. I heard him move across the floor, and there was a sudden spark from a flint. Then the blessed light of a candle shone out, sending the darkness back into the corners.

Feeling sick and shivery, I let out the breath I'd been holding. I stared at Gurdyman. He was standing in the middle of the room, quite still, his head slightly on one side. He was listening.

I could hear nothing but the rapid beat of my alarmed heart. Trying to calm myself, I slowed my breathing. *You're safe*, I told myself. *Nobody can find you down here.*

Who was looking for me? It did not even cross my mind that whoever it was could be after Gurdyman: I knew he wasn't. The giant must have found out that someone from the family he was targeting – *my* family – had come here to this house, and he had followed. Now he was about to break in, so that he could search through my belongings, just as he had everyone else's. Well, he'd be disappointed because . . .

How had Gurdyman known he was coming?

Hard on the heels of that question, bursting across my consciousness like a shooting star, came another: *Was Gurdyman's assumption right?*

He was still standing there; still listening.

I nerved myself to speak. I had to ask; he might be mistaken, and we could be huddling down here for nothing. I drew a breath, opened my mouth . . .

From above us, over beyond the far wall of the crypt – the direction of Gurdyman's twisty-turny house – I heard a bump, followed by the very faint sound of slow, stealthy footfalls.

Gurdyman was not mistaken. Somebody was in his house.

Desperate though I was to ask how he could possibly have realized the intruder was on his way, I dared not utter a sound. Instead, I tried to work it out for myself. Perhaps Gurdyman had been out on some mysterious nocturnal errand, and seen a suspicious stranger lurking nearby. He does go out at night, and I know better than to ask where he goes and what he does. He did once mention a sacred well, and a secret midnight meeting of black-cloaked magicians, but I'm all but sure he was teasing me.

I was comforting myself with this pleasantly reasonable solution when I realized something: the cot on which I sat was warm from Gurdyman's body. He had not been outside; he'd been right here in the crypt.

How else could he have known? Had he heard the intruder in the alley? No, that didn't seem likely, for down in the crypt we were deep underground. It was only just possible to hear the intruder above us now, as he paced through Gurdyman's house.

Something else occurred to me. The first sound made by the intruder had not come from the front of the house, where the stout wooden door opens on to the alley. It had come from the rear, where, between it and the narrow alleyway beyond, the little open courtyard is enclosed by a high wall.

A *very* high, thick wall, which merges on either side with the rear walls of the neighbouring houses, and which is even topped with thatch, as they are.

No man, surely, could have scaled it and dropped down into the courtyard without serious injury. Could he?

This man was a giant, I reminded myself. He was long-legged and very strong. Very probably, he was capable of feats beyond the scope of normal men.

My fear overcame me. I crawled to the back of the little cot and curled up with my back to the wall, draping my shawl over my head and face so that only my eyes were visible. It was a senseless act, really, for if the intruder found the hidden door, he'd be down here in a flash and no shawl in the world would hide me from him.

As if he had picked up my thoughts, Gurdyman turned to me, giving me a reassuring smile. Very quietly he whispered, 'Nobody yet has discovered the secret, child, although many have searched the house. Do not be afraid.'

I repeated those last four words, over and over again. After some time, I realized that the all-but-undetectable sounds from above had ceased.

Gurdyman looked at me. 'Can you sleep there, on my cot?' he asked softly.

I nodded. Now that the threat had gone – or so I hoped – I was appreciating how tired I was.

He came across to me, reaching for a folded blanket and covering me with it. 'Then do so,' he said. 'The intruder has gone, but he may still be outside, alert for any sound or movement within the house. It would be wise not to venture back up there until morning.'

I snuggled down under the blanket. 'What about you?' Fond as I am of Gurdyman, I did not welcome the thought of sharing a bed with him.

He grinned, as if he knew exactly what I was thinking. 'I have much to do,' he said. 'I shall be over there –' he pointed – 'at my work bench.' He reached out his hands, placing them either side of my head. His touch was warm and comforting, and I felt my mind fill with calm, gentle thoughts. 'Sleep, Lassair,' he intoned.

I slept.

SIX

Gurdyman and I went through his house together in the morning, both of us hawk-eyed as we hunted for clues to what our night-time intruder had been up to. It was all too obvious that someone had gone through the house and its contents very thoroughly. To the casual eye, Gurdyman does not own much – and, certainly, everything of any value or interest is kept safely, securely and secretly down in the crypt – but the overturned benches and tables, and the pots swept down off the shelves, told us that every last item had been picked up and examined. If only it had stopped there. As in the other dwellings he'd searched, the intruder had a heavy hand when it came to putting things back. A couple of pots were broken, and it looked as if a small stack of wooden platters had been trodden on. I watched as, with a small sigh, Gurdyman picked up the detritus.

'I'm so sorry,' I said impulsively, my heart torn at his expression.

He turned to me, a cracked platter in his hand, a kindly smile on his face. 'Why are you apologizing?'

I gestured at the turmoil. 'All this.'

'You didn't do it,' he pointed out.

'I know, but the intruder is searching the places where my kin live, and now he's come here, and I—'

'Hush, child.' Gurdyman put the platter down and came to stand beside me, a hand on my shoulder. 'We are not responsible for the acts of others. Only our own, and nothing *you* have done has invited the attentions of this intruder.' He gave my arm a pat. 'And it is only inanimate objects that have been damaged.'

He was right, and his words consoled me. Nevertheless, it was with great trepidation that I climbed the ladder into the little upper room to see what had happened to my own belongings.

The bed had been searched. The straw mattress sat slightly askew on the wooden bed frame, so presumably the intruder had lifted it to see if anything was hidden beneath it. It also looked sort of crushed, as if large hands had felt all over it for concealed treasures. The pillows and covers had been removed and left in a heap on the end of the bed. They, too, had received the squashing treatment. My few spare garments had been dragged from the bag in which I'd brought them from Aelf Fen, and now lay scattered on the floor. I felt sick as carefully I smoothed them out and folded them. The thought of a violent stranger's touch on my personal belongings shocked me deeply.

The leather satchel in which I carry the tools of my healer's craft had received the most thorough attention. He – I would have sworn on everything I hold dear that it was *he* – had emptied it and laid every last item out on the floor in three ragged lines.

Nothing was missing: I knew that with total certainty, for I had packed the satchel myself two days ago. I had removed nothing since, and nor had anyone else.

I sat down on the floor and set about repacking my belongings. Then I put the bed to rights. I sank down on to it, deep in thought.

Yet another family dwelling place had been searched. Again, nothing was missing. The conclusion was obvious: whatever the searcher was hunting for, he still hadn't found it.

What would he do next? Would he start all over again, revisiting us all, this time not stopping till he'd torn up floorboards, demolished houses? But that, surely, would be too risky, for this man had killed, twice, and must realize that it would not be nearly so easy a second time to catch his victims unaware, even assuming he continued to evade whatever forces of law and order were now on his trail.

I wondered fleetingly if Gurdyman would report this break-in to the authorities, and knew instantly that he would not. He was a man who valued his privacy, and it was not in the least likely that he would wish to draw attention to himself in that way.

If the intruder were to be caught, he would hang, having

committed murder as well as his other crimes. Would that not persuade him to be sensible?

Being sensible meant giving up. As I sat there on my bed in Gurdyman's house, I sent up a brief and heartfelt prayer that our intruder would do just that.

Gurdyman and I settled down to a period of intense work. My mind was kept fully occupied during the waking hours, and, exhausted, I slept soundlessly and dreamlessly every night. In consequence, I barely had time to think about the intruder. We had a swift visit from Hrype, who closeted himself with Gurdyman, emerged looking preoccupied, and only in what seemed like an afterthought remembered to tell me that my kin back at Aelf Fen were all safe and well. Morcar, he reported, slowly recovering from his grief and adjusting to the prospect of life without his mother, had gone back to the Breckland.

If Hrype was out and about again, I calculated, and Morcar had left, then presumably the threat to Edild had gone. I breathed a sigh of relief. It looked as if my prayer had been answered, and the big, red-bearded giant who had been terrorizing my family had indeed given up and gone away.

Gurdyman introduced a fresh field of study, concerning the extraordinary substance called quicksilver. I was fascinated by it from the start; by its surprising weight; by its shining, glittering appearance; by its ability to shatter itself into beautiful little silver balls, then, if you put those balls together, form itself back into a smooth whole. My fascination was certainly increased by the fact that Gurdyman treated it with such awe. It was, he told me firmly, toxic. In case I was still in any doubt about what toxic meant, he told me that, too.

Despite its poisonous qualities, Gurdyman told me that quicksilver is used in a particular area of healing; one which, he added, I would no doubt experience myself if I practised my healing craft in the town. Calmly, and without a hint of awkwardness, he explained about the diseases that spread through the act of love. Assuming me to be innocent of such matters, he told me about the sexual hunger of the male sex, whereby a man away from the comforts of his wife's bed will pay for sex with a town prostitute.

I knew of such things. Edild explained briefly to me, when we treated one of Lord Gilbert's visitors who had recently returned from a sojourn in London. Gurdyman, however, went into far more detail. By the time he had finished describing the skin lesions and the pus-filled sores, I was feeling quite faint. It was a huge relief when we turned from theory to practice, and he set about teaching me how to make the quicksilver ointment used in treatment.

Gurdyman might have been able to concentrate indefinitely, but I couldn't. After a gruelling week in which I didn't see daylight except when I was dispatched to go out and buy food and drink, my teacher finally noticed he had worn me out and announced that I might have a break from my studies.

While we had been closeted in the crypt, full-blossoming spring had at last arrived. We had passed the equinox and April had come in, full of sunny smiles interspersed with soft, warm rain. On my first free day, I hurried out of town and went to stand beside the river. Such was my pleasure in simply breathing in the cool, fragrant air that I might have been ingesting the best French wine.

Spring had enticed even Gurdyman out of his underground lair, and he had set up a small work bench out in the little courtyard. He was busy on his mapping again; a task for which my assistance was more of a hindrance than a help. After a morning in which I succeeded in doing nothing except irritate him, it occurred to me that now might be a good opportunity to slip home and see my family.

Gurdyman was so intent on his work that I had to repeat my request before he realized what I was saying. Looking up at me, a frown on his amiable face, he said, 'Yes, child, that is an extremely good idea!'

I hurried up to my room to fetch my satchel. I would not take anything else, since I'd only be gone for a couple of days; three at the most. It would make a pleasant change to make the familiar journey without having to carry a heavy bag; having my father to carry it for me had been a rare pleasure the last time I'd made the trip. I went back out to the courtyard to say farewell to Gurdyman, telling him I'd be back soon. He waved a vague hand in acknowledgement.

As I slipped out of the house, my spirits high as the spring-time sun in the brilliant blue sky, I was very grateful for Gurdyman's preoccupation. I'd been worried that, recalling how my father had insisted on escorting me on the way to Cambridge, Gurdyman might similarly stipulate that I wasn't to make the return journey unless someone went with me. That, I told myself firmly, was quite unnecessary. For one thing, spring had, as it always does, filled people with the need to get out into the good fresh air, and the roads, tracks and paths would be busy with traffic. There was safety in numbers. For another, the fact that Hrype had felt able to leave his beloved Edild unguarded while he came to visit Gurdyman indicated that he no longer sensed a threat. Hrype was one of the wisest people I knew. If he believed the giant had given up and gone away, then that was good enough for me.

They jumped me on a lonely stretch of track where there was nobody about to hear or see.

They must have been observing me for some time, for this part of the journey was a little-used short cut which, I'm sure, few people know about. *I* knew of it, however, and they knew I used it.

To begin with, I was so frightened that I couldn't think. I'd been striding along, reflecting happily how pleased my family would be to have a surprise visit from me, and hoping my mother would have something with which to make a special, celebratory meal. I wasn't aware of danger until it was almost upon me; I heard a faint sound, and was in the very act of spinning round to see if anyone was there when they attacked.

They. Yes, I was sure even then that there was more than one of them. Not that I could tell by looking, or by listening. A heavy sack was thrown over my head, effectively blinding me, and a rope was thrown round me just above my waist, pinning my arms to my sides. I heard scuffling sounds as they tried to suppress my struggles, and a sharp yell of pain as my wildly kicking feet caught someone in a tender spot.

Then I was lifted off the ground, one person supporting my head and shoulders, another, my legs. I yelled as loudly as I could, but the thick cloth bag must have muffled the sound. They can't have been worried about being overheard, or else they would have gagged me, and after a few moments this fact penetrated through my panic and I stopped shouting.

They did not carry me far. I tried to count their paces, and thought I reached perhaps two or three hundred. Then I heard water. One of my abductors called out something in a language that sounded vaguely familiar; just a few words, softly spoken, sounding like a query. From quite close and below, another voice answered. Then I felt myself being lowered, and I was set down on what felt to my questing hands like a surface of wooden planks.

For a moment, I was left alone. I heard them talking quietly and urgently, and thought I counted at least four voices. There was a splashing sound, then I sensed movement. The splashing settled down into a regular rhythm, like rowing.

Was I on a boat? Yes, I must be. It seemed highly likely, as the place where they had jumped on me was quite near a tributary of one of the main branches of the fenland river system. Were we even now setting out along the winding, twisting, secretive waterways of the fens? Oh, *oh*, if we were, then we were about to lose ourselves in one of the finest hiding places I knew. If a mist came down, as it frequently did towards the day's end, whatever craft we were on could glide right past my own village and nobody would be any the wiser.

The fear came back, a hundredfold. Nobody would come looking for me, because *nobody knew I was missing*. Gurdyman believed I was on my way home to Aelf Fen, where I'd stay for at least a couple of days and probably more. But, in my village, they didn't even know I was coming.

Beneath the heavy hood, my eyes filled with desperate tears. With my arms bound to my sides, I could only just manage to lift a hand up to wipe them away.

After quite a while, there was a gentle thud, as if the boat had bumped up against a jetty. Then I was lifted up and passed from one pair of arms to another, and I felt myself being carried up. Up a ladder? Oh, but supposing the person carrying me slipped, or dropped me? I gave a whimper of fear. Then I was laid down once more, this time on something woolly which had a faint smell that confirmed it was a sheepskin.

Presently the sounds of rowing started again. They had, I guessed, just transferred me from a small boat to a larger one.

Time passed. I wasn't sure how long; it seemed an eternity. At some point, one of the abductors came and put something soft beneath my head. Unless they were particularly cruel, and lulling me into feeling safe when I was far from it, then it looked as though they did not mean me harm.

Not yet, anyway.

I began to feel cold. Either the sun was going down, or we were somewhere in deep shade. I rather thought the former; I seemed to have been on the boat for ages. Someone put a cover over me. I explored it with my fingertips. It was heavy, and it felt like stiff, coarse wool. It stank, but nevertheless I was grateful for its warmth.

Then I sensed a change in the boat's movement. Our progress over the water had been smooth and not very fast, accompanied by the sound of the oars, but now the boat was rocking, and whoever had been rowing had stopped. It was hard to be sure under the sacking hood, but I sensed that there had been a great change in our surroundings. It felt very much as if a small, contained waterway had given way to something altogether bigger . . .

After quite a long time, someone approached me and I sensed him crouch down by my side. Then the hood was removed. I took a deep breath of fresh, moist, salty air, and turned to look at my abductor.

He was huge.

He was staring at me intently, his light eyes unblinking. His hair was long, thick and reddish-fair, reaching down below his shoulders. On either side of his face, two plaits hung down, braided with leather thongs. A broad band, consisting of precisely woven strands of different-coloured leather, was bound around his brow. His beard was luxurious, and redder in colour than his hair. He was dressed in a deep blue, sleeveless tunic, bordered at the neck, hem and cuffs with bands of

embroidery in a copper colour. Beneath it he wore close-fitting
breeches. His feet were bare.

I was very much afraid that I knew who he was.

His face was expressionless, giving me no clue as to what
he was thinking. Or what he wanted with me, although I was
trying hard not to speculate on that. He drew my eyes and all
my attention, and it was with an effort that I looked away
from him to see where I was.

I was on a ship, just as I'd thought. It was long and extremely
graceful, its narrow prow and stern flaring out to a broader
mid-section. I was lying in the stern – above me and to my
right, I could see a big man holding the end of what I assumed
was the steering oar; and in front of him, on the gunwale, I
made out the rowlocks. But nobody sat at the oars now; there
was no need.

From a tall mast in the middle of the ship billowed out a
huge, rectangular sail, which effectively blocked my view of
the front of the craft. A steady wind filled it. With a gasp
of horror I pushed myself up so that I could see over the
side of the ship.

We were out on the open sea, and the distant land was no
more than a low, dark line. Beyond it, the sun had set, going
down in a spectacular display of red, pink and gold.

I forced my shocked brain to concentrate. The land was to
my left, with the sun going down behind it, so that was west.
And that meant we were sailing north. Sailing very fast, in
fact, for a strong south-westerly wind was blowing hard and,
with the sail angled to receive it, our craft was flying over the
waves, sending silvery-white plumes of spray high in the air.

Shocked into protest, I turned back to the bearded giant and
screamed, 'What do you want with me?' I paused for breath.
'*Where are you taking me?*'

His lips spread in a grin, revealing white, even teeth. 'You
will find out,' he said. His voice was rich and deep, and he
spoke with a heavy accent. I knew that my language was not
his mother tongue.

He leaned towards me and I shrank from him, terrified.
Instantly he put up his hands in the universal gesture of peace,
pulling back again. He began to speak, in words I didn't

understand, then stopped, frowning in thought. He tried again. 'I will untie,' he said, indicating with a nod of his head the ropes still wound around my upper arms. 'Yes?'

'Yes,' I agreed. I was totally bemused. He had clearly seen that I was frightened, and he seemed to be asking my permission to approach me. Yet he and his crew had abducted me! It made no sense.

Unless – I shivered as the ghastly thought took hold and became the truth – unless they needed me alive and well. Because this red-bearded giant who had come among my kin to search and to kill had not given up at all. Instead, having failed to find whatever he was after by direct means, he now intended to force the location of the thing he sought out of a family member.

That family member being me, and I had absolutely no idea how I was going to answer him.

He was close to me now, reaching his long, powerfully muscled arms around me to untie the knot that secured the rope. His hair brushed my face, and the dying sun set alight the thick red highlights among the blond. I could see individual strands of hair, like fine, bright copper wires.

My mind appeared to have collapsed beneath the strain. Here I was, alone on a speeding ship heading the good Lord above knew where, with four – no, five, *six* – big, burly men. One or more of whom was about to inflict some awful sort of pain on me in order to make me tell them something I didn't even know, and all I could think about was *hair*.

He had unwound the rope and now he sat back on his heels, coiling it neatly. He was staring at me, and I felt he was concentrating as hard on me as I was on him.

I took a quick look at the darkening water stretching out on either side of us. The black line of the land seemed further away now. Then I returned my eyes to him. 'Where are we going?' I repeated, this time in a whisper.

Something was happening to me. I was feeling dizzy, and the first stirrings of nausea were beginning, as if I'd eaten a bad piece of fish. I swallowed, and that made it worse.

'Look at the horizon,' he said.

I must have appeared confused. He pointed one huge arm

out over the vast, empty sea to the east. 'Set – put your eyes
to a – a steady point that does not move,' he said, halting here
and there as if searching for words that I would understand.

I twisted my head to look out beyond the tall figure of the
man at the steering oar. Too fast: vertigo hit me hard, and it
seemed as if the whole world was spinning around me. I felt
the first rush of vomit come burning up my throat and into
my mouth.

Perhaps he guessed it would happen. Perhaps it always did,
when people were out on the open sea for the first time.
Anyway, he was ready. Even as I retched, he had a leather
bucket held ready under my mouth. As the convulsions
continued, I felt a strong, warm hand placed firmly on my
forehead. With the other hand, he pulled my hair back and
out of the way.

Presumably, I thought, before the suicidal misery of seasickness drove everything else out of my head, he preferred his
prisoners not to stink of vomit when he interrogated and
tortured them . . .

Someone gave me a cup of cool, refreshing water when I'd
finished. I batted away the big hand that held it – I could not
tolerate the thought of swallowing even a drop of water, since
I knew I'd bring it straight up again – but the hand was insistent.

'Drink,' a deep voice said. I raised my head a tiny fraction
and looked into the face of a stubble-headed, bronze-bearded
crewman whose bare upper arms were encircled by beautiful,
intricate tattoos. He mimed taking a sip of water, swishing it
around and then spitting it out, and I understood. I did as he
suggested, aiming into the bucket. Someone had emptied it.
To my surprise, the water felt good, and I risked swallowing
a little.

The tattooed man nodded his encouragement, and said something in a tongue that sounded a bit like singing. From behind
me, the red-haired giant spoke; I hadn't realized he was there.

'Thorben says it is good to drink,' he translated, 'for always
it is easier to be sick when there is something to bring up.'

It was not a particularly cheerful thought.

It was almost dark now, I noticed. A pair of lanterns had

been lit, well below the level of the gunwales. The moon was rising. Were we going to sail all night? Oh, dear Lord, was that *safe*? Supposing we ran into something?

The red-haired giant had brought more covers: a thick, soft wool blanket and another skin. He lifted me up, as if I weighed no more than a child, and, taking hold of the sheepskin that I had been lying on – rumpled up now from my twisting and turning – shook it out and spread it out on the boards of the deck. When I lay back down on it, it was warm from my body. Then he tucked me up in the thick blanket, putting the skin on top. The stinking, stiff cover he rolled up and thrust under one brawny arm. He sniffed at it, miming disgusted recoil, and, despite everything, I grinned.

He stood looking down at me. Then he said, 'Go to sleep.'

It was as if he had spoken a powerful charm. My eyelids were suddenly heavy, and I felt myself drifting. I was snug in my wrappings; the pillow under my head and the sheepskin on which I lay were soft and comfortable; the luxurious woolly blanket was wonderfully warm. My last thought, before I fell asleep, was that the ship's motion that before had made me so sick now felt like a mother's gentle rocking of her baby's crib.

SEVEN

It was a combination of light and hunger that woke me.

The rising sun was shining directly into my face and, when I raised myself on one elbow to look out at the sea flying past, it was as if tiny, golden fires had been lit on the top of every wave.

I was so hungry that my stomach was growling like an angry wolf.

A different crewman stood at the steering oar, and I did not like to disturb him. Other mariners were visible, all looking preoccupied with whatever they were doing, and I could hear sounds of activity from the fore part of the ship. Maybe that was where they ate? Hopefully, I stood up, intending to go and find out. They had taken care of me so far, I reasoned, and so it didn't seem likely that they were planning to starve me to death.

My legs felt like feathers. Staggering, I grasped hold of the top of the gunwale, standing quite still. Fully expecting the dreadful sickness to start again, I looked round for the bucket. It was there, just by where my head had lain all night, and, again, someone had rinsed it out. These men, whoever they were, kept a clean ship.

I waited. Nothing happened, except that, after a while, I sensed that my legs were actually going to hold me up. I risked a step. Two steps. To my amazement, I realized that, as if utilizing some latent skill I hadn't known I possessed, my body was reacting to the ship's motion. I have, on rare occasions, ridden a horse, and this new sensation felt in some ways similar. The beautiful ship beneath me was galloping over the waves, responding to every nuance of the sea's powerful restlessness. And I, standing on her narrow deck, was responding to *her*, my legs bending automatically to compensate for her movement, my body – my spirit, perhaps – in tune with that of the ship.

It was in that instant that I fell in love with her.

Buoyed up, exhilarated by my new confidence, I moved on along the deck, beneath the huge, full sail. In front of it, I spotted a small rowing boat, upturned and lashed to a thwart. It was, I guessed, the means by which the abductors had transported me from the narrow fenland waterways out to the ship. I went on towards the front of the ship. There were, indeed, crewmen up there, and they were sharing out food.

It was probably my hunger that made me take in that fact first. Then, in the same instant, I saw what reared up behind them and screamed.

The long, spiked neck of a dragon rose into the clear morning sky, soaring up, up, to the high, proud head, reddish in colour, the fierce mouth spouting a blaze of flame, the pale, wide eye staring out intently over the sea . . .

Somebody laughed, and as I unfroze from my terror, I saw what I should have seen instantly: this was not a real dragon, but a beautifully carved figurehead, up there above and in front of the ship, bravely leading the way through whatever perils the sea cast at it. At *him*, I corrected myself instantly. While the ship was undoubtedly *she*, the dragon could be nothing else but *he*.

The red-haired giant was beside me. The morning sun shone on his bare head, and in that bright, early light, he looked more fair than auburn. He was smiling. 'Behold, Nidhöggr,' he said, pointing up at the dragon. Then, frowning in thought, he added, 'In your tongue, Malice-striker.'

A deep shudder went through me. *Malice-striker*. The name of the ship I had twice seen in my visions. And now here I was, on board the very same vessel.

I tried desperately to ground myself, absorbing the good, solid wood of the deck planks beneath my feet; the feel of the fresh salt-tasting wind on my face. As the dream world receded, and I saw with the eye of reason, I understood that the craft on to which my abductors had brought me was subtly different from the vision ship. Lean and graceful though she was, the vision ship had been shaped like an arrow, and shields had been positioned along both gunwales. My vision ship was, without doubt, a war ship. Whereas this craft was . . .

I spun round to the giant. 'What do you call this ship?' I demanded.

'*Malice-striker*,' he repeated, grinning again, as if in amusement that I appeared to have lost my wits.

'No, I mean, what sort of ship is she?'

'Ah.' He nodded in understanding. 'This is what we call a knarr. A ship for carrying goods, people, horses, cattle – anything that has to be ferried over the sea.' He reached out a big hand and patted the gunwale behind him. 'Broad and strong, high-sided and robust, the knarr is built to be reliably seaworthy.'

A knarr, I repeated silently. This Malice-striker was a cargo ship. In that case, there must have been a predecessor that shared her name. In a flash of intuition, I knew I was right. Gathering all my courage, I forced myself to look the giant straight in the eye and said softly, for I wanted only him to hear, 'She is not the first ship to bear the name.'

His expression of astonishment gave me a brief but intoxicating moment of proud joy. He had captured me, bound me, made me his prisoner and was now speeding away with me on his ship, to God only knew what destination and for a purpose I didn't even dare guess at. It was high time I struck a return blow, if only the feeble, pointless one of taking him by surprise.

He recovered very quickly. Grabbing my arm, he led me a few paces away from the avid eyes and ears of his crew. Leaning down to speak right into my ear, he hissed, 'How do you know that?'

I pulled my arm out of his grasp, rubbing at it. There would be five little bruises there later. 'Because I saw her predecessor,' I said, forcing a calmness I was far from feeling.

Violently he shook his head, as if by so doing he could negate my statement. 'It is not possible,' he whispered.

I shrugged. 'Possible or not, I did.' I wondered fleetingly whether to go on, or to leave him guessing. I decided to tell him. 'I saw a vision,' I said. 'From the past. A long, slender ship, sailing very fast along a wild shore. The figurehead was a dragon, just like yours.' A little devil was prompting me to go on, and, dangerous though I knew it was, I did. 'That ship

was no knarr,' I whispered. 'No *cargo boat*.' I emphasized the
words, putting scorn into my voice. 'She was a warship, and
she carried fierce, brave warriors frantic for the fight.'

Dangerous did not begin to describe it. I saw the fury ignite
in his light eyes, and the fist that caught the side of my head
was so fast that it appeared to come out of nowhere. I fell,
awkwardly, collapsing in the angle between the deck and the
ship's side. I felt something wet and warm on my head: my
own blood. Then my view of the deck, the giant, the crew and
the sky was invaded by darkness, and my head fell with a
painful thump on to the deck.

It was night when I woke up. The moon rode high in the sky,
but she was partly obscured by cloud. I was back in my place
to the left of the steering oar, in the stern of the ship. Once again,
I was lying on sheepskin, my head – bound in a bandage – on
a pillow, blankets covering me. I had a terrible headache. I tried
to look round for my leather satchel – it must be here, since I'd
been carrying it slung across my body when they took me – but
I couldn't see it.

My movement alerted the broad figure sitting beside me,
visible as little more than a black shape. I caught a glint of
light from his bald head, and a deep voice said, 'Einar regrets
that he hit you so hard.'

Einar. The giant's name was Einar. 'He certainly did,' I
muttered.

'You should not have provoked him. He is very aware that
the glory days are no more, and he does not sail a longship
as did his ancestors.'

Yes, I thought, *that's precisely why I said what I did.*

I wriggled round to try to get a better look at the man beside
me. He was older than the other crewmen, with a wrinkled,
weatherbeaten face that told of years out in the rough elements.
'Who are you?' I asked.

He made a sort of bow, as much as anyone can when they're
sitting down. 'I am Olaf,' he said. 'I am, among other jobs,
the ship's cook.'

Cook. Food. Oh, I'd been hungry this morning, and had
been hoping to be fed when I'd gone exploring up to the prow.

Now, a whole day seemed to have gone by. My belly felt concave. 'Please could you find me something to eat?' I pleaded.

He leaned forward and put a spark to the wick of a lantern, lowering the flame so that the light was small. Then he waved a hand, and I saw a rough wooden platter loaded with bread, strips of dried meat, some sort of pie, and an apple. Beside it there was a stone jar.

Olaf handed me the jar. 'Drink first,' he said. 'Not too fast, or it will come back again.'

The water in the flask was cold, and only tasted faintly of the inside of the jar. I took some slow sips. My head throbbed even more now that I was sitting up. 'I always carry a satchel with me,' I said. 'Where is it?'

Olaf reached behind him. 'Here.'

I took it from him. To hold something from home, something from my normal life that belonged to me, was incredibly comforting. I unfastened the satchel's straps – tucked inside, where I had stowed it before I left Gurdyman's house, was my beloved shawl – and felt around for the remedy I sought: a strong painkiller made up of white willow, feverfew, valerian and just a touch of the powerful medicines that we extract from monkshood and poppy; the ones that are deadly if you are too heavy-handed. I put the bitter powder on my tongue, washing it down with a mouthful of water.

Olaf was watching me with interest. 'You travel well-prepared,' he remarked. Peering into my satchel, he added with a smile, 'You appear to anticipate many injuries and much sickness.'

'I'm a healer,' I said.

His eyes widened. 'A healer.' He nodded, as if something had just become clear. Then, before I had time to ask, he pushed the platter towards me and urged me to start eating.

'Of course,' I said through a mouthful, as the first sharp edge of my hunger eased off, 'I should have known better than to risk such a provocative remark to a man as violent as Einar.'

Olaf looked at me, and in the dim light I made out a quizzical expression. 'Violent?'

So that was the game we were going to play, I thought. The crew were going to pretend they had no idea what their captain had done; that he had broken his way into several dwellings and committed assaults and a couple of murders. 'Violent,' I repeated firmly. 'Two dead, one of them my aunt, one my sister's mother-in-law. I suppose,' I added with heavy sarcasm, 'he would say they got in the way. Perhaps they *provoked* him.'

Olaf opened his mouth as if to speak, muttered something and then stopped. 'Do not judge him until you know,' he said.

Oh, yes, there would no doubt be some justifying explanation, I reflected angrily. Einar would say that he'd been forced to act as he did, since finding whatever it was he sought was more important than any other considerations.

He still hadn't got his hands on it, I remembered. And now he seemed to be pinning his hopes on persuading the truth about the object's whereabouts out of me.

Which was going to be a problem, since I had no idea where or what it was.

I looked down at the last scraps of food on my plate. Suddenly I wasn't hungry any more.

I had been lulled into the illusion that I was going to be all right with this extraordinary band of mariners. Despite the fact that their leader, this Einar, had assaulted and killed in his quest for the object he sought, despite the fact that they had jumped on me, bundled me into their boat and were now sailing away with me, whether I liked it or not, they had treated me kindly. I had been fooled by soft sheepskins, warm blankets and decent food. Yet only that morning Einar had hit me so hard that I'd been unconscious all day.

From some dark hiding place, fear crept out and swirled around me, enclosing me in its tightening coils.

I must not let them see I was afraid. Must not even allow this Olaf, posing as a cheery, friendly ship's cook, to read my true mind.

I turned to him. Gathering my courage, praying that my voice would sound convincingly firm, I said coldly, 'And now, Olaf, I would like you to tell me who you all are, what you want from me and my family, and where you are taking me.'

He looked at me, and I thought I saw compassion in his eyes. 'You must not . . .' he began. Then he stopped. For a few moments he sat in frowning, silent thought. Then he said, 'There is a purpose. We—'

'A purpose, yes, of course there is!' I hissed furiously. 'You're going to try to beat out of me what you believe I know, which is the whereabouts of this *thing* that Einar's been hunting for!' A shaft of pure dread momentarily froze me, as images of that huge fist being raised against me again filled my mind. I clenched my jaws together against the wobbling. 'I'll tell you right now, it won't do any good, because I have no idea what it is you're after or where it is!'

'Hush.' He breathed out the word on a sort of soft whistle, like a man soothing a spooked horse. Suddenly I felt his hand take mine, giving it a reassuring squeeze. 'You have every right to feel afraid and angry,' he went on, his deep voice quiet and gentle, 'and to demand to know where we are taking you.' He paused, and for one wonderful instant I thought he was going to tell me.

I was wrong.

After a long moment, he said, with an unmistakable air of finality, 'I am not permitted to explain. But—' He broke off, and even from where I sat, I sensed the struggle between obeying his alarming captain's orders and answering my questions. Then he said, 'You are a clever young woman. Think about everything that has happened to you since we took you, and decide for yourself if we are—'

Again, he stopped. It was very strange: as if, from somewhere quite near at hand, someone – Einar? – was aware of the conversation and was somehow controlling how much Olaf was allowed to say to me.

Even stranger was that, on that beautiful ship flying over the waves in the silvery moonlight, I fully believed this to be possible. If the ship and her crew were indeed under the command of a man who had such power, then, I reasoned, the way in which I was most likely to guarantee my survival was to do exactly what I was told. And, if I was to avoid any more blows to the head, it would be wise to stop antagonizing the ship's captain.

Olaf stood up, stooping to collect my platter and mug. 'Sleep,' he said. 'We have a long way to go.'

I settled down, pulling the covers over me. The stiff, stinky cover had once again been spread over me, I noticed. The air was damp with spray, and I realized now that this topmost cover had been treated with animal fat – which accounted for the smell – for it was waterproof. My face was wet, but elsewhere I was fairly dry. There was no covered accommodation on board, unless you wanted to go down below the deck level into the hold. Better to be up here exposed to the elements than shoved in down there; I was vastly relieved that Einar hadn't felt it necessary to imprison me. There was no need, of course; there was no way to escape except by throwing myself into the sea. Whatever the future held, I was not that desperate. Not yet . . .

I thought about what Olaf had said. He'd told me to think over all that had happened, and decide for myself. Did he mean what I hoped he did – what, indeed, had already occurred to me? That making me comfortable, feeding me and refraining from shutting me up in the hold were significant? Was I to deduce from this treatment that I was more of a guest than a prisoner?

But they'd snatched me out of my pleasant existence against my will! And I knew without any doubt that Einar wanted something that he believed my family possessed. I was still very afraid that he intended to force me to lead him to it.

Why, then, asked the voice of reason in my head, *is he even now speeding away with you as fast as he can, leaving your home and your kin far behind?*

It was a question I just couldn't answer.

I closed my eyes, but sleep was a long way off. How long since I'd been taken? This was only my second night on board, so nobody I loved would be worrying about me yet. I thought of my mother, then my father, who had been so desperate to keep me safe that he'd escorted me back to Gurdyman's. What would my poor father suffer, once he knew I was missing? But that thought was far too painful, so I arrested it. Perhaps I'd be back again before anyone knew I was gone. Unlikely as it seemed, it was something to cling on to.

I slid a hand inside my under gown and my fingers found
the ring that Rollo gave me, which I wear on a leather thong
round my neck. Rollo: my mysterious stranger, who drops
into my life with no warning, and, equally unpredictably, out
of it again. Rollo: as of last year, my lover. Rollo: part of me
till I die. Shaped like a serpent devouring its own tail, the ring
is made of solid gold. I don't dare wear it on my hand because,
apart from being a constant temptation to thieves, it looks like
a very magical object. Rollo told me it belonged to his grandmother, and she was a witch. I thought he might have been
joking, because so far the ring had shown not the least sign
of magical power.

Now, grasping it in my hand, it comforted me simply because
Rollo had given it to me. He had carried it with him for many
years and through many dangers, this heirloom of his bloodline,
and the fact that he'd wanted me to have it filled my heart
with joy. I had no idea where he was, or when I would see
him again. I only knew that, as long as we both lived, our
lives were entwined and our fates lay together. Sooner or later,
he would find me. Or, perhaps, I thought as the ship sped me
along to an unknown future, *I* would find *him* . . .

I was drowsy now. In that half-state between waking and
sleeping, small fragments of dreams flitted through my mind.
I saw the village, and there was Edild, speaking softly to
Hrype. As if it had been an extension of that vision, all at
once I sensed a warm, furry body snuggling next to me. My
spirit animal had come to comfort me and, knowing Fox, he
would stay close all the time I needed him. Yes, he was probably part of my dream, but I didn't care.

The voyage went on, and I counted three more nights. There
was nothing much for me to do, although I did help Olaf with
some of his more straightforward tasks, such as doling out the
food and scrubbing the wooden platters with sea water after
the crew had eaten. As we worked together, he began to instruct
me in that strangely familiar language he and his crewmen
spoke, and I realized that I knew quite a lot of it already. There
have always been traders who visit the fens, and I'd come
across many more since spending so much of my life in

Cambridge; unwittingly, I must have been absorbing this alien tongue.

I think Olaf saw that time was hanging heavily for me, and took pity on me. When there was something for my hands or my mind to do, it was easier not to feel anxious and scared.

I studied Malice-striker and her crew. The ship was indeed a living thing, just as I had first suspected, and my initial rush of love for her did not diminish. She was some twenty paces long, perhaps five paces across at her widest, although she tapered gracefully fore and aft. It was as if whoever had built her kept in his mind and his heart a memory of her predecessor, that long, lean hound of a ship that I had seen in my dream vision. Her hull was strengthened by a series of fourteen ribs, with extra ones at the prow, stern and just before the mast. The cargo hold yawned in the gap between the fore and aft decks. As far as I could see, other than ballast there was nothing down there except for the crew's supplies and their small, well-wrapped bundles of personal belongings. Everyone slept as I did, up on deck in the meagre shelter afforded by the ship's high sides.

The crew totalled eight: five more in addition to Einar, Olaf and the tattooed man with the bronze beard whose name was Thorben. Nobody, apart from Olaf, paid much attention to me. They all looked much the same to my eyes, being to a man big, brawny and with a lot of light-coloured hair, blond-ish or auburn-ish. In age, they ranged from old Olaf down to a white-fair lad who was probably younger than me. Einar seemed to be making a particular effort to ignore me. I hoped it was because he felt bad about having hit me. I feared it was because he did not want to risk getting to know someone he was going to have to interrogate once we reached wherever it was we were going.

There was an awful day, perhaps halfway through the journey, when land was close at hand to our left (I'd learned from Olaf to refer to that as *port*). The wind was howling, the seas were huge, and half the crew, including me, were set to baling out the vast quantities of water flooding into the ship. Everything was soaking wet, and, on that exposed deck, there was nowhere to shelter.

I couldn't have been the only person on board to be frightened, and, indeed, I caught more than one of the crew muttering
prayers and casting hopeful eyes upwards towards the realms
of the gods and, more frequently, forward to that magnificent
dragon at the prow. They, however, had the advantage of
experience. Olaf – kindly Olaf – put it into words, taking a
precious moment's rest from working hard enough for three
men to take my hand and say, 'Einar is a skilled mariner, and
this is but a small storm. Together, he and Malice-striker will
bring us through.'

He was right. The storm blew itself out, the furious black
clouds melted away and the destructive waves slowly flattened.
The wind blew powerfully from behind us and to our left,
constantly and steadily filling the sail. Looking back, I saw
what I thought was a faint black smudge. If it was the last tip
of land, then already we had left it far behind.

More days passed. I felt anxious all the time, desperate to
know where we were going. If only I'd learned more from
Gurdyman and made more study of his map, I might have had
some idea. We had sailed north – that I knew – and now, to
judge by the sun's position, I guessed we had turned north-
west. If there was anything out there except sea, then I had
never heard of it. I took a glance at the food and water supplies
when I thought nobody was looking, and, at a rough estimate,
I calculated we had enough for a few more days. We were
living on dried fish and meat, both salty and strong, neither
very appetizing. The fresh water had run out, and now the
choice was weak beer or sour milk. It occurred to me that,
had it not been for my presence on board and the possibility
that I'd try to run away, the crew would surely have made
landfall while they still could to take on fresh supplies. That,
no doubt, would be what they usually did.

We sailed on for four more days. Early in the morning of
the fifth day, the young crewman on watch in the prow called
out something in a voice made high by excitement. All the
others took up the cry, yelling the same word repeatedly,
jumping around in a sort of heavy-footed dance, slapping each
other on the back and giving each other the sort of hugs that
could crack ribs. It was Olaf who thought to explain to me.

'Land is in sight!' he said, and I thought I saw the suspicion of tears in his eyes. He pointed, and, following his extended arm, I could make out a vague, dark hump on the horizon.

He muttered something, but softly; it sounded almost like an incantation. It would not have surprised me if it was, because what I *thought* he said was, 'The Land of the Silver Dragon.'

EIGHT

Gurdyman emerged from almost a fortnight of intense study. So profoundly had he lost himself in his work that it was as if he had been in a trance; as if he had gone through the veil into another world, leaving the concerns and emotions of normal existence far behind.

A part of him had truly seemed to detach and set off down the roads, paths and secret trackways that he was trying to plot. He had gone into the northern lands, where the ground is permanently frozen, where great white bears pad on silent feet, where the night sky lights up with sheets of brilliant pinks, reds and greens. He had gone south, to where the sun beats on the arid sand and men's skins burn brown and black.

It was with a considerable effort that he dragged himself out of his phantom world and back into the crypt beneath his house. It took him some time to ground himself, and for a time he was disorientated. He forced himself to eat – there was no food in the house that had not turned bad, and so he had to emerge and buy supplies – and, once his belly was full, he lay on his cot and slept dreamlessly for the remainder of the day and all of the following night.

He awoke in the morning refreshed and fully himself. It was only then that he wondered where Lassair was.

How long had she been gone? He thought back, and a stab of alarm went through him. She had said she would only be away for a few days . . .

Perhaps she had been detained in her village. All manner of things could have happened to make her stay longer than she had anticipated: some difficulty or, God forbid, sickness, in her family. A sudden crop of illness or injuries among the villagers, so that her aunt needed the girl's help. An injury to Lassair herself; you could not walk from Aelf Fen to Cambridge on, say, a sprained ankle.

But Gurdyman could not reassure himself. In his heart, he knew that something was wrong. What should he do? He could wait for Hrype to come visiting, which must surely happen soon, since it was some weeks since he had last arrived unheralded at Gurdyman's door. Hrype would probably say that Lassair was safe and well at home, and there would be no more need to worry.

Try as he might, Gurdyman could not make himself believe that she was in her village.

The alternative was for Gurdyman to make the journey to Aelf Fen to let Lassair's family know she was missing.

It was something from which he shrank. As his concern for his pupil grew, he sat down in his sunny courtyard and made himself confront the reasons why he did not want to leave the town.

He did not like walking; that was the main reason. It was years – decades, possibly – since he had ventured further than the busy quaysides of his own town. He did not feel at ease out in the open countryside, for he had become detached from the natural world.

He filled a pewter cup with cool, white wine, slowly sipping it. *Have I, then, made myself a prisoner within my own walls?* he wondered.

With a jolt of apprehension, he remembered the intruder. He saw again himself and Lassair, hiding in the crypt beyond the secret door. Supposing the intruder had been lying in wait for her? But she had thought it safe to set out alone for her village, believing that the man had given up and gone away, and Gurdyman recalled that he had seen no reason to dispute it.

But he had been very preoccupied, back then . . .

A painful stab of guilty fear touched cold against his heart.

The fear deepened as he thought back to what he and Hrype had discussed, the last time Hrype came to see him. *Is that what this is?* he wondered, dread chilling him. No: he must not allow himself to dwell on that. There were many possible reasons for Lassair's absence, and he should not think the worst until he had to.

I should have stopped her, Gurdyman thought. Had he not been so obsessed with his work, he would have realized she

might be going into danger, and reasoned with her to wait
until word could be sent to her father to come and fetch her.

He dropped his face into his hands.

After a short time, he stood up. Lassair was very possibly
in danger, and he was the only one who realized it. Her family
had not known she was on her way, and so would not appreciate that anything was amiss. Only he could raise the alarm.

He walked back inside the house and set about packing a
small bag with the necessities for the trip. As he did so, he
smiled grimly at the thought that he, who loved to pore over
maps and charts and the details of other people's travels to the
furthest corners of the world, should be so very reluctant to
leave his safe, secure house and undertake the half-day's journey,
along a very well-travelled route, to a small and doubtless
friendly fenland village. He who once had been willing – *eager*
– to go anywhere that anyone was prepared to take him . . .

He was ready. He had a light pack containing food and
drink on his back, and a staff in his hand. He stood just inside
the door, trying to still the rapid beating of his heart. *This is
for Lassair*, he told himself firmly. *She may be in peril, and
only I am aware of it. The sooner I raise the alarm, the sooner
we can set about finding where she is and what has happened
to her.*

He threw open the stout door and stepped out into the
sunshine.

He reached Aelf Fen as the sun was setting. He had made good
time, given a ride for much of the way by a trio of jolly farmers'
wives returning home from market. It had surprised him that
the journey had been so easy; it would, indeed, have been
enjoyable, he thought as he walked the last few miles to the
village, had it not been for his abiding concern for Lassair and
the guilt that was now gnawing at him. He should have realized
sooner that she had been gone for too long. *A couple of days
or so*, she had said. He knew her well enough now to realize
that she did not break her word. Yet so wrapped up had he been
that he had allowed almost two weeks to go by. If, as he was
increasingly fearing, someone had taken her away, then she
could be almost anywhere by now. She could even be . . .

Stop.

He drew a long breath, deliberately stilling his thoughts. There would be time enough to face that if it happened. Coming to a halt on the edge of the village, he closed his eyes and turned his concentration inwards, searching for the life force that was Lassair. *Where are you, child?* he asked silently. *Are you still with those of us who dwell in this world?*

After a while, he began to smile. Opening his eyes, he grasped his staff and, ignoring the blisters on both heels, strode on into Aelf Fen.

Far away, journeying on down the length of a sunny land that jutted out into the Central Sea like a booted leg, Rollo Guiscard drew his horse to an abrupt stop, his mind filled with sudden, sharp anxiety.

Lassair.

He had felt a dark cloud hovering in his mind for some time now. It had taken shape quite quickly, and, whenever he had been able to take the time without risking his own safety, he had sent his thoughts hunting for her. Periodically he would remove from his wrist the beautiful plaited leather bracelet she had given him, sometimes holding it tightly in one hand, sometimes pressing it to his breast.

He loved her. Had loved her since he had met her, and, as he had got to know her better, the love had grown. Early the previous summer, they had at last become lovers. Almost a year had passed, but he recalled every moment of their brief and enchanted time together. As far as he was concerned, they were bonded now. He hadn't needed the little handfasting ceremony she had performed, touching though it had been, to bind himself to her.

His horse shifted under him, made anxious, perhaps, by his unease. He reached down and patted the gelding's neck. He was a young horse, and Rollo had been riding him for only six months or so; horse and rider were still in the process of becoming acquainted.

With a sigh, Rollo tightened his knees on his horse's sides and they moved on. There was no question of turning back, no matter how much he might long to. He was travelling south in response to a command that he could not refuse. Besides, if what he felt was true, and Lassair was in danger, then he was much too far away to rush to her aid.

He kicked the gelding to a trot, then a canter. Needing both hands on the reins, he tucked the plaited wristband away beneath his tunic. Right over his heart.

'Be safe, Lassair,' he muttered.

Then, firmly, single-mindedly, he turned his thoughts to what awaited him at his destination.

The Land of the Silver Dragon.

Silently, I repeated the words to myself. The land was fast approaching, and I could make out white-covered mountains rising up behind a dark-coloured coastal strip. Here and there, rivers ran down into the sea, winding their way through low hills. As we drew nearer, I saw isolated farmsteads, usually consisting of one long structure and a few outbuildings. There did not seem to be any towns or villages; not even a hamlet or two . . .

I concentrated on the farmsteads. This place was inhabited, at least, I told myself, even if there were no settlements such as I knew in my homeland. It was a profound relief, to realize I was going to be among other people. Here and there, I noticed smoke rising from the farmsteads, and I spotted herds of sheep and even some cows. On a narrow strip of shore, I saw a small hut, its roof steeply pitched and apparently covered in turf. Outside it, three men and a boy were busy with fishing lines. The boy waved a friendly hand at us.

We had approached from the south, and now we were sailing north-westwards, following the curving line of the coast. We were close to land now, and suddenly two of the crew pushed past me and, with respectful bows, approached the dragon head rearing high above the prow. To my great surprise, they unfastened some hidden catch and the head came away in their hands. Reverently they wrapped it in the cloth that Olaf was holding out, and presented it to Einar, who stowed it away in what appeared to be a purpose-built space.

Olaf must have noticed my wide-eyed stare. He came to stand beside me, and, leaning down, murmured, '*Malice-striker* is an entity of the sea, where he rules in power and majesty. We remove his image as we draw near to land, lest we offend the benign earth spirits.'

I nodded dumbly. I did not dare think too much about that. Then, suddenly, I heard Gurdyman's voice in my head: *The dragon was a creature of the sea and drew his power from the water element. Approaching land, the figurehead had to be removed.*

It was unreasonable, but somehow I felt immensely comforted. Not just because of the vivid moment of memory, but because someone from my real life, someone from my home, had known and told me of something in this current, alarming new world in which I found myself.

The sail was furled, and now the crew sat at the oars. The coast came nearer, and I saw that we were rounding a headland jutting out westwards into the sea. We turned into a wide bay, around which the low-lying coastal plain was cupped in a semicircle of mountains, forming a dramatic backdrop to the pastoral scene. Several small settlements dotted the plain, widely spaced.

We were clearly heading for a wooden jetty, roughly halfway along the bay. We were still in deep water; looking over the ship's side, I could make out the sea bed, a long way down. I turned back to the jetty, and now saw that a group of people stood on it. One of them raised a hand, and called out something. Einar answered, his voice loud and deep as he pitched it so as to be heard over on the jetty.

We were, it seemed, expected. 'How did they know we were coming?' I whispered to Olaf, standing close beside me.

He smiled. 'The first lookout would have spotted us at dawn,' he replied. 'Ever since, successive watchers have reported our progress.'

'Reported?' I asked.

He shrugged. 'Sometimes messages are relayed by beacon fire. Sometimes a man will simply get on his horse and pass the word on in person.'

Slowly I nodded. Einar must, I reflected, be a man of some importance in this land, to merit such a homecoming.

We were near enough now for me to make out the individuals

who formed the group on the jetty. There were seven adults and three children, including a babe in arms. The adults appeared to have grouped themselves around a central figure, and I found my eyes drawn to him.

He was tall and broad, with a head of flowing silvery-white hair and a beard to match. A wide moustache curled above his mouth, its long ends twisting out from his face as if they had a life of their own. He was surely an old man, yet he stood straight and proud, his shoulders huge under the fur-trimmed cloak. In one hand he held a staff, but, even before I had seen him move, I was quite sure it was a symbol of authority and not a walking aid. For authority radiated from him; as if someone was yelling the words aloud, the whole scene and all the people in it seemed to proclaim: *This is our chieftain.*

With an effort, I turned away from his commanding face and looked at the men and women who flanked him. There were two tall men, resembling Einar both in looks and in the self-assured way they stood, and surely his brothers? I stared at the one on the chieftain's right, for, fleetingly, his expression had reminded me of someone . . . But it was gone, and there was far too much else to worry about for me to try to pursue it. Each brother stood with a woman, presumably his wife; one was willow-slender, her hair white-blonde, and the other – the one with a baby in her arms – was short and plump, with a cheerful face and apple cheeks. The man beside her bent down and said something that amused her, and I heard her merry laughter coming out to meet me over the water.

Beside this group, standing slightly apart, were two other women, possibly mother and daughter, or mistress and servant. The elder one wore a dark, concealing veil.

It looked as if a welcoming party awaited us. Moreover, they appeared to have dressed in their best, for every one of them wore flowing wool garments, tunics and heavy cloaks, for, although the sun shone out of a clear, pale blue sky, the air was chilly and a spiteful wind blew. The garments were unsoiled by sweat, mud or the usual marks of toil. Long, bright hair shone in the sunshine as if freshly brushed; even the children had clean faces. With dismay, I looked down at myself. My gown was filthy, stained with everything from sea water

– a lot of that – to sour milk. I stank, for I hadn't washed in getting on for a fortnight. I had been using my trusty bucket for my bodily functions – the crew had been discreet, and pretended not to notice – and I felt stale, rumpled and foul. I put up my hands to my hair, twisting it up and securing it beneath my cap. The cap had originally been white, and I dreaded to think what it must look like now.

Olaf nudged me. He must have observed my distress, for he said, 'Do not worry! Nobody expects us to look clean and fresh after being at sea for so long. Soon you will have the opportunity to wash.'

I nodded an acknowledgement. Washing my body would be a start, but I had no clean garments with me; not even a change of linen. Would I have to run around naked while my laundered clothes dried? I'd *freeze*, surely, never mind the question of modesty. I smothered a slightly hysterical laugh.

The men at the oars were rowing cautiously now. At a word from Einar, at the steering oar, they raised their oars out of the water and laid them down inside the gunwales. Einar had judged it to perfection: *Malice-striker* had just enough way to nudge up against the jetty, bumping gently against its wooden supports. The young man up in the bows leapt on to the jetty, his bare feet clumping on the boards, and quickly secured the rope he held to a post. From the stern, Einar threw a second rope, and the youth ran back just in time to catch it.

Even as the boy was tying it, Einar stepped ashore, straight into the open arms of the chieftain in the fur-trimmed cloak. They embraced, and then the older man broke away. Glancing at me, he asked something, his voice too quiet for me to hear. Einar, too, looked at me, then nodded and made a quiet reply. I shivered in sudden fear. Would it start, now? Would these huge men take me away and persuade me to tell them what they believed I knew?

Einar was coming back to the ship. He called out a series of orders – quite incomprehensible to me – and, working alongside his crew, set about the apparently numerous tasks that have to be completed when a ship reaches port. Not sure what to do, I stood by myself; Olaf had gone to see to whatever tasks were his responsibility.

I sensed eyes on me, and risked a glance towards the jetty. It was a mistake: everyone was looking at me. I dropped my head, ashamed to meet their eyes.

I heard a quick burst of chatter – someone sounded quite cross – and then a baby's cry, quickly soothed. There was a thump as one of the group jumped down on to the deck. I sensed someone very close to me.

I looked up, into the round, light brown eyes of the woman who had held the baby. Her arms were empty now and, looking swiftly, I saw that the infant was now cradled by one of the big men. The woman reached out and took my cold hands in her warm ones.

'I am Thyra,' she said slowly. 'I am elder son's wife. I . . .' She paused, frowning, then smiled again as she found the word she sought. 'I greet you,' she said. 'Welcome. Welcome to our land of Iceland!'

Iceland. I had heard of it, but it was a land of mystery, on the edge of the world where the ice reigned.

I was in *Iceland*?

The shock affected me deeply, and I was hardly aware of being helped ashore. My legs, having grown accustomed to the movement of the ship, did not work, and I stumbled and would have fallen, except for the quick, strong hand of one of the tall men.

The big chieftain led the way and, in twos and threes, we followed him up the track that wound away from the jetty. We crossed a stretch of pebbly shore – I saw strange stones that appeared almost black, and some other substance that looked sort of crumbly – and passed a big wooden rack, hung with gutted fish slowly drying in the sharp wind. Then we headed off over short, wiry grass. I saw a flock of sheep, in a meadow surrounded by low, roughly built walls of jagged stone. A small herd of cows in another field came across to look at us.

We walked on, the chieftain setting a brisk pace. As I had thought, he had no need of the support of his staff, which he swung by his side in an almost casual way. Presently, we reached the summit of a long, gentle slope. Looking down into the shallow valley on the far side, I saw within it, on a slight rise, a long, low building covered with turf. Crouched close to the ground, its roof was steeply pitched, punctuated by two large smoke holes. From the vantage point of being slightly above it, I could see that it was made up of two similar structures set together, from the rear of which protruded smaller wings. It was vast: you could have fitted my family's home within it five or six times, and that wasn't counting the rear wings.

The plump woman, who had reclaimed her baby for the walk, was beside me. 'That is the Jorund longhouse,' she said, a happy smile creasing her face. 'It was built by the forefathers when first they came to this land, seven generations ago. It is our home.' Then, with an encouraging nod, she urged me to follow the rest of the group down into the valley.

From somewhere, the women of the household had acquired hot water. Lots of it. I imagined a big fire burning, pots and pans set over the heat. I stood in the latrine room, and, behind the doors that closed it off from the passage leading into the main house, took off my stinking garments. One of the women – a young serving maid with a shy smile – instantly took them from me. In answer to my instinctive protest, she mimed washing. *She* was going to launder my clothes? I was aghast at the thought. It would be an unpleasant task, and I would far rather have done it myself. With a shake of her head, as if she understood my protest, she smiled again and hurried away.

Thyra and her companion – a girl of about ten – gave me a washcloth and a hard block of soap. Dirty as I was, I used it sparingly, for it was harsh. I had some soapwort leaves in my satchel; given the opportunity, I would boil some and prepare some of the gentle, foaming liquid that my people use for washing. Not that I was complaining about what they were offering me. Never before had I bathed in such generous amounts of hot water.

When at last I had finished, Thyra handed me a length of cloth to dry myself. Emerging from a vigorous rubbing of my hair, I saw that she was holding out garments for me. There was a fine linen under gown, and, to go over it, a long, pleated shift of soft wool, beautifully woven in a pattern of light and dark brown, highlighted with bands of cream. Over that, fastened to it just below the shoulders with two small silver brooches, went a long apron that hung down front and back, entirely covering the gown. It was a little like the scapular that my sister Elfritha wears over her habit, and, I guessed, served the same purpose of keeping the gown clean.

My hair was still damp, so I combed it out, twisted it in a knot and fastened it at the back of my head. Normally I would have covered it with one of my white caps, but the only one I had with me was probably even now being given a thorough wash by the little serving girl. The women of this house went bareheaded, and I would have to do the same.

Suddenly I remembered my shawl. When Elfritha gave it to me, she said it was to remind me of home and a sister who loved me. Hurriedly I opened my satchel and took it out, then draped it over the pleated shift. Elfritha had dyed the soft lambs' wool with shades of green, and the subtle colours looked well with the muted shades of the shift.

Thyra's eyes widened with interest. She took a fold of the shawl in her fingers, nodding in appreciation at the quality. Then, standing back to look at me, she said, 'Good. *Very* good!'

Then, beckoning to me, she turned and led the way along the short passage to the main house.

I heard the voices and the laughter even as we emerged from the passage. In front of us was the entrance room, with the building's big, wooden door standing ajar. To our right was a wooden partition, and in it were double doors. Thyra opened them and led the way into the main hall.

A long fire pit extended down the middle of the room, and on either side of it were benches. Some were occupied, but in general the people in the hall were on their feet, busy with food preparation. It looked as if the household were getting ready for a big feast. Several vast pots hung over the fire pit, suspended on chains from heavy iron tripods, and, at a work table close by, a group of women with their sleeves rolled up kneaded, rolled, chopped and stirred. One looked up at me and gave me a grin.

At the far end of the fire, on a raised platform, was set a

throne-like chair and several more, lower, chairs. The man in the fur-trimmed cloak sat on the throne. On his right sat the man I believed was Thyra's husband. On his left sat Einar. Another man sat beside Thyra's husband, talking quietly to the slim woman with white-blonde hair. Next to Einar sat a broad-shouldered, strong-looking woman with reddish-fair hair woven in a thick plait. Her light eyes were fixed on me. I could not read her expression; it was as if she had deliberately smoothed out her features so as not to give any clue to her thoughts.

Thyra took my hand and led me up to the dais. I made myself meet the eyes of the man in the cloak.

After a very long moment, he spoke. In a deep, resonant voice, he said, 'Well met, Lassair.' *He knew my name.* 'I am Thorfinn Ofnirsson, this is my farmstead, and these are my kinfolk.' He pointed to his right. 'My elder son Jorund, Jorund's wife Thyra –' he indicated the woman beside me, his wide mouth stretching in a quick smile – 'my daughter Asa and her husband, Njal.' He turned to his left. 'My second son Einar you have already met. Beside him sits my second daughter, Freydis.' Now he raised his arms, spreading them to include the rest of the men, women and children in his hall. 'These, too, are my people; my blood kin and those who serve us.' He paused, staring down at me from the dais. 'Come and sit beside me,' he commanded. 'You must—'

I'd had enough. I'd been abducted, borne away over the sea for nearly two weeks, then brought here, to this extraordinary place and the enforced company of people I'd never met in my life. I was quite sure I would be breaking some basic rule of courtesy, but I didn't let that hold me back. Drawing a deep breath, I marched right up to the dais, climbed on to it, and, standing over the man in the cloak, I said, loudly and firmly, '*No.* I will not sit beside you, or listen to one more word from you or anyone else, until you tell me why I have been brought here and what you want with me.' I paused, and swiftly all my grievances against this man and his family filled my mind. 'Your son and his men grabbed me, tied me up and slung me aboard their ship,' I cried, the words tumbling out, 'and they did it so cleverly that, to start with, nobody would realize I was gone, but I've been away so long that by now my friends and my family will be *really* worried about me, and my poor father will probably think I'm dead, and that will kill him too because he loves me very much and he'll be riddled with guilt and believe it's all his fault because he *knew* there was danger and he'll think he should have taken better care of me, and—'

Fear, panic, despair and misery had been flooding through me, but I'd been managing to control them. The thought of my beloved father, however, out of his mind with anxiety, going out every spare moment to waste his time searching for me, was my undoing. To my horror, I felt tears fill my eyes. In a voice that sounded more like a scream, I cried, '*I want to go home!*'

A sort of quiet groan echoed round the hall. As I'd feared, I had clearly done something very offensive. I hung my head, waiting for the reprisal. Would the man in the cloak – Thorfinn – have me forcibly removed? Would Einar leap to his feet and hit me again?

Nothing happened. I raised my head, to see Thorfinn studying me. Then, slowly, he nodded. 'Please, come here,' he said again.

I looked at him. The skin of his face was leathery and creased and, although in that moment his expression was sombre, I judged by the lines that he smiled a lot and was given to laughter. I stared into his eyes, searching for the threat I dreaded to find.

I went on staring, for what felt like a very long time. He did nothing: he did not speak, did not move. It was as if he was silently saying: *Look all you like. I have nothing to hide.*

My fear began to ebb away. I was still very apprehensive, and sick with worry about my family, but the sickening dread that these men were about to torture me to find out something I didn't know had, for the moment, almost gone. Every instinct – and I've learned to trust my instincts – was shouting out at me that this old man was not going to harm me, and I reasoned that, if he didn't want me hurt, nobody else would be allowed to do so either. Whoever and whatever he was, I appeared to be under his protection.

I went to sit in the chair beside him.

NINE

Presently, the sons and daughters sitting beside Thorfinn began to drift away. It was approaching the middle of the day, and I imagined they all had tasks to do. Last to go was Einar. He turned to look back at me before he left, and I thought he was about to speak. Almost imperceptibly, Thorfinn shook his head. Einar spun on his heel and strode away.

Thorfinn looked down at me. 'Just now, you asked me a couple of questions,' he said softly. 'Understandably, you wish to be told why you have been brought here and what we want of you.' I opened my mouth to ask the questions again, but he put up a hand for silence. 'Forgive me, my child,' he said. 'It is natural that you want to know these things, and you have my word that all will be explained to you in due course.' *When?* I cried silently. *And how soon will they take me home again?*

He nodded, as if he had heard. Then he said, 'It is my habit, on such days as this, to eat but sparingly during the day, so as to have the best appetite for later.' I was right, then, about the feast. I wondered what they were celebrating, and how long into the night they'd go on carousing. I wouldn't be getting any sleep till they'd finished . . . But he was still speaking, so I stopped feeling sorry for myself and listened. 'It would please me if you would now eat with me,' he was saying, 'and perhaps you will tell me about yourself?'

It wasn't *fair*! He had put off answering my questions, yet now he was expecting me to satisfy his curiosity! 'Apparently you already know my name,' I said stiffly. 'You also seem to know where I live, where my kinsfolk live, and the fact that I regularly travel to and fro between my village and Camb— er, a big town nearby.'

'Cambridge,' Thorfinn murmured.

I barely heard. My anger rising again, I hissed, 'Your son

killed my sister's mother-in-law and my aunt! He came hunting
for something, either on your instructions or on his own behalf,
and he—'

'Stop.' The single word, quietly spoken, had an instant
effect: I felt as if the words lining up to tumble out of my
mouth had been pushed back down my throat. 'Have patience,
Lassair,' he went on. 'For now, do not speak of what you do
not understand.'

*I understand that my people have been killed, wounded and
suffered the distress of having their homes ransacked!* I wanted
to shout. But there was an unseen power emanating from the
huge man beside me, and I did not dare.

Food was brought – flat bread, dried cod, pots of a cool,
slightly sharp substance that I guessed was some sort of coagu-
lated milk, and that proved to be delicious – and Thorfinn
made sure I took my share. As we ate, he asked me about my
village, about Cambridge, about my training as a healer.
Although we only spoke in fairly general terms, I had the
feeling he already knew much of what I was telling him.

It was very strange, and I still had absolutely no idea why
he was interested in my kinsfolk and me, nor what it was he
believed we possessed, and that he was going to such extraordinary lengths to find.

The food was all gone. Thorfinn sat quietly beside me.
Suddenly I yawned, hugely and uncontrollably. Recalling
where I was, belatedly I put a hand in front of my mouth and
muttered an apology.

'Would you like to sleep?' he asked. I nodded. Despite
everything, I could hardly keep my eyes open.

Thorfinn beckoned, and one of the women busy preparing
food came across to us, wiping her hands on her apron. He
said something to her in their own tongue – thanks to my
lessons with Olaf, I could pretty much understand the words
– and, with a smile, she held out her hand to me. I got up,
and she led me away.

We went on down the hall, then through a narrow doorway
into another, smaller room. I remembered that, from the
outside, the homestead looked like two buildings set end to
end, so this must be the second one. There was a central hearth,

and around it wide platforms set around the inside of the walls, strewn with furs and bedding. A group of four or five women sat together close to the hearth, quietly talking. They looked up, nodding to my companion and staring with interest at me. My companion led me to the far end of the room, indicating a cosy corner of the platform, tucked deep beneath the steeply sloping roof. She patted the heavy sheepskins spread out ready, miming sleep by putting her face down sideways on to her joined hands.

I needed no further invitation. I got up on to the platform, crawled inside the nest of sheepskins and curled up. I was aware of the woman's soft footfalls as she went back to the main hall, and of the gentle, murmuring voices of the women beside the hearth as they resumed their conversation. Then sleep took a firm hold of me, and that was that.

I woke to a babble of muted chatter, interspersed with bursts of laughter and a voice suddenly raised in song. There seemed to be a lot of people in the main hall, and it sounded as if the feast had begun. I looked up at the bit of sky visible through the smoke hole, and saw that it was deep, twilight blue.

I got up, carefully tidying the sheepskins, then straightened my borrowed gown. I smoothed back some loose strands of hair, retied my shawl, then crept across the room and along the short, narrow passage till I was standing in the doorway of the main hall.

Trestle tables had been set out, one each side of the fire pit and one up on the dais. People were seated, on benches and, up on the dais, on chairs. Thorfinn sat on his throne, his back to me. The food smells were wonderful, making my stomach growl. It seemed a long time since I had shared Thorfinn's light meal. I hoped they hadn't forgotten about me; perhaps someone – friendly Thyra, maybe – would bring me a platter of varied delicacies . . .

A man's voice, deep and strong, rose up above the others. He was singing, and, from the shouts of male laughter and loud guffaws, I guessed it was a ribald song. It was ever the way, my Granny Cordeilla once informed me, to concentrate on the bawdy, light-hearted songs and tales before and during

the feast. *When people's minds are on filling their bellies*,
she used to say with a wicked grin, *it's no use trying to make
them concentrate on some deep, serious and significant tale
of the ancestors; save that for when they're replete, my girl,
and you'll have their full attention.*

Would a bard tell a tale later tonight? Would anyone notice
if I stayed there, crouched in the doorway, and shared it? I
noticed again, as I stood listening, that I could understand
quite a lot of what people were saying. It was more than
curiosity that prompted my interest: when my granny died,
she bequeathed to me the role of family bard. Professionally,
I am always interested to hear how a fellow storyteller sets
about it.

People were striding up and down the tables now, brawny-
armed men and women with bulging biceps, carrying vats of
food and ladling it out on to the waiting platters. I smelt a
variety of delicious aromas, some familiar, some new to me.
Among the servers strode a huge man with white-fair hair,
carrying an enormous jug in each hand. His job, it appeared,
was to keep the drinking mugs full.

I shivered. It was cold, standing there well away from the
heat of the two hearths. My exclusion was making me feel
miserable, although I realized it was unreasonable. Yes, they
had been friendly – welcoming, even – but I was still their
prisoner, and prisoners didn't get invited to feasts.

Just as I was firmly reminding myself of that fact, a tall,
slender figure stood up from a chair on the dais, descended
and walked elegantly over to me. It was the elder daughter
– Asa – and her expression was cool. Fully expecting to be
curtly ordered back to the room where I'd slept, I turned away
from her.

She *did* issue an order, but it wasn't the one I was anticipating. In a voice as chilly as her ice-maiden appearance, she
said, 'My father invites you to come to the feast. Please,
accompany me.'

She turned and walked away, and I hurried after her.
Bemused, I hoped they would have set a place for me well
away from the dais, where I would be out of the eagle eyes
of Thorfinn and his immediate family. They hadn't: Asa led

the way right back up on to the dais, where, on Thorfinn's left hand, Einar stood up to give me his place.

As he began to move away – I saw that another seat had been brought for him – Thorfinn shot out an arm, and clutched at his son's wrist. Einar's wrist was huge, yet his father's hand easily encompassed it, holding him firm. 'Einar has something to say to you,' Thorfinn said, very softly.

I didn't realize he meant me until, bending to crouch beside my chair, Einar spoke. 'I regret that I hit you,' he muttered.

Astounded, it took me a moment to think how to respond. I'd been about to say, *Oh, that's all right, I realize I provoked you*. But then I met Einar's eyes.

My aunt Edild has been trying to teach me how to read people. I'm not very good at it yet. But in that instant, I saw something in Einar that told me to stand up to him. If I meekly crumpled now, effectively letting him get away with what had been a hard and surely unnecessary blow, then he would make up his mind about me and never change it, probably writing me off as a weak and timid little girl who had no guts.

I did have guts; I do. I am descended from many generations of fen people, and life has never been easy. Among my ancestors are wise women, bards and warriors: Ligach the Pearl Maiden sang before kings; my namesake forebear walked with the spirits; and three of my Granny Cordeilla's brothers fought at Hastings, two of them to the death.

Keeping my eyes on Einar's, I lifted my chin and said coldly, 'You hit me hard enough that I was unconscious for a day.' It was a bit of an exaggeration, but not much. 'Next time, either give me fair warning and a weapon, or pick on someone your own size.'

I thought I'd provoked him too far. There was dead silence on the dais, and I knew the others were all closely observing. I'd unwittingly spoken so loudly that I guessed some of the people sitting closest at the other tables had heard, too. Einar's eyes narrowed, and I thought he had gone pale.

The tension was broken by a chuckle, not quite muffled. A male voice said, 'Sounds fair enough to me, Einar.' I spun round, to see that the white-fair giant with the jugs was standing at one side of the dais.

Someone else laughed, and others joined in. My eyes flashed back to Einar, and I saw the struggle between lashing out at me – which would surely only serve to increase the company's enjoyment of his discomfiture – or joining in the laughter. To my relief, he began to smile.

'I'll find you a sword,' he said, holding out his hand, 'unless you would prefer a battle axe.' I took his hand, and my own was engulfed. The he let me go and went to take his seat.

I let out the breath I'd been holding. The giant filled my mug, and Thorfinn himself dug his eating knife into the communal dishes, set down before him on the table, and loaded my platter till it overflowed.

As far as I could judge, it seemed that the people here ate anything that the natural world put in their way: salmon, cod, water fowl, swans, puffins, ptarmigan, all featured in the feast. Some of the meats had been fried in what I thought was butter, except, when I asked, Thyra said it was seal blubber. Other meats had been roasted or stewed, and there were also sausages made of liver and blood, appetizingly seasoned, as well as salted fish. More of the soured milk stuff was served, and I learned it was called *skyr*. I ate everything I was offered, and only stopped when I was starting to feel slightly sick.

Everyone else in Thorfinn's hall had a greater capacity than I, and for some time I sat back and watched as the feast slowly wound down. From time to time one of the family would speak to me, but I sensed it was more for the sake of politeness than because they really wanted to.

Eventually, even the giants had finished eating; the white-haired one who had carried the ale and mead jugs celebrated the moment with a resounding belch so loud that it caused a round of applause. Then there was a burst of activity as pots, dishes and platters were cleared and the trestles dismantled and stowed away. Somebody threw a huge log on the fire, cups and mugs were topped up, and all the oil lamps were extinguished. Apart from a couple of flares set in the walls, the hall was lit only by the light from the long fire.

I knew what would happen next. I had never in my life been to such a feast as this, but I knew the general form. Now, as well-fed, slightly inebriated people sat back, warm, secure and comfortable, it was the turn of the bard to step forward. I wondered who served that function in Thorfinn's household. One of his sons? Some long-serving retainer, such as Olaf who sailed with Einar? A wise woman or cunning man, or whatever they were called here?

None of those: the figure who stepped forward into the firelight was broad-shouldered, like so many of these people, and had dark blonde hair whose reddish tones shone bright in the light from the flames. The hair had been plaited earlier; now it flowed in long waves, reaching to the waist.

The bard held up one hand, which I saw held a staff tipped with a brownish crystal shaped to a point. The base of the staff struck the floor, twice, three times. There was absolute silence in the hall.

Then Thorfinn's daughter Freydis began to speak.

'In the days of King Harald Fairhair, when brave men in their longboats ever pushed back the boundaries of this world, our forefathers came to this land,' she said. 'They were proud and independent, and desired to make a new dwelling place. Despite the dangers and the hardships, which were many and various, they preferred life in a new land that was theirs alone to existence under the tyranny of a king who sought to impose his own wishes on to his subjects.' She paused, her eyes raking around the intent circle of listeners. 'Thus it was, or so say the wise, that the perilous, seductive spirit of adventure entered the blood of our ancestors. From that time forward, each generation would throw up one whose feet ever itched to walk upon new shores, and who, despite the love of wife, children and kinsmen, despite the hard-won security and comfort of this our homeland, always wished to seek for more.

'In the days of our fathers' forefathers, there lived a mariner whose name was Thorkel Jorundsson.' The name fell like a spell, and I thought I heard a soft, collective gasp. 'And his indomitable courage was such that he ventured everywhere that the sun, moon and stars shed light.' A pause, and once more her gaze swept slowly around her audience. 'Thorkel knew his destiny from an early age, for it was foretold to him by his mother that he would cross the endless seas and,

in time, come to a land of liquid fire where men say time
began.'

She had only been speaking for a matter of moments but
already she had grabbed her audience, and I knew she would
not let them go until she had finished. Freydis was a born
storyteller; her very bearing – standing straight, tall and strong,
dressed in a beautiful gown of pale wool with silver glittering
at her shoulders, pacing slowly, hypnotically, to and fro in
front of the fire – commanded her listeners' respectful attention. Willingly, helplessly, I gave her mine.

Her tale might have been one her people had heard before,
but to me its powerful impact was heightened by its novelty.
She told of a man who was driven, by his fearsome mother's
predictions and by his own dangerous recklessness, to sail
behind the sun; to venture on, when sense and self-preservation
pleaded with him to turn back, until he reached his goal and,
unwittingly, the seeds of his own ultimate destruction.

Behind the sun. It was an emotive phrase, and I wondered
what it meant. Gurdyman had told me of the travels of the
Norsemen; how they had ventured far away, crossing unknown
seas, penetrating deep inside alien continents, following the
never-ending rivers. Hrype's jade stones had come out of the
east – was that what was meant by *behind the sun*? The east
was, after all, where the sun rose . . .

But Freydis was well into her stride now, and I focused my
attention on her strong, melodious voice.

'Thorkel's crew were loyal and courageous, and at first their
souls yearned for adventure just as his did. Yet, as the days
and the weeks went by, and as the last familiar landmarks
were passed and left far behind, even the doughtiest sailor
began to feel the shivers of doubt in his heart. "Where are we
going, Thorkel?" asked the bravest of them. "Have you some
goal in mind, which you do not choose to share with us? Or
do we sail merely in the hope of finding whatever land it is
that you see in your dreams?" But Thorkel made no answer.'

Freydis looked around, holding first one pair of eyes, then
another. 'For Thorkel was indeed a dreamer,' she said, her
voice dropping to a whisper. Such was the silence in the hall,
however, and such the carrying quality of her voice, that every

word was audible. 'He saw visions, and his visions had an uncanny way of turning into reality. He had not told his crew, but it was true that his quest was driven ever onwards by what his inner eye had revealed to him: a place of brilliant light and colour; a city of hundreds of thousands of souls; a land where they worshipped strange deities under a sun that burned so hot that men's skins had turned brown; a land where the fierce gods were appeased by the very lifeblood of the people.

'Now there came a day when Thorkel's crew would go no further. Home and hearth were but distant memories; the land now visible, when the concealing mists permitted a glimpse, was a strange one, and full of the cries of unknown birds and animals. For many days now, the ship had made no landfall but sailed ever on, day and night. When the winds failed, men took to the oars. "We are tired, Master," said the crewmen. "We are afraid, we fear that we are lost, and we despair because we do not believe we shall see our loved ones and our home-land again."

'Then at last Thorkel broke his silence. "My loyal sailors," he said, opening his arms as if to embrace them all, "indeed, my dear friends, each and every one of whom is like a brother to me, would I take you into a place from which there was no return? We are not lost: banish that thought from your hearts and your minds. Why, is it not always said among us that a good ship always finds her own way home to port? And a good ship is what we have, my friends" – he paused to put his mighty hand on the neck of the figurehead, rearing high above him – "the very best of ships!"

'Encouraged by his words, one of his crew – his oldest, most trusted companion – ventured to say, "But will you not tell us where we are bound and why we are going there?" Thorkel looked at him for a long moment, and then, with a slow nod, he said, "I will, for you are worthy men and it is only fair that you should now be told for what purpose we have come so far."

'Then Thorkel seemed to go into a trance, and, when at last he broke his silence, it was as if another was using his mouth, lips and tongue to speak for him, for his voice had altered. "Our honoured ancestors have sailed all over the known world," he intoned, the words falling on the enchanted air like the slow beats of a deep bass drum, "and, for we who follow in their footsteps and would emulate their high, brave courage, and experience the eternal thrill of discovering new shores, there is little left to find. But the spirits came to me in a dream." A shudder went through his crewmen at the mention of the spirits, and not a few grasped at the crosses or the Thor's hammers they wore round their necks, many murmuring swift prayers. "The spirits spoke to me," Thorkel went on, his eyes alight with the flame of passion, "and they told me that there was one more voyage to make; a voyage of exploration open to every man who could force himself to face the perils of the journey."

"'And that is *this* voyage, Master?" a crewman asked nervously. Thorkel smiled, and he said, "No, my friend. It is the journey inside ourselves.'"

Freydis paused, once more turning to rest her eyes on the circle of her audience. 'They did not know what Thorkel meant and, indeed, some feared that the long voyage and its many perils and privations had caused him to lose his reason. Perhaps Thorkel understood this, for no further word did he speak of this strange inner voyage.

'The ship sailed on, and in the alien waters in which the crew now found themselves, they saw many marvels and many horrors. A fleet of small boats disappeared before their very eyes. A water spout erupted out of a flat calm, as tall as the highest mountain. Unknown creatures followed the ship, and the crewmen sensed an intelligence behind the curious eyes that studied them. And then, without warning, Thorkel gave the order to make landfall.'

Freydis paused again, long enough for her entranced listeners to turn and glance at each other, their eyes wide in the firelight. But then she spoke again, and instantly her audience's attention was back with her.

'The ship entered a busy, vibrant port where men of varied tongues bartered and traded,' she said. 'The harbour was filled with crafts of all sizes, although none had come so far as Thorkel and his crew. Their appearance caused much interest, and both men and women approached, wanting to touch their pale skins and stroke their long, fair hair. Leaving instructions for his crew to trade their skins and their walrus ivory for fresh food and good water, Thorkel went ashore alone and he did not return until early the next morning. When his crew saw him, they blanched.'

Freydis stopped. She stood quite still, looking down at the ground, for several heartbeats. The tension mounted, and it seemed as if everyone in the hall, including me, held their breath.

Then into the silence came Freydis's cool, clear voice, and as I heard her words, I felt a deep chill run up my back. 'For Thorkel Jorundsson,' she said, 'was not the same man he had been when he went ashore.'

TEN

lways leave them wanting more, my Granny Cordeilla used to say. I knew, even before Freydis turned away and melted into the shadows, that she would not complete her tale that night. Her audience did not appreciate that she had gone, however; several of them sat, bemused expressions on their faces, staring round as if she was suddenly going to reappear and tell them the conclusion.

I wondered, suddenly, if there would *be* a conclusion. As if some inner part of me knew better than my conscious mind, I was quite sure there wouldn't . . .

But it was a fleeting thought, there and gone before it had time to lodge.

It seemed to take Freydis's audience some time to return from the imaginary world to which she'd transported them. I wasn't the only one to sit blinking stupidly as I came back to reality. Around me, people began to make desultory efforts at clearing up, and I went to help.

I wondered where I would be taken to sleep. I guessed it would be back to the second, smaller room, where I'd rested in the afternoon, since it seemed to be exclusively for women; presumably, the unmarried ones. I was right, and presently Thyra came to escort me back to the place where I'd slept earlier. Settling down in the warm, soft sheepskins, the light from the hearth gently illuminating the room, I was vaguely aware of other women and girls coming to bed. I was on the very edge of sleep when a sudden, frightening thought struck me.

These strangers might have been welcoming and hospitable to me. I might have just spent a most enjoyable evening with fine food and drink, entertained by an exceptional storyteller. Yet one of these people – apparently a high-ranking one – had come to my faraway home and committed very grave crimes, including two murders. If, as it appeared, Einar had gone on his mission with his father's full knowledge and approval, then surely it made them all guilty.

I realized, with a sick sense of fear, that I could not allow myself to relax my guard. With a great effort, I forced my anxious thoughts to grow still and finally fell asleep.

Sometime in the night I was thrown awake by a vivid and disturbing dream about a tall, light-haired, bearded man who went ashore as one person and came back as someone different. After that, sleep was a long time returning. When it did, the dreams were even worse.

Gurdyman had decided it would be best not to alarm Lassair's family by bursting in and announcing he was very worried about her because she appeared to be missing. Instead, he found a place beneath an ancient oak tree from which he could watch the village unobserved, and then sat down to wait for Hrype to appear.

He hoped fervently that his old friend was nearby. If not, he could be in for a very long wait.

As it transpired, however, he did not have to restrain his impatience for long. Quite soon, he saw Hrype emerge from behind a small, well-kept house on the edge of the settlement, whose garden was full of tidy herb beds: Lassair's aunt's house, he guessed. Standing up, he put his hands to his lips and blew a hooting whistle.

'Not the most unobtrusive of calls to make in daylight hours,' Hrype observed, reaching the top of the incline and coming to join Gurdyman under the oak. 'Had there been any of my fellow villagers within earshot, it might have penetrated even their dull and unobservant minds that it's rare to hear an owl in the daytime.'

Then, catching a good look at Gurdyman's face, he stopped. The levity, and the surprised pleasure at unexpectedly seeing his friend, drained away. 'What's wrong?' he demanded urgently.

Gurdyman told him. 'She's not here, then,' he added. There was no need to ask; Hrype's reaction told him that what he had so dreaded was true.

Hrype was standing a little apart from him, half turned away, looking down towards the village. 'I might have known nothing that wasn't life-threatening would have prised you out of your house and brought you into the country,' he muttered. Then, spinning round, 'Please, don't think I don't appreciate it.'

'I don't,' Gurdyman said quietly.

There was silence. Gurdyman observed his friend, watching him go through the possibilities. Dismissing, probably, the easy answers. The ones that said, *there'll be an obvious explanation; she'll have run into that Norman of hers and gone off with him for a few days.* Or, *she'll have met some poor soul on the road in need of healing, and gone back with them to their home to take care of them.*

For one thing, Lassair would not have done either of those things without getting word to her loved ones. For another, it wasn't *a few days.* It was more or less a fortnight.

Gurdyman sighed. He knew, even before Hrype spoke, that his friend would have reached the same conclusion that he had. Nevertheless, he waited for Hrype to admit it.

'I believe,' Hrype said eventually, 'that you and I might have prevented this.'

Gurdyman nodded. 'I believe that, too.' He met Hrype's eyes. 'It is not easy to live with.'

The silence resumed.

The next day, some of the young women whose accommodation I was sharing took it upon themselves to look after me. The morning was bright and sunny and, I guessed, as warm as it got up in those northern latitudes at that time of year. Which in fact wasn't really very warm at all, for the sun's strength was feeble up here. In the girls' cheerful, giggling company, I was led away into the low hills behind the farmstead, to where, to my amazed delight, a spring of natural hot water came bubbling up out of the black ground, forming a steaming, broiling lake. The girls shed their clothes and their inhibitions, plunging in mother-naked with squeals of mock-horror at the temperature of the water, urging me to join them. I didn't need much urging.

There must have been some code of conduct that reserved specific times for the two sexes, for no men or boys came to join us. After a while, however, I was feeling so relaxed, and enjoying the experience so much, that I wouldn't have minded if they had.

Back at the farmstead, one of the older women approached, bearing my own clothes, laundered and neatly folded. Taking them and thanking her, my first instinct was to go and change into them immediately. But, by the time I was back at my sleeping place, I was no longer so sure. Sensing someone watching me, I turned, to see Asa standing in the doorway.

Her cool, aloof expression was momentarily softened into a smile, and I saw how beautiful she was. 'The gown which Thyra gave you becomes you,' she said. 'It, and the other garments, is a gift, and yours to keep. We will understand, though, if you prefer to put on your own clothes once more.'

I looked down at myself. The cream and brown robe was lovely; probably the best-quality garment I'd ever worn. It, and the apron and under linen, felt right, somehow. I felt very comfortable in them, and, in a strange way, it was as if I was used to wearing them. It occurred to me suddenly that it wasn't only the clothes that felt familiar; or, possibly, they were a symptom of something larger. The fact was, I felt at home here in the farmstead. I got on with these people; I seemed to understand them, although I had no idea why. In some unfathomable way, they were familiar.

I had already resolved the question of how it was that, with Olaf's help, I had managed so quickly to pick up a working knowledge of their speech. From all that I had observed, it was clear that these people regularly visited my own country. Einar and his crew, for example, obviously knew the waters around the fens, and Thorfinn appeared to have heard of Cambridge. These facts did not surprise me, for the Norsemen had long traded with my own countrymen, and it seemed quite possible that I had been absorbing speech and accents similar to those of my hosts since I'd first been able to hear and understand.

I still had no idea why I was there or what they wanted from me. Yet, some time during the day and the night since my arrival, and despite my constant efforts to remind myself what Einar had done, it occurred to me that I'd stopped being afraid. I felt almost that I was one of them. Under the circumstances, it seemed right to go on wearing my new finery. Then, I would *look* like one of them, too.

Still, the fact remained that I had been brought here against my will and without my agreement.

As all this flashed swiftly through my mind, I realized I hadn't answered Asa. I returned her smile, and said, 'I am most grateful for the gift. I will pack my own garments away, and continue to dress as my hosts do.'

She gave a quick nod of acknowledgement (of approval?) then turned and slipped away.

Later in the day, Thorfinn sent for me. He greeted me courteously, and I had the sense that his swift glance took in quite a lot. He proposed a ride; two tough-looking, shaggy ponies stood ready outside the homestead.

We crossed the valley, surmounted the gentle slope at its lip and then rode off along the coastal plain. Reaching a place where a small river flowed out from the hills to meet the sea, we turned inland. As we jogged along, Thorfinn spoke of many things: the landscape, the climate, the problems of growing enough food during the short season to feed the people in the long winter months. I guessed he hadn't brought me out there to discuss the weather and food production, and, sure enough, presently he drew rein at the top of a low rise, turned to me and said, 'Did you enjoy Freydis's story?'

'Yes, very much,' I replied. 'Although I confess it gave me bad dreams.'

'*Bad* dreams?' he shot back.

It was as if he knew. 'Well, powerful dreams,' I amended. That was putting it mildly; in my sleeping self, I had experienced a voyage such as Thorkel's, and in nightmare visions I had travelled inside my soul and been forced face to face with aspects of myself and my past that were neither nice nor welcome.

'Powerful dreams,' Thorfinn repeated thoughtfully. He was staring at me, right inside me. I had the sense that he was seeing me very clearly.

It was not a comfortable feeling. 'What happened to Thorkel?' I asked, more to stop his probing than because I thought he'd tell me. 'Did he manage to get his ship and his crew safely home?'

'He did,' Thorfinn said. I sensed a heaviness in his tone, as if some ancient memory disturbed him. 'In time, he married, and his wife bore him a son.' He shot me a quick glance, his light eyes holding mine for only an instant. 'His son, too, was a mariner, and that son's daughter in her turn bore a son who followed his forefathers to sea.'

I worked it out. 'So that man was Thorkel's great-grandson.'

'He was,' Thorfinn agreed. Again, he looked quickly at me. It was as if he was constantly gauging my reaction. 'He was called the Silver Dragon,' he murmured, 'and this was his land.'

He must have been a mighty figure, I reflected, for his people still called their land by the same name.

'What was he like?' I asked.

Thorfinn looked up into the sky. 'It is warm today,' he observed. Only relatively so, I could have added. I wrapped my borrowed sheepskin jerkin more closely around me. 'We shall dismount,' he went on, 'and sit here on the headland, looking out over the sea.'

I settled beside him. The ponies wandered away, and I heard the sound of their strong teeth tearing at the short, tough grass. I'd imagined we would sit there a while, and he would tell me some more about life up there in that inhospitable land. But I was wrong. When, at last, he began to speak, it was to tell me a story that precisely answered my question: the story of the Silver Dragon.

'You asked what he was like,' he began. 'He was, like most of us, a mixture of good and bad. He was a big man; tall, broad-shouldered, heavily bearded, with a head of thick, fair hair streaked white by the sun, the wind and the salt sea spray. That was why they gave him the nickname: they said he looked like a dragon wreathed in its own silvery-white smoke.' He smiled, as if reflecting on some fond memory.

'To begin with, he was fearless and intrepid, leading his

loyal crew into many adventures as they followed the routes discovered by the forefathers and, extending them, always pushing on, on, discovered new lands. The Dragon had faith in his own abilities: was he not the descendant of great men, mariners who feared nothing and risked every peril in order to push out the boundaries of their world? Besides, the Dragon believed that he carried his own luck with him.' A shadow crossed the lined old face. In a softer tone, he murmured, 'It is ever so, that the gods observe those who are brash and overconfident, and, in time, remind them forcefully and painfully that they are but human.'

I nodded. Gurdyman had told me legends from out of the unimaginably distant lands in the hot south, beside the Middle Sea. In the tales, men who began to believe they were gods always suffered. I pictured Gurdyman's face, trying to recall the word: *hubris*.

'What happened to the Dragon?' I prompted Thorfinn.

He smiled sadly. 'Knowing that a . . . a certain path was becoming increasingly perilous, he persisted in following it when he should have turned back.'

'Like his great-grandfather Thorkel,' I butted in, remembering Freydis's tale.

'Yes,' he said. The word was barely above a whisper. 'The result was very painful for him,' he went on, resuming his story, 'and for a while he feared he was losing his reason. He—'

'What about his crew and his ship?' I interrupted. 'They must have been in danger, too.'

Thorfinn turned to me. 'A good question,' he remarked. 'The Dragon at that time was a long way from treating his crew in the way that good, loyal sailors deserve to be treated. There was indeed danger for them, for the Dragon's mind had turned inwards, and he was not as alert to the ever-present perils of the sea as he should have been.'

'Did he . . .?' I began, but Thorfinn did not let me speak.

'The Dragon returned to his senses just in time,' he went on, 'and, understanding at last the desperate chasm that yawned at his feet, he tried to save himself. Abandoning his wild ways, he ceased to sail his ship in anything but the safest, best-known waters, restricting himself and his crew to the tried and tested routes. He, who had been a seafarer in the finest tradition of our people, became a *trader*.'

The amount of venom that Thorfinn put into that one innocuous word had to be heard to be believed.

'One spring, when the travelling days had just begun again,' he said, continuing with his tale, 'the Dragon took his ship on a long voyage, leaving the home waters and returning to familiar shores, his hold full of wool and ivory to trade for the many things not found in his own land. In a backwater of a port, far away, he went ashore and, still deeply disturbed and not in his right mind, he got very drunk. He began to see visions: terrible images that attacked him like a cloud of demons, causing him to lash out blindly and wildly. His huge fist encountered a local man, and, in short, a ferocious fight broke out, leaving the Dragon badly beaten. Strong and indomitable though he was, he had been set on by ten men, and had come off very much the worse.'

I could well imagine. I shuddered, my healer's imagination seeing the likely damage.

'The men felt guilty afterwards, however,' Thorfinn continued, 'for they knew who he was – his reputation, indeed, had spread far and wide – and recognized that he was not in his right mind. They had some affection for him, and would not have harmed him had it not been necessary to restrain him and prevent him hurting others. One of them knew of a local woman who was skilled at healing –' (*How strange*, I reflected, *for that was just what I'd been thinking about*) – 'and fetched her to tend the Dragon.' He paused, his eyes staring into the distance. 'In stature, she was a small woman – tiny, in comparison to the Dragon – yet her heart was brave as a she-wolf's. She was slender and slight, with deep, dark eyes full of laughter, rosy cheeks and a smile that made men go weak at the knees.' He paused, a faint frown on his face, as if trying to recall what came next in the tale.

It seemed to take him quite an effort to pick up his narrative. Then, as if the pause had not happened, he said casually, 'Or so it was said. She was skilled in her craft, and with quick, nimble little hands, she patched up the Dragon's wounds and,

using the painful but efficient method of a round stone under
the arm and a hard push, put back his dislocated shoulder.
Realizing that he would not be fit to sail for many days, she
sent one of the men he had fought to inform his crew, and
had four of the others bear him away to her small house, on
the edge of a nearby village. There she tended him, bathing
his forehead when he sweated in his fever – for, despite her
care, one of his cuts had become inflamed – and sitting on
his chest when, in his delirium, he would have risen up and
fled out into the darkness.

'She was more than a patcher-up of cuts and a setter of
bones, this little healer,' he went on, his deep voice seeming
to thrum in the still air. 'Her ability to see inside another's
mind, and, moreover, to understand what she saw there,
amounted almost to magic. She perceived that the Dragon was
troubled by something that ran far deeper than cuts and bruises.
For all that she was yet young, she possessed the wisdom of
her ancestors, and she understood that it would not be easy
to make a man like the Dragon, who prided himself on his
great courage, open up to her and reveal what darkened his
heart. She bided her time, and gradually, over the days and
the long nights, she gained his confidence.'

I imagined how that might have been. How would I have
done it? Quietly, calmly, I thought; asking careful, apparently
casual, questions; always making sure I disguised what I was
really trying to do. It would take a great deal of patience,
when your healer's instinct was telling you in no uncertain
terms that a patient was suffering badly and needed your
help . . .

'In time,' Thorfinn went on, 'the Dragon began to trust this
bright, funny, confident little woman, who refused to be intim-
idated by him and who presumed to order him around in a
way that nobody, especially anyone female, had dared to do
since he was a child in the care of his indomitable mother. As
the days went on, his resentment of her began to lessen, and
he no longer had to grit his teeth at her chattering. He—'

'What about her?' I interrupted, no longer able to contain
myself. 'What did *she* feel about *him*?'

Thorfinn turned and grinned at me, as if to say: *typical*

woman's question. 'She, too, was warming to him, and starting to overcome her initial aversion to the big, brutal stranger who had lost his temper so spectacularly.' He paused, perhaps made awkward by this talk of feelings. 'It would not be exaggerating,' he said eventually, 'to say that she was growing quite fond of him.'

The healer falling for her patient – yes, it was not unheard of. Edild had warned me to be on my guard, if ever I were to share the intimacy of treatment with an attractive man made temporarily dependent on me, to watch myself carefully. So far, the only time I had encountered those conditions was in caring for Rollo, and *fond* did not begin to describe my feelings. I'd already been deeply in love with him.

In a vivid flash of memory, I recalled our hand-fasting. *There is no need for this, sweeting,* he had said, his expression soft with love, *for I am bound to you already.* Nevertheless – perhaps because he saw that it mattered to me – he had allowed me to proceed. I'd done it the old way, with our right hands bound by a strip of ribbon and a stub of precious beeswax candle lit by the flames of our two rush lights, symbolizing that what we made together was greater than the sum of our two selves.

Rollo. *Where are you?* I asked him silently. There was no answer.

I forced my mind back to the present, and to what else Edild had told me on the subject of the healer's relationship with her charge. She had explained how to deal with attractive male patients who believed they were in love with me. *Be brusque,* she had said, in the sort of tone that brooked no argument; I could hear her words now, stored within my memory. *Leave the man in no doubt whatsoever that you are there to tend his wounds or his sickness, and nothing more.*

'What did the little healer do?' I asked.

Thorfinn, prompted, went on with his story. 'She asked him outright what was worrying him. At first, he denied that anything was, but she persisted, and finally, exhausted by pain and distress, he gave in. He was tired that day – it was nightfall after his first attempt at walking further than to the latrine and back – and worn down by the weight he had carried for so long. She fed him strong ale, and, lying there by the hearth, finally he opened himself to her.'

I waited, hardly daring to breathe. There was something in the air . . . a nervous tension, as if the forbidden was about to be spoken, and the elements of the natural world around us – the black rocks, the wiry grass, the wide blue sky – were anxious with anticipation.

'The Dragon had in his possession a certain object,' Thorfinn said heavily, 'which had been passed down through the generations since the days of Thorkel Jorundsson, the Dragon's great-grandfather, and was first acquired when Thorkel went ashore in that far land behind the sun.'

I suppressed a gasp: unless I was mistaken, it appeared that Thorfinn was about to continue the tale that Freydis had begun last night. I'd been right, it seemed, when I'd instinctively felt that she would not conclude it. She wasn't going to, but her father was.

'In that strange port in a faraway land,' Thorfinn was saying, 'a man with dark skin and feathers in his hair offered him a strange ball made of a substance that he said was divine. It was a gift, he claimed, from the gods of his land. In colour it was black, but, held up to the flame of a candle or to sunlight, it would flash out green and gold lights that at times dazzled the eye.'

Thorfinn glanced at me, and then resumed his narrative, slipped so swiftly and easily into storyteller mode that I barely noticed the transition.

'"What is it?" Thorkel asked the dark-skinned man in an awed whisper.

'"It is a shining mirror," answered the man, "and it is very powerful, recognizing no boundaries or limitations. It permits a man to see the stark truth, for nothing may be hidden from it, and it does not hesitate to reveal everything it knows. It is ruthless; it is an object that only the strongest, bravest man may consult."

'Thorkel, while sorely tempted by an object described as only fit for the strongest and the bravest, nevertheless was cautious. After all, he knew nothing of this stranger with the feathers in his hair, and it was well known that busy trading ports attracted the unscrupulous and the devious, willing to use any trick to make money. "And what benefit is it to a man, this ability to see within himself?" he demanded. "What advantage would that bring to a mariner like me?"

'The stranger gave a mysterious smile. "The shining mirror is a stone of divination," he murmured. "It bestows upon its owner the gift of prophecy." He nodded at the Dragon's instinctive gasp. "Moreover," he continued, "if a man has the strength, it allows his conscious will to search out and harness the unseen forces of the spirit world, so that their immeasurable powers are at his disposal." Leaning forward, dropping his voice to an intimate whisper, the dark man added, "You could manifest the energies of the spirit world here on earth. What then, mariner, could you not achieve?"'

I shuddered. Thorfinn had conjured up the mood too well. I did not like the sound of this magical stone; not at all. Although I am still a novice in the arts that Gurdyman and Hrype are trying to teach me, already I knew enough to fear anything that offers the power of the spirit world as a tool at the disposal of a mere human being. Over and over again, Gurdyman stresses that the spirits must be treated with deep respect: *keep well away unless there is absolutely no alternative*, is his constant advice. He doesn't follow the advice himself, but I suppose – ancient and experienced in his craft as he is – that is his prerogative.

'And so Thorkel acquired the magic stone,' I breathed. He must have done, for, had he had the good sense to turn and walk away, this story would never have happened.

'He did,' Thorfinn agreed. 'He gave the stranger with the feathers in his hair a bag of hard-earned gold, and the stranger wrapped the shining mirror in its soft leather cloth, and Thorkel bore it away.'

He was a fool, I thought. 'What happened?'

'At first, Thorkel was thrilled with his purchase, and he did not begin to suspect that, from the moment it came into his possession, it had begun to alter him.'

'His crew saw the change in him,' I said, remembering Freydis's tale. *He was not the same man he had been when he went ashore*, she had said.

Thorfinn nodded. 'Indeed they did,' he agreed. 'But he was their captain; their leader. They were far from their own land, and they knew that they depended on his courage and his skill to get them safely home. And, indeed, the alterations that they observed in Thorkel were but subtle, and did not appear to diminish his abilities as a mariner. It was . . .' He paused, apparently searching for the right word. 'It was his character that had changed.'

He did not elucidate. I wanted to probe, but, almost as if he wanted to forestall my questions, he ploughed on with his tale. 'The ship and her crew returned to their homeland, and the people welcomed them with great joy, for they were long overdue. After a time, Thorkel withdrew to a small hut up in the hills, where he stayed, suffering great privations, through a long and ferocious winter. He was entirely alone, and to this day nobody can say what he endured. What he endured in his *mind*,' he amended. 'Physically, the damage was all too visible, for Thorkel lost a foot and half of his right hand to the biting cold that stops the blood and kills the flesh.'

I shuddered. I had heard of the condition, but never seen it. 'What was he like?' I asked, although part of me felt I would really rather not know. 'Was he himself again?'

Thorfinn smiled. 'He was, child. It is likely he understood by then that it was the shining stone that had so affected him, and it seems that he wrapped it up and hid it away.'

I frowned. 'But it didn't—'

'But it did not stay hidden?' Thorfinn finished my question, quirking an eyebrow at me. 'No, it did not, for its powers are seductive and it does not give up its hold so easily. Thorkel's son grew to manhood, and in time he inherited his father's black stone. It passed on to his daughter, and in all that time the stone was no more than an object of fascination, for its beauty was undiminished. But, for some reason, its powers slept; perhaps, indeed, it was that no one during those long years awoke them.'

'Until it came into the Dragon's hands,' I whispered. 'And he reacted just as his great-grandfather had done.'

'He did,' Thorfinn said heavily. 'He fell deep under its enchantment, and it took him, helpless, on a terrible journey inside himself. So affected was he by what was revealed to him there that his mind was all but destroyed.'

He fell silent. Deeply shaken by the horror of what he had just said, I dared not speak.

After a moment, he resumed. 'Had it not been for a chance meeting with a dark-eyed, laughing healer,' he said softly, 'the Dragon would have torn himself apart.'

ELEVEN

Thorfinn and I sat for some time, both of us deep in our thoughts. I guessed he was still lost in the Dragon's tale, perhaps grateful that this kinsman of his had had such a timely rescue from the powerful object that was slowly stealing his soul. I had heard of such things. Gurdyman, who enlightened me, left me in no doubt as to their danger.

Even while I was thinking about Thorfinn, something was batting at the edge of my mind, trying to attract my attention. I did as I've been taught in such situations, deliberately slowing my breathing, relaxing my body and stilling my thoughts. Quite soon, I understood.

I understood a lot; it was as if a mist had cleared, revealing the sun shining on a bright image. I maintained my silence for a little longer while I worked out how best to tell Thorfinn what I now believed I knew.

'It seems to me,' I said quietly, 'that the Dragon could not risk continued possession of his shining stone.' I sensed Thorfinn stiffen as his attention flew back to me, but he did not speak. 'He knew that it was too dangerous an object; for him, anyway. He realized that his only hope was to abandon it.'

'*Abandon* is the wrong word.' Thorfinn's tone was harsh. 'He could never have done that, for the stone was far too important to him. It was,' he added heavily, 'an heirloom, and it belonged to his line until the end of days.' He paused, as if about to pursue that thought, but evidently changed his mind. He shook his head, muttered something, then turned back to me. 'But yes, you are right. He understood that it was too powerful for him, and he had no option but to leave it in the safe keeping of another. Not for ever,' he added urgently, as if I had protested, 'but until such time as he should have a son, and that son would be ready to take possession of the stone. To try his own strength against it,' he murmured, his voice dropping to a whisper.

Until he had a son, I repeated to myself. Yes, that would be the way of it. Already the stone had passed through the hands of four generations, and family tradition would no doubt insist that the Dragon's son had his turn.

'The Dragon left it with the little healer, didn't he?' I said. I suppose I was guessing, but I felt the confidence that comes when you're right. 'And . . .' Something else occurred to me, and it was all I could do not to yell in triumph. 'And the *long trading mission to familiar shores* that you spoke of was to somewhere in the fens, wasn't it?' He didn't answer, but I sensed an easing of tension in him, as if, for some reason, he was pleased I'd worked it out. 'The healer lived somewhere near where I live, and she took the shining stone and hid it in a safe place. Now the Dragon's son must have grown to manhood, and he wants it, and so your people sent Einar to go and look for it, and he broke into the places where members of my family live and . . . and . . .'

I stopped, for my bright confidence had cracked and broken, and my clever theory fell in ruins at my feet. Two things about it deeply disturbed me: first, no matter how I tried, and bearing in mind that I knew from first-hand experience that Einar had a terrible temper and readily lashed out with his huge fists, I found all at once that I could no longer see him as the ruthless killer of Goda's mother-in-law and my aunt Alvela.

Was *this* the reason why I'd had to work so hard to remind myself he was a murderer? Because I'd been wrong about him, and deep down I knew it?

His people would not have sent him out to perpetrate such violence, no matter what the goal. I just couldn't believe it. It was always possible that they did not know he was a killer, but I couldn't really make myself believe that, either. They were clannish, here. Younger generations revered their honoured elder and did what he told them.

But *somebody* had come looking. The other shocking thing about my theory was that, whoever the searcher was, he had concentrated his hunt on the dwellings of my own kin. Which meant . . .

Who was she? I am the family's bard, the keeper of the traditions, the one whose job it is to memorize the long kinship lists, the family trees. Where, among all those people, was there a healer? Edild, of course, but the description of the young woman did not really fit her.

I spun round to Thorfinn. 'How many years ago did this happen?' I demanded. 'When did the Dragon leave his precious shining stone in the fens?'

Thorfinn looked at me steadily. 'Some sixteen, seventeen years before Duke William arrived,' he said. His voice, I thought, was carefully neutral.

So that was 1049 or 1050. Definitely not Edild, then; she hadn't been born. Who were the healers in my Granny's generation? She was the bard, the storyteller, and I couldn't recall her ever having mentioned a healer. She'd had two elder sisters, but they hadn't had any particular talents beyond those that everyone needs to survive out in the fenland. What of my mother's kin? She had come from shepherding stock, and her family had worked a compact but thriving smallholding. She came from a long line of big, fair women just like her, but there could easily have been a small, dark one among them. Had this unknown woman been the healer summoned to tend the Dragon when he'd been so badly beaten? It was the best I could come up with. It fitted, since the dwelling places where the giant had searched were as closely attached to my mother's kin as to my father's: Goda, Elfritha and I were her daughters, and poor Alvela had been her sister-in-law.

I tried to think which of my mother's aunts had been a healer, and I thought I recalled her speaking of a woman who had been skilled with plants and the preparation of medicines. Ama? Aeda? Cross with myself, I could not bring it to mind.

Thorfinn was waiting. I drew a breath, and said, 'I believe that the woman who healed the Dragon was an ancestor of mine, on my mother's side. While she tended him, he learned to care for her and to trust her, so that, when he made the momentous decision to part from his magic stone, he left it in her keeping. She hid it away in such a secure place that it has lain there ever since. Except now, the Dragon's son wants to claim his inheritance, and, on his behalf, Einar –' no, not Einar, I was sure of it – '*someone* has been to the fens to search for it.'

I was not entirely pleased with my account. I knew I was right in essence; it was just in the details that it threatened to fall apart.

Thorfinn studied me for a long moment. Then, nodding, he said, 'You have made deductions, and leapt from what you know to what seem to you reasonable conclusions. You are right in some things, for it was indeed to the fenland that the Dragon travelled, and, as you surmise, there that he left his treasure in the hands of the woman who healed him.'

'But was she . . .?' *Was she my mother's aunt?* I wanted to ask.

Thorfinn, it seemed, wasn't going to tell me. 'The stone has been hidden these many years,' he went on, 'and now it is sought, most urgently.' He closed his eyes, as if suddenly weary. 'Not, however, by the son of the Dragon; for, having grown up with the story of what the shining mirror almost did to his father, the son has, until now, been content to leave it where it lies.' Opening his eyes, he turned to me.

The look in his eyes made me shrink away.

'The stone's existence is known of outside the Dragon's immediate kin,' he said. There was despair in his voice. 'A feud has been waged, through three generations, between two siblings and their descendants. The Dragon's mother – Thorkel's granddaughter – had a younger brother, who was a lesser being than his sister in every quality save malice and spite, and who grew up resenting his sister to the point of loathing. Two generations later, his grandson believes it is his sacred mission to restore his branch of the family to what he sees as their rightful position, in ascendancy over the Dragon's line. To this end, he has embarked on a search for the stone, which we hope and pray with all our hearts will not succeed.'

I was shivering, and it wasn't from the cold. 'Is he big, bearded and red-haired?' I whispered.

'He is,' Thorfinn said solemnly. 'His name is Skuli, and he is warped by evil.'

And, I could have added, *he broke his way into our homes and killed my kinswomen.*

My triumph over having deduced correctly was short-lived.

I remembered, far too graphically, what this man warped by evil had done to my kin.

Oh – *oh* – was he still there, casting his huge and threatening shadow over everyone I loved? Here was I, so far away, made impotent by distance; I might now know what he'd been looking for, but that was no help whatsoever to my family, because there was no way of telling them. He believed that they stood between him and what he so powerfully desired. The fact that they had no idea about either the stone or its whereabouts wasn't going to be any protection at all . . .

I leapt up. I would have run to my pony and galloped away, except that Thorfinn grabbed a fold of my skirt and held me back.

'Where are you going?' he asked.

'*I'm going home!*' I cried. 'They need me – I'm the only one who has any idea what this is about! I've got to go *home!*'

His hold tightened, and slowly he pulled me back to sit down beside him. 'You are full of courage, little one,' he said, and I heard the very edge of amusement in his tone.

'They're in danger,' I whispered. To my shame, I felt tears well up in my eyes.

What happened next was entirely unexpected: Thorfinn made a quiet sound, almost of distress, and, putting his great arms round me, drew me down against his mighty chest. It was the sort of all-embracing, enfolding hug that my father used to give me when I was a child and had fallen over – when, come to think of it, I was a young woman, secretly crying in the night because the man she loved was far away and she had no idea when she would see him again.

For a while, I just surrendered to it. Thorfinn might not be my beloved father, but, in that moment, he was a good substitute. Some faint, soft, tender chime of memory was ringing . . . prompted by a small, comforting movement, or some smell common to all big, fatherly men? I didn't know. Before I could isolate it and pin it down, it was gone.

'It was not out of malice that I had you brought here,' Thorfinn said presently. 'It was, child, for your own safety.'

My head shot up at that. 'My *safety*?' I cried incredulously.

'All those miles in Einar's ship, and his fist to keep me in my place?'

'I regret the fact that he hit you more than I can express,' Thorfinn said, and I sensed the anger simmering in him. 'Einar is repentant, and in time I believe he will find a way to make recompense. You . . . it is no excuse for what he did, Lassair, but unwittingly your words to him touched a very raw spot.'

It was a time for honesty. 'It wasn't unwitting at all,' I muttered. 'Einar had just abducted me, and I was very scared. I really needed a way of hitting back at him, and that taunt about him sailing a cargo boat instead of a longship was the best I could think of.'

Thorfinn gave a rueful laugh. 'You could not have come up with a more piercing thrust had you tried,' he observed. Then he added, so softly that I only just heard, 'The original *Malice-striker* was my ship.'

Yes, I thought. *Of course.* 'What was she like?'

'She was long and lean, and she rode the wave tops like a sea bird gliding on wide wings,' he said, the love and the longing very evident in his voice. 'She was light, with a shallow draught, and her high courage and adventurous spirit were daunted neither by fierce seas nor by winding rivers leading into unspeakable darkness.' He paused. 'I drove her too hard,' he muttered. 'I used her unkindly, for I . . .' Abruptly he broke off. He was silent for a moment, and I sensed he was undergoing some internal struggle. When he spoke again, there was a cheerfulness in his tone that even a child would have known to be forced.

'Well, Einar's craft has inherited her great spirit,' he said with an unconvincing smile. 'The dragon head now rises up over his knarr, and a fine ship she is.'

It was, I felt, time – and not only for my sake – to return to what he'd just been saying, about the reason I'd been taken there. 'You were about to tell me why you had me brought to you,' I said.

He looked down at me. 'I was,' he agreed. 'Child, as you will have surmised, Skuli Ondarson knows the general location of the shining stone. He has two very powerful motives for

finding it: first, he believes that the precious inheritance should
have passed down the male line, in which case it would have
gone to his grandfather and not his great-aunt, and now he
would be the rightful keeper.'

'Why didn't it?' I asked.

'Because Thorkel and his son Ondar perceived too clearly
the relative merits of Ondar's daughter and son,' Thorfinn said,
'and, while the one – his daughter Gudrun – was a worthy
keeper of the magic stone, there was no doubt that the other
– Ondar's son Arnor – would have turned its dangerous and
formidable power to further his own dark ambition.'

'And this son, this Arnor, was the red-headed giant's grandfather.' I was trying to get the lines of the family clear in my
mind.

'Yes, Lassair. Arnor is dead, but Skuli is very much alive,
although it would be better for many people – not only us – if
it were not so.'

'I saw him,' I said faintly. 'I'm sure I did.' In my mind I
relived that moment on the edge of the village, when I'd seen
a man, or perhaps a vision-man, on my way back from checking
Granny's grave.

A real-life man, it now appeared. And one who presented
a grave danger to me and mine . . .

'It's very possible,' Thorfinn agreed, 'for he was close on
your tail, and he would have taken you if the chance had
presented itself.' From his grave tone, I understood that being
taken by this Skuli was something to be avoided at all costs.
'It is also possible that it was Einar you saw, for he too had
been watching you.'

'Einar was . . .' I wasn't sure I understood.

'We knew that Skuli had gone in search of the shining stone,'
Thorfinn said patiently. 'We knew too that he would be totally
ruthless, and let nothing get in the way. He would fight, despoil,
kill; he would, if he got his hands on someone he believed
was aware of the stone's whereabouts, torture the truth out of
them.'

'I thought that was why I'd been brought here,' I said in a
small voice. 'I thought Einar was going to force me to tell
him something I don't even know.' The echo of that fear

shivered up through me. I tried to dismiss it. 'I was nearly right!' I added, trying to laugh.

'No you were not, child,' he said gravely. 'It was no part of our plan to do you harm.'

But I barely heard. My mind was racing, trying to absorb all I'd been told. Something occurred to me: 'You said just now there were two reasons why Skuli wants the stone. What's the second one?'

Thorfinn gave a deep sigh, as if the burden was suddenly too much to bear. 'Because of one specific quality which it possesses,' he said heavily. 'There is a particular journey he desperately wishes to embark upon, and he has convinced himself that only by possessing the shining stone, and harnessing its power, will he find the way.'

I frowned. 'But I thought – didn't you say that the stone's main quality was that it helped you look inside yourself?'

'Yes, I did,' Thorfinn confirmed. 'But that, as I'm sure you realize, is not the voyage Skuli has in mind. No, child – it is another of its powers that he desires.' His voice dropped to a whisper and, leaning towards me, he murmured, 'He believes that the place where he is bound can only be reached with the aid of the spirits, and he intends to use the stone to manifest them to help him.'

He must be mad, was my first, violent reaction. No man in his right mind would even consider something so dangerous. Fleetingly I wondered where this place was that Skuli so desperately wanted to go, and what he hoped to achieve by finding it at such peril. Then, slowly, it dawned on me: he had to be stopped. Whatever it took, Skuli must not be allowed to get his hands on the shining stone.

I even began to view my own abduction in a slightly different light.

'Do you understand now?' Thorfinn asked. 'Skuli had located your village, and he knew where the rest of your family lived. He knew about your wizard friend in Cambridge, and he was waiting to grab you as soon as you ventured out alone. But he had reckoned without Einar, who already knew much of what Skuli had to work to discover, and who, perhaps with the might of right on his side, succeeded in getting to you before Skuli did. It was, I understand, a close-run race.'

I saw myself in memory, blithely striding along, thinking about home and food. Not one but two giant-sized men had been stalking me, and the only, tiny, sound I'd heard to give away the fact of their presence had come just before I was taken.

'They walk softly on the ground, for such big men,' I said. I was still trying to suppress thoughts of what Skuli might have done to me, and it helped to think about something else.

'They do,' Thorfinn agreed. 'Both are hunters, and learned young how to tread without making a sound.'

Hunters: arrows, knives, blood, pain, guts, death. Not a good image. 'So Einar brought me all the way here to keep me safe from . . . er, to keep me safe,' I said quickly. 'Couldn't he just have taken me on board his ship and sailed up and down the coast for a while? Why did he have to bring me so far?'

Thorfinn did not immediately answer. When eventually he spoke, it was as if he was replying to a different question entirely.

'Tonight, Freydis will continue with her storytelling,' he said. 'Now, child, I am growing cold. Fetch the ponies, and we will return to the homestead.'

'Now,' Freydis began, 'I shall tell the tale of the Perilous Voyage, for it is a journey that many of our kinsmen have made, and one that many did not survive.'

It was late in the evening. The tables had been cleared of everything except the mugs and the flagons of ale, and two or three torches had been set in the walls. The fire in the long hearth was glowing, shedding soft light on the attentive faces sitting on either side. As Freydis announced the subject of her tale, there were one or two murmurs, and some of her audience turned to look at her in surprise. Had they expected her to pick up Thorkel's story? The previous night, after all, she had left us with that disturbing image of a man visiting a strange port and returning to his crew not the same man. Not that it mattered to me, of course . . .

I sensed someone watching me. Turning, I saw it was Thorfinn. He gave an almost imperceptible nod.

Then I understood. Freydis's tales were for my benefit, for I was the stranger; I was probably the only one who had never heard the stories before. As far as I was concerned, there was no need for Freydis to relate the end of Thorkel's tale and its aftermath, for Thorfinn had already done so.

I settled back to hear about the Perilous Voyage.

'They went to trade their furs, their amber and their walrus ivory,' Freydis said, her eyes glittering in the firelight as she looked around the circle of her audience, 'but, for many, that was merely a pretext: in their hearts, they knew that what they sought was adventure. And where better place to seek it than the vast continent that spread out to the south and east? In their light, nimble ships, they had the means of penetrating deep into its secrets, returning home with tales of giants and river monsters, whirlpools and rapids, and cities sparkling with jewels beneath a sun that burned like fire.' In a whisper judged perfectly to reach the intimate circle around her and no further, she added, 'Who, after all, can resist the summons of the unknown?'

She told of the men who discovered the inland route from the northern seas to those of the south; of how, when the waterways petered out, the brave sailors got out of their craft and carried them overland to the next river. Bending to the oars once more, they rowed until they were exhausted, then did it all over again the next day. They fought hunger, fatigue, homesickness, as well as more tangible enemies such as starving wolves and hostile tribesmen. On they went, travelling almost due south now, until the great northern forests thinned and disappeared and they emerged on to the steppes.

'Then, when they had already travelled so far that home was but a memory,' she went on, her voice strengthening, 'they came to the most terrifying obstacle of all: forty miles of rapids, formed of no fewer than seven cataracts; fearsome chasms between high rock walls where the river plunged like a rip tide condensed into a narrow funnel.' She spun slowly round, letting the image sink in. 'They gave them names, those brave sailors,' she said, respect very evident in her voice. 'The Gulper. The Sleepless. The Island Force. The Yeller. And, when each had been overcome and the men were desperate for rest, they came to the fiercest of all. Some called him Ever-fierce; some, simply, Impassable.'

Impassable. Could there be, I wondered, a more daunting name?

'If they managed to do the impossible and come safely through Impassable,' Freydis continued, 'still more swirling waterfalls, rapids and unexpected descents awaited them, until they began to fear they had passed unwittingly into some watery hell from which the only escape was death.'

Again, she fell silent, slowly looking round at us all. 'There was only one way to survive the rapids,' she said matter-of-factly, 'and that was to do as they had done between the waters of the northern rivers and carry their craft, around the wild white waves. The prudent followed the portage tracks all the way. The adventurous – some would say the foolhardy – chose only to avoid the hungry maws and the sharp teeth of the waterfalls, opting to shoot their slender ships like arrows down the broiling white water, riding the angry waves like fierce, brave horses.'

I tried to imagine it, but my heart quaked at the very thought. How had they found the courage to risk their ships – the only means by which they could hope one day to return to their distant homes – amid those thundering waters? How could they dare risk their lives?

As if she had picked up my thought, Freydis was nodding. 'Many perished,' she said, her voice low. 'The survivors set up a great stone, on which they marked in runes the names of the dead. That stone,' she added softly, 'is still in use today.'

Into my mind flew an image of a bearded giant, wet, spent, knife in hand as he carefully picked out the rune marks that stood for his dead friend. He was muttering under his breath – a prayer, no doubt – and he had tears in his pale blue eyes . . .

'Now, at last, the way became easier,' Freydis was saying, calling my attention back to her tale, 'for the river broadened out and slowed its hectic pace, and the sailors could raise their sail and have a rest from the oars. In time, the river emptied into the smaller inland sea, and from there it was an unchallenging trip down the western shore until, finally, the Great City came into view.'

The Great City. I had heard the name. In fact, quite a lot of what Freydis had just recounted seemed vaguely familiar. I closed my eyes – she was now describing the city's wonders – and let my mind go blank.

Almost instantly, I heard Gurdyman's voice inside my head as, together, we pored over his map: *One such voyage led to their Great City.*

Its name, I remembered, was Miklagard.

The frustration bubbled up as, once again, I wondered why Gurdyman had elected to tell me of these matters just before I was abducted and brought here. It surely was not simply coincidence. But how had he known? Had he somehow been preparing me? For what?

Somehow (could it be, was it possible?) he had foretold that this would happen; that I'd be stolen away from my home, my family and my friends and deposited here, far in the north, for reasons I was only starting to understand.

'Shining stone.'

The words slithered into my awareness like a glittering serpent. Freydis had spoken them. Snapping to attention, I listened.

She was telling the story of a man who had not survived the cataracts; who, alone in his vessel while his companions had portaged their own craft, had risked one too many sets of rapids, and been thrown into the hungry, turbulent water as his frail ship broke up into firewood.

'His kinsmen mourned him long and deeply,' she said, sounding now as if she was chanting, 'for, although his heart had begun to turn to the dark, he had led them well and they trusted him. As they stood around the marker stone on which they had carved his name, they vowed their loyalty, and they swore that they would not rest until he had been avenged.'

Avenged? It sounded as if the man's kin believed his death had been no accident, unless they were planning vengeance on the very cataracts themselves . . .

'For it was Arnor's claim that he had been deprived of what was rightfully his by birth,' Freydis said, very quietly, 'and both he and his kin believed that it would have protected them all from the dangers of the Perilous Voyage.'

Arnor. I knew I'd heard the name. Arnor . . . Yes; he was the younger brother, deemed unsuitable to receive the shining stone. The one who, in Thorfinn's words, *would have turned its dangerous and formidable power to further his own dark ambition.* It was as if Thorfinn was repeating his words of earlier, directly into my mind.

So Arnor had not been appointed guardian of his family's great treasure, because that honour had gone to his sister, I reflected, and he had believed himself robbed of its powers as protective talisman. Yet he had gone on the dangerous voyage anyway, and his life had been lost.

I tried to recall everything that Thorfinn had told me about the stone. I couldn't actually remember him mentioning it could protect its bearer, but he had said that it allowed the harnessing of the unseen forces of the spirit world. With those at your disposal, I realized, what more protection would you need?

Freydis was winding down to the conclusion of her tale; I was a bard myself, and I recognized the change in her voice, which was gradually turning from stimulating to hypnotic. I felt I could safely miss the end of the story; I had more important things to think about.

I was trying to put it all together: to discover, in truth, what it all had to do with me. Skuli, clearly, wanted to succeed where his grandfather Arnor had failed; this voyage to the Great City must surely be his goal, and he believed that, to make it safely, he needed the shining stone. Yet the Dragon's side of the family line were equally determined he should not get his hands on the treasure; presumably, they had good reason for not wanting him to reach that goal . . .

My head was bursting; I could no longer think straight. It was so hard, I reflected crossly, when they were feeding me information so grudgingly.

Around me, people were standing up, stretching, draining their mugs and heading off for bed. There was nothing else to do but join them. With the fervent hope that I would see more clearly after a night's rest, I headed for my sheepskins and a well-earned sleep.

TWELVE

I was finishing a tasty breakfast the next morning – fresh-baked bread and a cup of *skyr* flavoured with honey – and laughing with Thyra as we watched her second-youngest child attempt to lick out his bowl for the last, sweet dregs, when Thorfinn approached.

Dropping a hand on my shoulder, he leaned down and murmured in my ear. 'Come and walk with me, Lassair.'

He wasn't someone you disobeyed. In any case, the prospect of another outing with him was appealing. I might well discover the answers to some of the questions that kept tormenting me.

I fetched my shawl, then hurried outside to join him. We set off towards the headland out to the west of the homestead, and, when the time extended and still he did not speak, I glanced at his face and guessed he was deep in thought. We climbed to the top of a low cliff, and suddenly the brilliant blue sea was spread out below us, the early sun sending up dancing sparks of reflected light that dazzled the eyes.

'It is time for you to go home, child,' Thorfinn said without preamble. 'Einar has been watching the weather, and his ship will sail at midday.'

Joy flooded through me. In that first moment, I felt nothing but relief; it was only as the surprising news sank in that other considerations occurred to me.

The first was that, if I was bundled up and dispatched back to my fenland home this very day, then there would be no chance for me to find out what I so desperately wanted to know: why I'd been brought here, and how my family and I were connected with the Dragon and his shining stone. Einar was a taciturn man, and I knew without a doubt that he would be as unforthcoming on the journey home as he had been on the way here.

I looked at Thorfinn, standing still as stone beside me. The second consideration was to do with him; well, it *was* him.

As the prospect of parting from him became a reality, I discovered I'd grown rather fond of him. It was illogical, and I knew it; his son had abducted me, hit me, brought me here, hundreds of miles from my home and without one word of explanation, on Thorfinn's orders – not the hitting bit, I quickly corrected myself. Thorfinn would never have sanctioned that. Nevertheless, far from being fond of the old man, I should resent and loathe him.

But I didn't.

He seemed to be expecting some reaction to his announcement. When none came, he turned, looking down at me with a half-smile. 'Are you not pleased to be going home?' he asked.

It was a moment where nothing but the truth would serve. 'Yes, of course. But I don't want to leave you,' I added, half under my breath.

He did not reply, and I wondered if he'd heard. He was old, after all, and old people usually get a bit deaf. He cleared his throat a couple of times, and, when he spoke, I still wasn't entirely sure.

'Skuli has to be stopped,' he began, 'for he is bent on a mission that has already caused death and distress, and many more people will suffer if he succeeds in finding what he seeks.' I opened my mouth to ask if he meant Skuli's ruthless hunt for the stone, or the dream of succeeding where his grandfather failed, or perhaps both, but he pressed on, not letting me speak. 'To this end, I am sending a band of fighting men, including my son Jorund, my daughter's husband Njal, and others of my close kindred, as well as Einar and his crew.'

'To stop one man?' I asked, surprised.

Thorfinn smiled. 'Skuli is not alone, child. He has his own group of loyal followers, who have sworn in blood to go wherever he leads.' He sighed deeply, looking suddenly careworn and old. 'This is a kin feud, Lassair, for it originates with the destructive resentment of a brother for his elder sister; an evil, corrosive emotion that has come down two generations and has descended into malignant hatred.' He sighed again, slowly shaking his head. 'The fact remains, however, that Skuli and his headstrong young men are my kinsmen, and, no matter

what they have done and intend to do, I am head of the family
and they are my concern. If they kill, if they should die, the
responsibility is mine.'

No wonder he looked so careworn; Skuli had already slain
two defenceless women. My heart went out to him. I guessed
he longed to lead his sons and his kinsmen into the fray, as
he would have done in his prime.

Maybe he read that thought; I wouldn't have been surprised
if he had. For, very quietly, he said, 'You and I need not yet
be parted, child, for I am coming with you.'

The reaction was instinctive. I spun round and flung my
arms round him, and, after a moment, he gave a chuckle and
hugged me back.

'There is one more place I would show you, before we
return to the farmstead and prepare for departure,' he said.
'Come with me.'

He led the way along the low cliff, following a crumbling
path that followed the contours of the land. Presently another
cove opened up below us, and in it, beached high above the
water line, was the skeleton of a long, slender ship. Her mast
had gone, leaving a broken stump, and her figurehead was
missing, but neither absence marred her beauty.

I knew I'd seen her before, when she was in her prime: she
was the ship of my dream vision. I had seen her running before
the wind, and I had feared she was coming for me. Why – *how*
– had I had that foreknowledge of her?

It was frightening, and I felt my skin contract into goose
bumps. The spirits were near . . .

Thorfinn was heading off down the path to the shore, and
I hurried after him. Just then I didn't want to be alone. He
strode across the dark sand and gravel of the beach, stopping
under the bows of the ship.

'That is where a proud dragon once reared up,' he said,
pointing up at the prow. 'A dragon who breathed fire and silver
smoke, who always brought the ship safe home to port; whose
fearless heart kept the crew from harm, and who struck malice
into any foe who dared raise a hand in anger.'

'A dragon with a long, graceful neck and a snout ended in
a curling swirl of fire and smoke,' I murmured, 'set high on

a proud ship that flew over the waves as if the dragon had
spread its wings.'

'Yes, yes, all of that,' he said eagerly. He did not ask me
how I knew. 'Fearless, trustworthy, beautiful as the sunrise.'
He paused. 'This,' he added in a whisper, 'was my ship.'

Words were dancing in my head, weaving together to make
a new sense. A dragon that exhaled silver smoke. A giant of
a man, with a silvery moustache curving like breath. A ship
whose figurehead struck malice in the hearts of her foes.

'This was the original *Malice-striker,*' I said very softly. *He
was called the Silver Dragon*, he had once said to me, *and
this was his land.* 'And you, Thorfinn, are the Dragon.'

In the utter silence, I thought he held his breath.

'Why didn't you tell me who you were?' I asked. 'Why did
both you and Freydis tell the story as if it was about another
man? As if the Dragon was some long-gone kinsman, remembered only by his deeds?'

'Freydis acted on my orders. As for me . . .' He hesitated.
'The Dragon is no hero of his own tale. He – I – faced the
great test, and failed. The shining stone was the rightful inheritance of my line, yet its power was too much for me and I
had to give it up.'

'It was slowly killing you!' I protested. I heard his voice,
speaking, as I now knew, of himself: *he fell deep under its
enchantment, and it took him on a terrible journey*. And, even
worse: *the Dragon would have torn himself apart. His mind
was all but destroyed*. 'You had no choice, and you acted out
of pure self-preservation.'

He shrugged. 'Perhaps. But a better man than I would have
found some way to confront the power of the shining stone,
as others had done before him.'

'Maybe – maybe . . .' I tried to think. 'Maybe they weren't
as sensitive as you.'

He laughed, a short, bitter laugh. 'Sensitivity is not a quality
much prized in a fighting man.'

'*I* prize it,' I muttered. Then, turning so that I was looking him
in the eye, determined to have an answer, I repeated, '*Why* didn't
you tell me who the Dragon really was? That the beaten, hurt,
desperate man who was healed by my mother's aunt was you?'

His eyes slid away. I knew then that I wasn't going to get an answer. I was right: he simply said, 'I had my reasons.' Then he strode away.

We did not speak on the way back to the homestead. He, I think, was tired after telling his tale. He was, after all, an old man. For my part, I was trying to deal with yet another mystery, and failing as miserably as I was with all the other questions that were perplexing me. It was quite a relief to part from him, and, hurrying to pack up my few belongings and prepare for departure, I was glad to have something to do.

The farewells were accomplished quickly – I supposed that departures and homecomings were a regular occurrence for these people – and I was happily surprised when Thyra, Freydis and even cool, distant Asa came to bid me calm seas, a following wind and safe homecoming. Although everyone must have known the task that the men faced, there was little evident emotion. Some good-hearted ribbing, even the occasional burst of hearty laughter, set the general tone. Perhaps they regarded this as an exciting adventure.

There was one exception. Thorfinn was last to board his son's ship, and he stood on the jetty, embracing a woman of around his own age whom I had seen in the homestead, although she always kept to the shadows. She was weeping, her poor face turned up to look into his, and the pleading in her eyes was evident even from where I stood, on deck. She clung to him, and in the end he had to gently disentangle himself, patting her on the arm as he did so. 'I will do all I can, Gytha,' I heard him say. 'You have my word.'

She nodded, and I could see the effort it took her to attempt a small, brave smile. Even as Thorfinn paced along the jetty and boarded the ship, she was already turning away and hurrying back towards the farmstead.

Old Olaf was beside me. I heard him give a heavy sigh. 'What's the matter with her?' I whispered.

'She is Thorfinn's sister-in-law; the kinswoman of his late wife,' he whispered back. 'She is widowed, and alone in the world save for her two sons, and both of them sail with Skuli.'

I remembered Thorfinn's bitter words concerning the feud

that had split his family. Here it was, translated into human
terms, as a mother pleaded for the safe return of the sons she
loved; who were, through the evils of that old hatred, now in
opposition to the very man she was begging to save them.

It was yet another twisted strand in this unfathomable tangle.
Heartsick suddenly, I turned away.

At a word from Einar, the crew set about manoeuvring the
ship away from her berth. Their quick efficiency spoke of a task
performed a hundred times, and soon we were out of the little
bay and heading for open water. Men bent to the oars, and our
speed picked up. We rounded a great headland on our port side,
and all at once the wind caught us. The big, rectangular sail
was unfurled, the oars were laid aside, and Einar took up the
wonderful dragon's head and set it in place on the prow.

Malice-striker was back in her natural element, and the spray
from her swift passage was fresh on my face. The wind picked
up as we left the shelter of land, and now we were flying.

Putting everything else out of my mind, I settled down in
my accustomed place and prepared to enjoy the voyage.

Rollo had reached his destination. In the castle where he had
spent most of his childhood, he was enjoying the rare luxury
of being spoiled. The castle was still the stronghold he remembered: built for defence, tall and mighty, with no money wasted
on such fripperies as comfort or decoration. A few of its
residents, however, had begun to tire of life inside a military
fortress, and the private quarters of some of the higher-ranking
women now showed the civilizing, eastern influence of the
island's previous masters.

Rollo was housed in one such set of apartments. It was
separated from the main body of the castle by a narrow courtyard in which shrubs and small trees grew in pots, and a
fountain splashed into a blue-tiled pool. Walking from the
forcefully masculine fortress into the sweet-smelling, richly
furnished rooms was like moving from the grey tones of dusk
into brilliant midday. Colour was everywhere, from the silk-
covered divans with their jewel-toned cushions to the tray of
sapphire-dyed glasses and the crystal jug of sunshine-bright
sherbet in which sprigs of fresh, green mint floated.

He lay back on the soft silk, gazing out through the decorated archway on to the plain far below. The castle was well sited, affording views in every direction. Not that attack was likely now, since the island's Saracen rulers had conceded defeat three years ago. The mood was, as far as Rollo could tell from the short time he had been there, one of resignation, just beginning to border on content. Count Roger Guiscard, it was rumoured, was ruling his new territory wisely, retaining many of the administrative methods that had worked well for his predecessors, both Byzantine and Muslim. Trade was flourishing, and people were making money. In Rollo's experience, little was better guaranteed to make men settle down under a new ruler than more money in their purses.

He took another sip of his drink, revelling in the feel of sunshine on his back. For the first time in weeks, he was clean, having indulged himself extensively with hot, scented water in the baths. He was dressed in new clothes – a gift to celebrate his homecoming – and he was still enjoying the novelty of rich silk against his skin. The various small hurts of a long journey were healing, and, no longer having to watch his back, he could allow the tension of perpetual vigilance to seep away.

He thought back to what – *who* – had sent him south. The king, of course; always the king.

Here, so far away, he was able to consider the nature of King William with detached, impartial eyes. Increasingly, men spoke of him as if he was no more than a short, fat fool presiding over an increasingly debauched court; a man who was fond of jokes and silly japes, prone to fits of temper that reduced him to stammering impotence, and more concerned with grooming his long hair and wavering over which pair of ridiculously long-toed shoes to wear that day than with vital affairs of state. It was understandable, for the king appeared to cultivate that image, playing up to it by surrounding himself with fashionable, frivolous, fatuous young men who, according to the most malicious of the gossips, inclined only to their own sex.

Was it all subterfuge? Rollo believed it was. He had seen the sharp, calculating intelligence behind the facade; he knew that William was far from being a fool. Perhaps, like the Emperor Claudius, he chose to conceal his true nature behind

an amiable, shallow exterior. It fitted with an expression Rollo
had heard his own formidable father use: *never permit those
who would judge you to perceive your true nature.*

Leaning back into the accommodating silk cushions, Rollo
went back in his mind over the missions he had carried out
for William. Each had been deeply clandestine; receiving his
orders in secret, Rollo had obeyed them in a similar manner.
Very few people, he was sure, would ever begin to suspect
some of the things he had done for his king.

And that, of course, was why he was now here, back in the
country of his birth, letting the sun warm and relax him while
the potently alcoholic drink in the beautiful crystal glass slid
gently down this throat . . .

He remembered every detail of that secret meeting with King
William. The two of them had been alone, although, aware of
the king's careful habits of self-preservation, Rollo was in no
doubt that armed guards would have been close by, ready to
rush to the king's side should William so much as raise an
ironic, aristocratic eyebrow.

It had been just before Easter that the king had summoned
him. Plunging straight to the point – as, in Rollo's experience,
he usually did – William said, 'You have kin in Sicily?'

'I have, sire,' Rollo agreed.

The king waved an impatient hand, clearly inviting him to
expand on his brief answer. 'Go on. Guiscards, yes?'

'Yes. My late father was a distant cousin of Robert and Roger.'

'Roger Guiscard, now styling himself Count Roger of Sicily.'
It was a statement. Knowing the king as he believed he was
beginning to, Rollo was not surprised that he had such facts
at his fingertips. 'Now that the last Saracen stronghold has
fallen,' William went on, 'the Normans hold the whole island.
Roger rules Sicily, and Robert holds the southern mainland.
They have Malta too. Between them, those adventurous
Normans are steadily expanding their control over the sea
lanes and the trade routes of the whole area.'

Rollo detected a note of admiration in the king's voice.
'They have . . . achieved their goal, sire,' he said with diplo-
matic tact.

'Indeed they have,' the king agreed, 'and, from what I am told, Roger is setting about the task of governing his new possession with rare good sense. They don't call your kinsmen "the Resourceful" for nothing.'

Rollo lowered his eyes. The king was privy to intelligence that had not made its way to him. Nevertheless, it was heartening to hear of his kinsman's success.

He sensed keen eyes on him, and, looking up, met the king's stare. 'Some time since you have been home, Rollo?' he asked softly.

'Er – some years, yes, sire.' Seven years: seven long years. An image of dry, sunlit slopes formed in his mind, an azure sea lapping on rocks far below. He smelt lemons, and the sweet, dizzying perfume of jasmine.

'How would you like to return there? Not for long,' William added, 'just time enough to test the mood regarding a certain situation.'

Intrigued, his head still full of the seductive sights, sounds and smells of home, Rollo said, 'Sire, I am, as ever, at your disposal.'

Then, drawing close and dropping his voice to a mere breath, William described to Rollo the rumour that he had extracted, seemingly out of the air, and what, if it had any foundation, it might predict for the not-too-distant future.

Rollo felt the shock run through him as the implications sank in. 'Is it . . . can it be so, sire? Sicily is one thing, but to speak of the Land Over the Seas as a similar goal . . .' He did not dare go on.

William studied him, one eyebrow raised, a cynical amusement in his eyes. 'That, Rollo, is precisely what I want you to discover.'

So here he was, once more on the king's business. As soon as he was fully restored after the trials of travel, he would set about the task. He had, he reflected, the perfect cover: a long-absent son of the island returning to visit his kin and the land of his birth.

He wished his father was still alive, for his assistance would have been invaluable. Rainulf Guiscard, dead these fourteen

years, had died as he had lived: throwing himself wholeheart-
edly into everything he did in this life that he had so loved.
One of the younger men had challenged him to see who could
climb first to the top of the castle's tallest tower, and Rainulf,
many years the man's senior, had accepted with alacrity. He
had won the challenge, and would have enjoyed the champion's
seat at the feast that was to follow, except that, celebrating
victory in his usual exuberant style, he had let go of both
handholds to raise his arms in triumph. A piece of stone had
broken away beneath his foot, and he had fallen to his death.
Witnesses claimed he had still been yelling his triumph as he
hit the ground. It seemed highly likely.

One parent dead, one still very much alive; Rollo's fiery,
dark-eyed mother had retained her devastating beauty, and
they said men queued up to take Rainulf's place in her bed.
None, the rumour-mongers had to add, had ever been admitted;
Giuliana was a one-man woman, and the fact that the man
was dead made no difference.

It was in Giuliana's apartments that Rollo now resided, and
it was she who was spoiling him so thoroughly, as only a
mother can when her son returns home after a long absence.
There was, however, more to her than a passionate wife, an
adoring mother and a lover of costly fabrics, good food and
fine wine: she had been Rainulf's partner and helpmeet in the
turbulent years, and fought alongside him as he and his fellow
adventurers carved out their kingdom in the south. She might
now be relaxing in the new peace of her land, but Rollo doubted
if she had turned soft. The old skills would still be there, and
he intended to invite her to utilize them.

Rainulf was gone and lost to his son, but Giuliana would
be a very good alternative. She always knew what was going
on; she had a rare ability to keep her eyes and ears open, and
to remember even the smallest detail of what she observed.
Moreover, she had a whole army of contacts in virtually every
sphere of activity on the island. What she didn't know, one of
her contacts would.

Frowning in thought, letting his mind run over a network
of ideas and possibilities, Rollo took another sip of the drink
and wondered how best to phrase his initial approach.

THIRTEEN

G urdyman was back in his house. Although ashamed to admit it, he found it a vast relief. *I do not like the outside world*, he thought. It really was ironic, he reflected once more, that a man who was devoting so much effort to trying to map out the far places never willingly ventured further than the pie stall at the end of the alley.

Perhaps it was because he had travelled so far in his childhood and as a young man – all the way to Santiago de Compostela, although he'd been too young to appreciate the place. Then, as soon as he was old enough to begin exploring the world by himself, all over Spain, both the Muslim and the Catholic regions; out to the wild trio of islands off Spain's eastern coast, and thence on to North Africa. On, always on, to Egypt, to the Holy Land and far beyond; away from his parents' hearth for more than a decade, so that they gave him up for lost and erupted into tears of joy when finally he returned.

He smiled, shaking his head as if to deny that the young man who wanted to see *everything* should have changed so conclusively into an old sage more than content with his own walls. To whom even the short journey to an obscure fenland village had taken so much effort that, home again, he felt both physically and mentally exhausted.

But perhaps that was due to the harrowing nature of his mission. Lassair was not at Aelf Fen, and she had not been waiting for him when he returned to Cambridge. It was enough to make anyone depressed and anxious . . .

He and Hrype had agreed not to say anything to the girl's family; Hrype had even undertaken not to tell Edild, and Gurdyman appreciated how hard *that* was going to be. They had reasoned that there was no point in worrying anybody else. 'Not,' Hrype had said bitterly, 'when the two of us can worry enough for all.' There had been no word from Lassair;

as far as her kin were concerned, she was safely in Cambridge, working hard with her wizard mentor.

If only she was, Gurdyman thought sadly.

He was sitting out in his little courtyard, face turned up to the early summer sun, when there was a knock on his door. Hurrying along the passage, his heart leaping with hope, he opened the door to reveal Hrype. One look at his expression answered Gurdyman's unspoken question: Lassair had not returned.

In his face Gurdyman also read guilt. Recognizing it, he felt the same emotion burn through him.

'He's been seen again,' Hrype said baldly.

'The red-headed giant.' Gurdyman nodded slowly. 'Yes. And . . .?'

'No news of her.'

'Is that a hopeful sign, do you think?' Gurdyman asked.

Hrype shrugged. 'Those who have been keeping watch on my behalf report that he has at least five brawny young men with him; very likely more. I have not managed to locate the secret place where he's moored his ship, and it is possible that he's keeping her aboard. However, I do not think so, for by all accounts he is still searching.'

'It could be that she is his captive and he has not yet managed to make her tell him what he wants to know.' Putting his worst fear into words made Gurdyman feel sick to the heart, but it was surely better to face up to the possibility than pretend it did not exist.

'She cannot tell him what she does not know,' Hrype said softly. 'Nevertheless, I am confident that he does not have her. Yet,' he added ominously.

Unconsciously, his hand had gone to the small leather bag hanging from his belt, in which, Gurdyman knew, he kept his precious rune stones. Gurdyman nodded. 'And do the stones tell you where she is?' he murmured.

Hrype gave a twisted smile. 'I see locations, Gurdyman, and I sense that, although she was at first terrified, she is no longer in fear of her life. In fact –' his brows drew together in a puzzled frown – 'if I read the stones aright, it would seem she is actually . . . excited – even, could I make myself believe it, *happy*,' he finished. He shrugged. 'I am not even sure if either is the right word. I cannot perceive what the runes are telling me.' He shook his head violently, obviously angry with himself. He would never blame the stones, Gurdyman reflected; only his own failure to understand the message.

'Are we to think, then,' Gurdyman said cautiously after quite a long silence, 'that the person on whose orders she was taken is someone altogether more – ah – benign?'

Hrype's head shot up, and his strange silvery eyes met Gurdyman's. 'I pray that is so,' he whispered fervently.

There was another silence. Again the one to break it, Gurdyman said, 'How much, do you think, does Edild know?'

Hrype grimaced, a look of pain on his face that was caused, Gurdyman guessed, by the reminder of having to keep the terrible secret of Lassair's abduction from the woman he loved so deeply. 'Her instincts tell her what is true,' he said, 'and in her head I believe she accepts it. But in her heart . . .' He did not go on.

Gurdyman nodded. 'The old woman spoke only to you, then.'

'Yes. She trusted that I would know what to do with the information. Although now I doubt very much that her trust was justified,' he added bitterly.

'This is not over yet, my friend,' Gurdyman said calmly. 'Do not judge either her wisdom or your own until every outcome is known.'

Hrype turned to him, frustrated fury in his face. 'Not *over*?' he echoed. 'How can it ever be over when the whole picture is not known to any one of us?'

He had a point, Gurdyman acknowledged. 'Can you not reveal to Edild what *you* know?'

'I wish I could,' Hrype replied fervently. 'But the secret is not mine to tell.'

Silence fell once more. The sun moved a few degrees through the heavens, and then Gurdyman said, 'What will you do now?'

Hrype gave a sort of snort. 'What *can* I do? Go home, wait for Lassair to come back.' His face contracted in a fierce scowl. 'I have never felt so impotent!'

'Will you send word as soon as there is news?' Gurdyman asked, getting to his feet to see his visitor to the door.

'Of course. And you too, notify me if . . . if anything happens?'

'I will,' Gurdyman promised.

He watched Hrype reach the end of the narrow alley and turn the corner, out of sight. Then he closed and locked the door and returned to his sunny courtyard.

Einar and two of his crew rowed me up the winding waterway and dropped me in exactly the same spot that we had started from – or so I guessed. I'd had a sack over my head when they bundled me aboard *Malice-striker's* little boat and rowed off with me.

Now that the moment had come, I discovered it was going to be hard to part from them. Despite our inauspicious start, Einar and I had become friends. He was the tough, silent type; bound by all sorts of obligations – to his kin, to his home, to pride and honour, to his father's expectations – and, knowing him a little now, I understood just why my jibe about *his Malice-striker* being a cargo ship and not a warlike longboat out of the age of heroes had wounded him so deeply. He had apologized again for hitting me, and this time, perhaps feeling that he knew me better too, it had been sincere. I'd been prompted to say sorry for what I had said. 'I did not mean to hurt you,' I added.

He'd given me a wide, true smile. 'Nor I you.'

We grinned at each other, and I knew we would not say another word about it.

I stood on the low bank and watched the little boat disappear round a bend in the river. I started to raise a hand to wave, but made myself stop. I wasn't at all sure that big, brawny Norsemen went in for sentimental farewell gestures.

I shouldered my satchel and turned for home. I was dressed in my own clothes, and I had bundled up my new gown and apron into a tight roll, which I'd tied on top of my bag. With no idea of how I'd begin to explain my finery, I hoped nobody would see it and ask where it came from.

I was heading for home, but I wasn't going to tell anyone what had happened. I'm not sure why: I was obeying an imperative instinct that was commanding me not to reveal where I'd been and what I had learned. Somehow I knew this wasn't over. For one thing, this Skuli, who had been so desperate to find the shining stone that he had been prepared even to kill, was still out there. The thought had given me a shudder of fear, although Thorfinn and his tough band of warriors had promised that they would be watching over me.

Thorfinn had held me by the shoulders as we'd said goodbye on board *Malice-striker*, staring down intently into my eyes. 'We shall meet again,' he had said. I believed him.

There was still something he wanted from me, although he had not told me what it was. Now, trudging home to my village, I felt as if I were on some secret mission for him. I didn't mind; in fact, I relished the prospect. It appeared that, some time over the past days, I had come to trust him. With any luck, my family would assume I was arriving home from Cambridge, and I would let them. It wouldn't exactly be lying; merely allowing them to believe something that wasn't actually true. I thought I could probably cope with that.

My homecoming was exactly as I had foreseen it. My father's face lit up in his usual smile of pleasure when he saw me. My mother, preparing food, remarked that, true to form, I had arrived just in time for a meal. But she also gave me a quick, tight hug.

Assuming, just as I had hoped, that I was fresh from Cambridge and my studies, my brother Squeak asked if I could turn him into a frog yet.

I stayed for four days – I was, after all, pretending to be on a visit to see my family, so I could hardly depart again before I'd spent some time with them – and I was constantly troubled by the vague, uneasy sense that I was waiting for something. My instincts told me that there were invisible patterns shifting just below the surface, and I did not understand. The one person I really wanted to see was Hrype, and he was not in the village. I spent a day with Edild, working on the suddenly abundant supplies of plants now available, and making large quantities of the remedies we used most. She was clearly on edge, although, when I cautiously asked, she gave me such a short answer that I did not dare pursue it.

I did screw up my courage and ask where Hrype was, to which a terse 'No idea' was the reply.

Oh, dear . . .

I was out searching for dew-fresh blackberry leaves – they stop wounds bleeding and are also useful to lessen diarrhoea – early the next morning, when it happened again.

Someone jumped me.

I could not believe it.

At first I was just so *angry* that it drove out fear. Whoever held me was yet another huge man, and when I beat my fists against his broad, bare arms, it felt like striking hard old oak.

He carried me away from the track into a small stand of hazel trees, my face thrust into his chest so that my cries were muffled and I could barely see. Just as on the previous occasion, he – they – had chosen the spot well: there was nobody around.

The man carrying me dumped me on the ground. I stumbled and fell, then leapt to my feet, spinning round to stare in panic at the circle of hairy, heavily armed giants surrounding me.

One of them had long, flowing hair and a thick, abundant beard. Both hair and beard were light, coppery red.

His blue eyes were on me and they burned as if he had a fever. Even in that very first moment, my healer's instinct told me there was something deeply amiss with him. Not thinking what I was doing – I was far too terrified to think at all – I sent out a feeler towards him, and in return got such a jolt of *wrongness* that it made me stagger backwards away from him.

He was like a flying arrow, directed with furious purpose in one direction. His fanaticism bordered on madness, and I was at his mercy.

A sob rose in my throat, and I only just managed to suppress it.

'You know who I am,' he said, his voice a low, guttural growl. I nodded. 'They have told you, my kinsmen, what I search for and why I want it.' Again, I nodded. He knew I knew, it seemed,

so there was no point in denying it. The last thing I wanted to
do was antagonize him.

'I must get to Miklagard, you see.' Now he sounded reasonable, as if he was stating something that everyone ought to
understand. 'The Great City,' he added, 'which you may know
as Constantinople.'

I barely knew it as anything. It was a word on Gurdyman's
map. 'Yes,' I whispered. It sounded more like a whimper.

'I cannot make the journey without the stone,' he went on,
pacing to and fro before me as if he could not contain the
destructive energy coursing through him. 'My grandfather
tried, you know, and he failed. He is no more now than a
name on the stone that marks the death place of so many brave
men. *I will not be one of them!*' he shouted, his voice rising
alarmingly. 'I will not,' he added, softly now. 'But I need the
shining stone. It is mine – it should have been passed down
to my grandfather and my father, and, had events turned out
as they should, it would now be in my hands.' He raised those
great hands, turning them this way and that, then clasping
them close together as if they held a round object. It did not
take much imagination to know what that object was.

His eyes were on me again, burning into me. 'You know
where it is,' he said, and the sudden chill in his voice made
me shiver. 'You will take me to it.'

'I can't!' I cried. 'I don't know where it is – truly, I don't!'

Slowly he shook his head. 'I do not believe you. My kinsmen
did not go to all that trouble with you merely to have you tell
them *I don't know where it is.*' His parody of my high-pitched
voice, shaking with fear, was cruelly accurate.

'But I—'

He cut off my protest. 'I do not know where Einar took
you, but it is not important. You have revealed to them everything you know, no doubt convincing them that the precious
object is perfectly safe wherever it is that it lies. Now you
will tell me, and then we will go to where my stone is hidden
and I will take possession of it.'

'I don't know *anything*!' I squeaked. 'I can't find the stone
for you because I have no idea where it is.'

If I'd believed repetition would work, I was wrong. Skuli

drew a long knife from his belt and slid his finger along its brilliant edge. A thin scarlet line appeared in the fleshy pad of his fingertip. I felt sick.

'I could cut you,' he mused, 'or I could cut that pretty little brother of yours – Leir, I believe, is his name. Or, tenderer flesh still, your baby nephew, the child that your brother and his dark-haired wife dote on.'

He knew all about us! Well, I thought, my mind racing, of course he did. He had broken into all our homes. Searched the graveyard where he thought my Granny Cordeilla lay interred. Killed my sister's mother-in-law and my aunt.

'I cannot tell you what I do not know.' My mouth had gone so dry that I could hardly get the words out.

He moved as fast as a snake. His arm was round my chest, the knife tip pushing into my face just under my left eye. I froze.

'Thorfinn was treated by a young woman who lived here-abouts,' he hissed right in my ear. 'She was a kinsman of yours. He left my stone in her care.'

And Skuli had burst into the places where my family lived, searching for what he believed was his, not caring what he broke, whom he hurt or killed, in the process.

The sharp little point was a constant pressure against my skin, not exactly hurting but, as it were, just about to. Quick as a flash, he moved it to my right eye, then back to the left. Into my mind flew the dreadful image of what it could do to me if he pushed a little harder.

'I don't know who she was,' I whispered. 'I've been trying to work it out,' I added in panic as I felt the muscles tense in the arm that was holding the knife.

'Try harder,' he commanded.

'I believe the healer might well have been an aunt of my mother's,' I said, the words tumbling out of me. I thought I was about to wet myself. 'But I don't know who she is or where she lives!'

There was a moment of utter stillness. I closed my eyes, committing to memory what might be my last sight of the world. Then, as if my own terror had somehow made him do what I so desperately wanted, the knife point was lowered.

He removed his arm from my throat and shoved me away from him, so hard that I fell flat on my face.

I lay panting, trying to work out which part of me hurt the most and if any bones were broken.

Then he spoke. 'Find out where this woman is,' he ordered. 'Then go and fetch my stone.'

I tried to get up on to my hands and knees, but the pain stopped me.

I felt a foot in the small of my back. 'I will be watching you,' he said, the cold words like a judgement. 'If you fail or if you try to deceive me, I will cut off your baby nephew's face before his parents, bring your little brother's eyes to you, and then I will kill you.'

The vomit rose in a hot surge, up my throat and into my mouth, and I retched into the grass. When it was over, I raised my head and wiped the tears away.

They had gone. I was all alone in the hazel grove, and I wanted to die.

It was a long time before I dared go home. I've seen the effects of shock in others, and I knew very well what I must look like. I made myself collect more blackberry leaves, the familiar, routine task helping to calm me, but still I did not dare risk my aunt's piercing glance. Like the coward I was, I waited till she was busy with a patient and left the basket of leaves by the door, calling out that I was off home now, to see my mother, and would return later.

It would be light for some time yet, and most of the villagers were still out working, up in the fields on the higher, dry ground or down by the water. Fortunately for me, in my family's house everyone was absent except for my mother. She sat by the door in the sunshine, spinning wool and watching her sleeping grandson.

I went to sit on the ground beside her, leaning back against the sun-warmed wall of the house and closing my eyes. I hadn't realized how exhausted I was. I could easily have fallen asleep, but I must not even think about it. I had a task to carry out; one which I dared not fail. I glanced over at the sweet little face of my brother's baby son, and had to fight down another bout of nausea as Skuli's words tried to force themselves into my mind. Ruthlessly I shut them out, and a spasm of pain shot through my head.

'You all right, Lassair?' my mother asked.

I opened my eyes. She was looking down at me, an expression of concern on her face. If I'd thought that she was a safer option than my keen-sighted, professional-healer aunt, I had underestimated her. Or maybe it was just that I looked even worse than I thought I did.

'I'm fine,' I said. 'A bit tired. It's warm today, and I must have walked for miles.'

'Yes, you were out a long time.' There was a pause. 'Want some nice, cold water?'

It was a long time since my constantly busy mother had offered to get up and fetch me a drink. On the few occasions in the course of a day that she actually manages to sit down, she tends to stay there. I smiled. 'You're occupied with your wool,' I said, getting to my feet. 'I'll do it.'

I sat sipping at the water, working out how to ask her what I had to know without raising her suspicions. I must not let out even the smallest hint of what this was really about, for my mother would tell my father, he'd get a band of kinsmen and neighbours together, and the next thing we knew, there would be a battle between my family and Skuli's band of well-armed giants, and you didn't need rune stones to work out how *that* would end.

After a while, I knew what to do.

I said, putting concern into my voice, 'Mother, we've had all these awful attacks and assaults on us and on Father's poor sister Alvela. But I've been thinking – do you know if any of your side of the family have also had their homes searched? After all, it's—'

My mother's scornful snort interrupted me. 'Do you think *we* didn't think of that?' she asked shortly. 'We've not been idle while you've been tucked up safe and sound in Cambridge with your wizard!' The irony of that, when you considered what had really been happening to me, struck me quite forcibly. I suppressed a wry smile. 'We all realized that my kin would likely be also at risk too,' my mother went on, 'but there's not many of them left now and nobody living that close.'

Yes. I brought to mind our family history. My mother had not originally been a local woman. Her family were all shepherds, living inland from the wet fenlands, on the firmer, dryer ground where the right sort of grazing is found. Her parents were long dead.

'I've only the one brother,' she mused, 'and he and his family live over to the east, out beyond Thetford. My aunt Ama, too – that's my mother's sister – moved right way, to Fulbeach.' She glanced at me. 'You won't have heard of it – it's a tiny place, by all accounts, down south of Cambridge.'

I was tingling with excitement. *My aunt Ama.* Yes, Ama, that was her name; the name I didn't think I remembered. Well, I *had* remembered it. She must be the little healer – Thorfinn's saviour, the woman who brought him back when he was about to lose himself.

It *must* be her. Surely it was . . .

Feigning nonchalance, I said casually, 'I'm not sure I can picture her. Have we ever met?'

'No,' my mother replied. She gave a short laugh. 'And if you met her in the road, you'd never know she and I were close kin, it's that different we look.'

Yes! Inside my head, I gave a cheer

Silence fell between us. I could just make out the soft, rhythmic sound of my mother's spindle as it spun this way and that through the still air, twisting the raw strands of wool into yarn. Presently, she started to hum.

I was thinking hard. My mother was wrong about Fulbeach's obscurity: I *had* heard of it. It was half a day's walk from Cambridge, south-east of the town, and its inhabitants frequently brought their wool into Cambridge, both to the town's own market and to be shipped away from the quays. It was probably a day's walk from Aelf Fen, yet my mother spoke as if the distance was an insurmountable barrier. It was the way of it, I reflected, when people lived each and every day in the same small place. In their minds, they created tall, insurmountable walls around them that became as forbidding as the real thing.

My mother had started talking again, remarking on how long it was since she'd seen her brother, and wasn't it strange, how you all got so busy within your own lives that you just didn't seem to find the time for the things you'd like to do, but I was barely listening.

I was thinking about my mother's aunt Ama, the healer.

Given the unthinkable alternative, it looked as if I would have to go and find her.

I set out very early the next morning, on the pretext of more plant gathering. I had surreptitiously packed up some food and a flask of water, for I knew I would be gone all day. It would take some explaining, but I'd worry about that when I returned.

If I returned. An image of Skuli and his knife floated before my vision, and I tried to banish it. If he was having me watched – I was quite sure he was – then surely he would realize I was doing my best and let me get on with it? That would be the logical reaction. The trouble was, I was not at all sure Skuli was the least bit logical.

As I trudged along, keeping up a good pace, I thought about what I would do when I got to Fulbeach and located my mother's aunt Ama. How would I persuade her to give up the treasure that a long-ago patient had left in her care? Dear Lord, would she remember that she even *had* it, let alone where she might have hidden it? I turned the questions this way and that, exploring possibilities. Could I get her out of her house on some pretext and search it? Could I pretend an interest in magical stones, and persuade her that I was just itching to have a look at the one I'd been told she possessed? Could I just tell her the truth?

I stopped before midday to eat. I was ravenous, having used up most of my energy in walking so hard. Then I got up and went on. I had reached the conclusion that I would just have to appeal to Ama's healer's instincts to save lives, and convince her that members of my family – hers too, since they were her niece's kin – would suffer terribly and die if she did not help me.

With that feeble plan the best I could do, in the middle of the afternoon I walked into her village.

'I'm looking for Ama. Ama the healer?' I asked, over and over again.

I should have asked my mother more questions before I set out on my quest. I would have saved myself a long walk.

My mother's aunt Ama wasn't a healer at all. Like the rest of my mother's family, she was a shepherd. Friendly people trying to be helpful pointed out her tiny house – on the edge of the village – and I saw the fields where her small flock had grazed; even, hanging on a nail in a tumbledown lean-to, the heavy shears she'd used to remove their thick fleeces. The shears were rusty now; the little house empty.

My mother's aunt was dead. If she'd even known anything about a sick Norseman and a magic stone – which I now very much doubted – then she'd taken her secrets to the grave.

The best I could do was stand in the village's burial ground and grind my teeth. Somewhere under my feet, her bones were rotting back into the earth.

Which was absolutely no good whatsoever to my family and me.

FOURTEEN

'The thing to do,' Giuliana Guiscard said firmly to her son, 'is for you and Roger to have a private little chat.'

Rollo absorbed the shock of her announcement without moving a muscle, and he was pretty sure he had given no hint of his surprise. While it was true that such a meeting was the best thing he could have hoped for, he had thought it so far beyond what he might realistically expect that he'd dismissed it.

He met his mother's dark eyes. 'This private little chat could be arranged?'

She waved a long-nailed hand. 'Of course. I wouldn't have suggested it otherwise.'

Intrigued now, he said, 'How well do you know the Great Count?'

She smiled. 'Bosso was very fond of your father.' Her casual use of Count Roger's nickname underlined her intimacy with him. 'Well, what else would you expect of cousins?'

Rollo smiled to himself. *Cousins* was stretching it, since his father and Roger were really no more than distant relations who happened to share a family name. In any case, there was no rule that said cousins had to like each other. The two men had apparently been close, however, and Count Roger was renowned for being loyal to those within his private circle. It looked as if this meeting might actually take place . . .

'What's he like, now he's lord of all Sicily?' Rollo asked.

Giuliana turned to look at him, her expression intent. 'He is as you recall. He's still handsome, tall and elegant. He has much charm, and is courteous and cheerful with all men. He is also very clever and extremely sharp-witted.' She paused. Then, staring straight into Rollo's eyes, said quietly, '*Never* try to deceive him, for the repercussions would be unthinkable. His own son Jordan once tried to rebel against him, and Roger had all the leaders of the revolt blinded. He pardoned Jordan

only at the very last moment, to remind him to have more
respect for authority.'

Rollo nodded. The story was well known. The last-minute
reprieve had been predictable – although possibly not by Jordan
himself – for the Count's love for his eldest son was legendary.
Jordan was cast in the Count's precise mould, as fierce and
brave a fighter as his father, and would, but for his illegitimacy,
have been his natural successor. The younger man had died
of fever the previous September, and it was said that Roger
had at first been inconsolable. 'Is the Count beginning to
overcome his grief?' Rollo asked.

Giuliana shrugged. 'I expect so. He has a country to rule.
Besides, his new little wife has already achieved the miracle
and borne him a healthy boy child, and there will no doubt
be more to come.'

'I thought it was widely known that, while his mistresses
gave him sons, his wives bore only girls?'

Giuliana laughed. 'That is largely true. Eleven daughters
and one sickly son by the first two wives, and, even among
the mistresses, only Jordan and poor Godfrey.'

Poor Godfrey indeed. The man was a leper, and not even
his father's wealth and devoted love could heal him. He had
retired to an isolated monastery, where men said he spent his
days in prayer while he waited for death.

'The baby is only weeks old,' Giuliana mused. 'It will be
years – decades – before he is ready to take his place at his
father's side, even providing he turns out to be like Jordan
and not a shy little girl in boy's clothing like his only legiti-
mate half-brother.' She gave a dramatic sigh, as if sincerely
pitying the count's lack of sons.

Rollo smiled again. The seven-year absence had not in any
way reduced his ability to follow the leaps that her agile mind
made.

'And here you are!' She opened her eyes wide, as if in
amazement to see him there sitting beside her. 'Son of his
dear cousin, living flesh and blood of the man he loved more
than any other!'

'Steady, Mother,' Rollo murmured. 'Let's keep the exag-
gerations credible.'

'You shall go to visit him, this very day,' she went on as if she hadn't heard. 'I will send a message, he will summon you, and then the rest is up to you.' She closed one large, dark eye in a wink.

He studied her, loving her, deeply entertained by her. For a brief instant, he forgot about his mission and simply reflected how good it was to see her again. Then, as if waiting for such a moment, the image of Lassair slipped into his mind. What would she think of his mother? What, indeed, would Giuliana think of her?

His mother's eyes narrowed fleetingly, and then a sly smile spread across her generous mouth. Silently and vehemently, Rollo cursed his own carelessness. He had vowed not to permit himself one single thought of Lassair when with his mother; her mind-reading ability was just too good. She was, after all, daughter and granddaughter of the *strega*. Or so the wide-eyed, credulous peasants said, crossing themselves and gabbling their furtive prayers when Giuliana swept past.

And now he'd let her in. Only for a heartbeat, but he had a feeling that was all she needed . . .

That events turned out just as Giuliana had predicted was no surprise at all. The summons had come, he had spruced himself up and ridden his beautifully groomed horse the short distance to Roger's castle, and now he was waiting in a lofty anteroom, to be ushered into the Great Count's presence.

A man clad in a leather breastplate over his tunic emerged through an archway to Rollo's left, standing silently before him while he looked him up and down. 'Weapons?' he demanded curtly.

Rollo raised his hands away from his sides, displaying his unarmed status. There was a long, narrow and very sharp blade tucked in a scabbard hidden in the inside seam of his left boot, but nobody had found it yet. He did not anticipate having to use it here, but you could never be entirely sure.

The guard jerked his head, indicating the room beyond the archway. 'Go in.'

Rollo walked through the arch and into the Great Count's private chamber. Fur rugs partially covered the flagged floor, and the walls – built of huge blocks of rough-hewn stone – were hung here and there with beautifully worked tapestries. A curtained bed stood to one side, and there were several large iron-bound wooden chests set back against the walls. Roger's armour hung on a rail, as if even here, in his private retreat from the rest of the castle, he must be ready at a moment's notice to revert into a fighting man.

He sat in a vast chair, beautifully carved, and was dressed in a simple woollen tunic over which was draped a rich cloak lined with vivid brocade. As Rollo paused inside the doorway, he stood up and, extending both hands, came to greet him.

'Welcome to the returning son of the family!' he said, smiling with what seemed to be genuine pleasure.

'Thank you, my lord.' Rollo went to make a bow, but Roger caught his hands and prevented it.

'You are my kinsman; the son of my late, dear cousin,' he said. 'Besides, we are alone and unobserved.'

Yes, Rollo reflected. It would have been a different matter had their reunion been public. He studied the Count. He was much as he had been seven years ago; perhaps more lines around the eyes and mouth, and grey hairs among the blond. He still stood tall and straight. He was the great-great-grandson of Hiallt the Norseman, who had set out to win himself quite a large portion of the land later called Normandy, and his ancestry showed.

As if, on inspecting Rollo, his thoughts ran along the same lines, Roger said, 'You carry your Norman blood like a banner.' He was studying Rollo closely. 'You resemble your father, even down to that smooth fair hair. Yet your eyes are of the south.'

Rollo was aware of that. He had been looking into a pair of eyes exactly like his own that morning. He bowed his head, unsure how to reply.

Roger returned to his seat, waving to a smaller, lower, but no less skilfully carved wooden chair placed just beside it. 'Sit, Rollo.'

Rollo sat. He waited, as was only right, for Roger to speak.

'You have come from King William,' he said after a moment.

'Who I don't suppose for an instant has sent you here just to
be reunited with your southern kinsmen.'

'No,' Rollo agreed. He hesitated, arranging his words.
'Nevertheless, it is good to see them. Especially my mother.'
Another pause. 'Thank you for looking after her.'

Roger burst out laughing. 'I won't tell her you said that,'
he remarked. 'Rollo, *nobody* looks after Giuliana. She's a
fierce woman, and I do not envy the man who would try.' He
leaned closer. 'She is a great asset,' he said quietly, although
he did not elaborate. Rollo guessed he was referring to his
mother's highly efficient spy network, something which would
indeed be very valuable to the ruler of a newly won kingdom.

Roger's soft words interrupted Rollo's thoughts. 'Like
mother, like son, eh, Rollo?' he murmured.

He knows, Rollo thought. *He knows exactly what role I fulfil
for my king.* 'Yes,' he agreed.

'And here you are, sitting with another Norman lord in the
midst of a very different realm,' Roger went on. Then, sharp
as a knife point: 'I trust there is no conflict of interest here?'

'None that I can see,' Rollo answered. 'Unless you are
aware of something that I am not.'

There was no answer. After a short pause, Roger said, 'Why
are you here?'

I have to tell him, Rollo thought. He took a breath, tried to
calm his fast heartbeat and said, 'Your successes here in Sicily
and, just recently, in Malta, are known of back in the north.
The time of the Saracens here is over, and the Normans rule
the kingdom in the south. King William applauds your achieve-
ments. He . . .' Rollo paused, thinking hard. 'There are other
lands where the Saracens still rule,' he went on slowly. 'Lands
with great ports over on the eastern shores of the Mediterranean
which, besides being invaluable for trade, are ripe for strong
fortifications from which a ruler might protect and defend his
territory. Once these lands were open to all, and men of different
faiths who shared the desire to visit the holy places of their
religious leaders and prophets were free to make pilgrimage.
Yet now the Holy Land is in the hands of the Seljuk Turks,
and these nomad warriors have lost none of their ferocity. Their
capital is a mere hundred miles from Constantinople.'

Roger nodded. 'Emperor Alexius Comnenus rightly mistrusts their proximity,' he observed. 'He no doubt fears they have their eyes on his Byzantine empire.'

'Indeed,' Rollo agreed. 'There are in addition these wild tales that tell of mistreatment of Christian pilgrims in the Holy Land. There is an Amiens priest called Peter the Hermit who, attempting to reach Jerusalem, claims to have been kicked out like a hungry dog from a kitchen. There are rumours that the Turks mistreated him, possibly tortured him.'

'Is that true?'

'I do not know, my lord. What is relevant is that, throughout the Christian community, people *believe* it is true.' Rollo paused, letting that sink in. 'The outrage of a skinny old monk on a donkey being barred from visiting the holy places where his Saviour suffered, died and was resurrected, will act like the spark to the kindling.'

'The kindling being what?'

Rollo met the Count's steady gaze. 'The awareness of those rich and extensive lands of the eastern Mediterranean,' he replied.

'With those aforementioned strategically placed ports all ready for strong Norman castles,' Roger added quietly. 'So, you see religious fervour – the desire to free the holy sites from the Turks' jealous and exclusive possession – as the excuse for a land-grabbing invasion?'

'King William wonders if it is not rather likely,' Rollo said cautiously.

Roger grinned. 'They say he is not a God-fearing man,' he remarked.

Rollo thought swiftly. 'He is a king, my lord,' he said. 'He cannot afford the luxury of simple faith, for the well-being of his realm is in his hands, and he must always do what is best for his country and his people.'

Roger's smile widened. 'Nicely put, Rollo. What you would like to say, I imagine, is that your realistic and sensible king is not the man to set off in the vanguard of a vast and costly fleet, with his head full of dreams of ousting the infidel and delivering the entire Holy Land back into Christian hands. He'll leave that to more hotheaded lords, and wait calmly at home to pick over the best of their territories when they fail to come back.'

Rollo lowered his eyes. He had nothing to add, for Roger was quite right.

Presently the Count spoke again. 'Twenty years ago, Pope Gregory contemplated an expedition to help the beleaguered Byzantines, and matters were less serious back then. It's rumoured he approached the leaders of the west, although no such expedition ensued. Not then,' he added. 'And it's said that our present pontiff is strongly influenced by Gregory.' He paused. 'That was back in the time of the Conqueror,' he remarked. 'What, do you think, would be his son's reaction to such an appeal, were it to come?'

Rollo recalled King William's words: *These men who would set off on this venture will waste their time, their trouble and their money.* He had laughed at them; he had called them *brain-washed dupes of the Church.* But Rollo wasn't going to pass that on to Count Roger. 'He is, as you earlier surmised, hardly champing at the bit to join in any rescue mission, my lord.'

'Unlike my nephew Bohemond, then,' Roger said.

Bohemond. Rollo recalled what he knew of the man. He was the son of Roger's sister, and, even among a race of tall, strongly built Normans, he was a giant of a man. His real name was Mark, but even in the womb he had been so large that his sobriquet had been attached to him before birth. Being called after a legendary creature of fabulous power and size would be, Rollo thought, quite a lot to live up to.

Bohemond had always been a man ever spoiling for a fight. Others would flock to follow him on this new venture, once he decided to go, for the restless Normans had won the kingdom in the south and were now looking round for the next conquest. They would—

Rollo's train of thought broke off. He had a succession of visions, one after the other, quick as blinking, and every one was of blood: sharp sword blades flashing under a brilliant sun; men wide-mouthed as they screamed their agony; bodies falling, legless, armless, headless, under the onslaught; women, running for their lives, wailing, desperately clutching the hands of their terrified children . . .

He tried to take a hold of himself, and the visions drew back a little.

'If they launch a campaign against the Turks in the Holy Land,' he heard himself saying, 'they will start a conflict that will have no end. When the honour of their deity is at stake, men know no reason.'

The echo of his softly spoken words slowly died in the utter silence of the room. Then Roger said, very quietly, 'Is that a prediction?'

'I – I do not know.' Confused, troubled, Rollo was still fighting to regain control.

Roger was watching him. 'Your mother is said to come from a long line of witches,' he murmured, 'and many believe she herself is a *strega*.'

Rollo suppressed a shiver. To have Count Roger echo so faithfully his own recent thoughts was alarming.

He realized, his unease deepening, that he had been in a light trance. *Had* he made a prediction? Had he seen true, and were those blood-soaked, brutal, and endlessly enduring events really lying in wait for the peoples of the eastern Mediterranean? With an effort, he brought himself firmly and ruthlessly back into the present. Swiftly he went through what had just passed between him and the Count; had he said more than he should? Had that strange moment of foresight lowered his defences, so that he revealed what he should have kept secret?

No. He risked a glance at Count Roger, whose demeanour remained alert, interested but benign. Rollo felt the tension in him fade away. No; it was all right. When he felt he could safely speak, he smiled easily and said, 'My mother is very intelligent and she keeps her eyes and ears ever open. It is therefore no surprise that on occasions she is able to foresee the turn of events.' He paused. 'If I have inherited the tail end of her gift, then it is my good fortune.'

He hoped he sounded sufficiently modest. The Count's ironically raised eyebrow suggested that maybe he hoped in vain.

There was a long, reflective silence. Then the Count said, 'You do not ask, Rollo, what my own views are on this matter.'

Rollo bowed his head. 'I am curious to know, naturally, my lord, but it is not my place to ask.'

The count gave a sort of snort, which could have been suppressed laughter. 'Quite,' he murmured. 'Well, Rollo, I shall satisfy your curiosity. If the summons should come for me to participate in this . . . enterprise, then I shall decline it. I have many Saracen subjects, whose loyalty I am busy cultivating. You will readily appreciate, Rollo, that for me to join in a Christian attack on their brethren in the Holy Land will hardly help me to achieve my aim. Sicily has had its own troubles, and the scars are still painful. A lengthy period of further years of dissension, division and strife is the last thing I want.'

His voice had risen as he spoke, and Rollo sensed the passionate determination behind the urbane facade.

'Besides,' Roger added after a moment, his handsome face creasing in a smile, 'here in Sicily we are in the ideal spot: a bridge between the west and the east. Should these events come to pass, and a great army call in on its way east, it is my merchants, my traders, my innkeepers and brothel masters, who will benefit.' His clever eyes met Rollo's. 'In times of strife, kinsman, there are fortunes to be won and lost. I intend my people to be the winners.'

As he mounted his horse and set off from the Count's castle, Rollo's thoughts returned to that strange moment of near-trance, keen to reassure himself once more that he had not revealed anything he should have kept back.

For, in addition to what he had told Count Roger concerning King William, there was something more; something he must not at any price share with the Count, kinsman though he was. For King William had told Rollo his innermost, carefully calculated conclusion, based, Rollo was certain, on a lifetime's astute observation of his fellow men. Especially those closest to him.

What the king had said was this: 'My brother Robert is not content to be Duke of Normandy; he wants more, and his ambition blinds him. He has the light of idealism in his eyes, and if the call comes for the leaders of men to form an army and take it to capture Jerusalem, he will leap to respond. But, as always, my brother will lack money, for his wealth has been squandered; frittered away on skirmishes and piddling wars with disgruntled neighbours.

'When the call comes – and I do believe, Rollo, that it is *when*, not *if* – Duke Robert will need a banker. He will look no further than his little brother, safe in his kingdom across the Narrow Seas. And when his little brother requires security for the loan, what will Robert have to offer but Normandy?'

The king's features had spread in a great grin of delight. 'If matters play out as I believe they well might, I shall be handed Normandy on a platter, without having to lift a finger or wave a sword. And the conquest of the Holy Places will be no pleasant walk in the sunshine; they will have to battle for every inch, and many will not return.'

He had not said any more. But then, Rollo thought now, he hadn't really needed to . . .

Halfway back to the castle where his mother had made her luxurious home, Rollo was suddenly struck with such a sharp stab of terror for Lassair that it forced him to draw rein and stop.

He felt his horse shift uneasily beneath him; was the horse also picking it up?

She was in deadly peril. She was going to be dreadfully hurt – she, or someone she loved. She had to do a task that was beyond her, or else she would die . . .

She was calling out to him, in desperate need of him.

The sensations ran through him with such power that he almost turned his horse's head for home there and then. The successive stages of the long journey flashed through his mind: over the Messina Straits, up through Calabria, Naples, Rome, on north towards the Apennines and the Alps, then the long trudge across the northern half of Europe and, at last, over the Narrow Seas to England.

Why not? He had done as King William asked; he'd actually talked to the man who ruled Sicily, and he had an answer to give his king. Of sorts.

He knew it was not enough. Yes, he could try to palm William off by convincing him there was no more to find out, but that would not work. William was not a man to be palmed

off. If Rollo wanted to go on being one of the king's spies
– and he did, for the role suited him like a skin – then he
knew what he must now do.

Reluctantly he loosened his hold on the reins and nudged
his horse onwards.

He wanted to be alone, for he had a great deal to think about.
He had fully expected to be; his mother did not usually appear
in the afternoon, preferring to rest in her luxurious bedchamber,
with the breeze off the sea stirring the light muslins that hung
at the windows.

He poured out a glass of the sherbet drink, and went to lie
on the divan. He closed his eyes. Lassair filled his mind, and
he gave a low moan of pain.

A voice said softly, 'I would love it if you'd tell me about her.'

His eyes shot open. His mother was sitting in a high-backed
chair, in a dark corner where the deep shadows had hidden
her from view.

As the silence extended, she said calmly, 'I knew, Rollo,
the moment I set eyes on you. You have changed.'

He thought hard. Lassair and his mother were so very
different that he was not at all sure he could describe Lassair
in terms that would do her justice and, moreover, make his
mother understand why he loved her. His mother was sophisticated, glamorous, beautiful, rich, clever, quick-witted, a
survivor with some strange and uncanny powers and a very
tough fighter.

Lassair was a village healer.

But she was more than that, he thought, realization flooding
through him. She might not be glamorous or rich, and her sort
of sophistication was of the mind rather than of the environ-
ment in which she lived, but, apart from that, the adjectives
he had applied to his mother also applied to her.

He swung his feet down, turned round to face Giuliana and,
with a smile, began. 'Her name's Lassair, and she's a very
gifted healer who can also dowse and, on occasion, pick my
thoughts right out of my head,' he said.

After that, it was easy.

*   *   *

In the twisty-turny house in Cambridge, Gurdyman sat in his sunny courtyard with an old scrap of parchment in his hand. The rolled parchment's rough seal had been broken, and there were fragments of wax scattered on the ground. Several people had helped it on its way from fenland village to town: a peddler, a ferryman, a merchant carrying herbal supplies, and a herbalist's young apprentice, who had brought the parchment to Gurdyman's door.

Written on the parchment were a few lines in a beautiful, regular hand. The message read: *She has returned to the village.* Below the lines was a single initial *H*.

Gurdyman wondered why he did not feel as relieved as he should . . .

FIFTEEN

The sense of hopeless despair slowly beat me down as I made my way back towards Aelf Fen. I did not know what I was going to do. I had set out for Fulbeach that morning so full of optimism, quite convinced that I would find my mother's aunt Ama and that she would calmly hand over the magic, shining stone the instant I asked her for it. I had been wrong, on every single point: my great aunt was a shepherd, not a healer, and had undoubtedly never met Thorfinn in her life, never mind been entrusted with the care of a precious, potent, magic stone. Besides, she was dead. Now I was returning to my home and my beloved family, no more able to save my little brother and my baby nephew from their terrible fate than I had been when I left. The whole day had been a total waste of time.

I felt like crying. Silently I called out to Rollo, even though I had no idea where he might be. Brave, an excellent fighter with fists, knife and sword, intelligent, full of good ideas and helpful suggestions . . . yes, I could really have done with him. But wherever he was, he wasn't *here*; that was all that concerned me just then. What use, I asked myself bitterly, was a strong, resourceful lover when he wasn't there when I needed him?

I dried my futile, stupid tears and went on. I stumbled occasionally; it was starting to get dark. I knew I was being very foolish in trying to get home tonight. I had lingered far too long in Fulbeach, sitting slumped in the graveyard as if I could summon up what I so desperately needed by sheer willpower. I should have found some sympathetic villager there and begged a bite to eat and a corner of a lean-to to sleep in. It was foolhardy in any case to travel alone at night, especially for a woman. It was more than foolhardy for me to do so, when I knew full well I had a mad Norseman with a crew of hairy giants at his disposal, all of them watching me like a hawk eyeing a sparrow.

I made myself go on, fresh tears rolling down my face and all but blinding me. Would Skuli find me this night? Knowing, somehow, where I'd been – I fully believed that was likely – and confident I was returning to seek him out with his treasure in my hands, was he even now waiting for me?

The night came down, and my apparently endless trudge went on. Soon I had convinced myself that Skuli would be lurking on the edge of my village, staring at me with those mad eyes and barring my way. He'd be standing there, huge chest thrown out, hair and beard shining like fire in the first rays of dawn, surrounded by that ever-watchful semicircle of big, tough, well-armed men.

And there I would cower, empty-handed and hopeless.

A sudden thought occurred to me. There would be, I realized, no point in Skuli torturing my family once I was beyond persuasion. Once I could no longer watch, whatever horrors he inflicted on Leir and little Ailsi would be futile.

When the moment came, and Skuli and his band of fighters surrounded me with their weapons in their hands, it would be better all round if I simply ran on to one of the outstretched knives. I gritted my teeth, forcing back the instinctive cry of protest as my panicky, terror-induced resolve to seek death hardened.

I did not want to die! Of course I didn't. But my thoughts just ran round and round inside my head, coming always back to the one conclusion.

Oh, but death! The end of all that I knew! It was intolerable. There was so much I still wanted to do. I had the best teachers in the world in my aunt Edild and Gurdyman – Hrype, too – all of whom would never stop working as hard as they could in order to pass on to me what they knew. I had a niece and two nephews, and I was only at the very start of getting to know them. I had a loving family – my eyes misted over as I thought of my father's agony when he learned I was dead – and my mother would never get over the loss of a child. I had friends, very good, close friends . . . Unbidden, unexpectedly, an image of Sibert popped into my head. Once I'd thought I'd been in love with Sibert, although it turned out not to be love after all but a very close affection. We had each saved the other's life, once.

Rollo. I thought of him last, but he certainly wasn't last in importance. I was in no doubt that I loved Rollo. We were lovers, and, one day, I hoped we would mix my Saxon and his Norman blood and breed a son who would fight for the rights of the whole world.

I could almost see him, this child. His fair hair had reddish lights in it, and he'd clearly inherited something of me. His eyes were dark like his father's. He . . .

A shadowy shape materialized out of the band of trees beside the track.

So this is it, I thought. It was sooner than I had expected, for I was still some way from Aelf Fen. I was surprised at how calm I felt. I closed my eyes and said a profoundly heart-felt goodbye to all those I loved. In that moment of utter despair, it really did seem the only way out.

My anguish had driven me far, far away from my normal self . . .

Opening my eyes again, I prepared to tell Skuli I hadn't found his stone.

It was very dark; the moon was up, but obscured just then by cloud. I'd been out all night, however, and my eyes were adjusted to the lack of light. In any case, I'd have known from the slight smell of perfumed smoke that it wasn't Skuli, not to mention the difference in height and bulk. This man was far from small, but Skuli and his crew were bigger and broader than most other men.

Hrype stood before me, his silvery eyes glittering in the starlight.

I said, 'I thought you were Skuli.'

'The red-haired giant,' he said.

'Yes. He wants me to . . . I've got to . . . Oh, Hrype, he's going to cut little Leir's eyes out!'

The tears took me by surprise, overcoming me before I had a chance to hold them back. My anxiety and my grief over-whelmed me, and for a moment I abandoned myself to my distress.

I've never thought of Hrype as a demonstrative person. I

know he is a loving man: he loves my aunt Edild, and I am sure he also loves Sibert; even poor, needy Froya, in his way. He stays with her, anyway, when in his heart he longs to be with Edild, because once, when he and Froya were grieving for his dying brother who was also her husband, they took the age-old comfort and they made love. Sibert was the result: my friend Sibert, who everyone except Froya, Hrype, Edild, Sibert and I believe is Hrype's nephew.

I was about to see another facet of this austere, distant man, who wore the clothes of a poor peasant and yet bore himself like a king. For Hrype – cool, detached Hrype, who often looked with disdain on the dullards with whom he shared his village life – took me in his arms and held me close to him as if I were a child who had had a bad dream.

I could feel his heartbeat. Strong, steady, unrushed. And then he spoke, soft, simple words of reassurance. 'You're safe now, child. No harm will come to you. You're safe.' And all the time his hand was stroking my hair, soothing me, calming me. In a sudden flash of memory, I felt Rollo's hands performing the same action, and another sob broke out of me.

And, very gently, Hrype said, 'Rollo would be here if he could.'

I have long known Hrype could read minds. I sometimes think he could do it any time he likes but he usually refrains, except when it's really important, because it's not very nice for him or the other person if he can hear everything they're thinking.

Now, in that awful moment, it was like a cold draught of water when you're parched.

'Would he?' I asked. Then – and I despised myself for the feeble tone: 'Couldn't he come, then?'

'No, Lassair.' Hrype had resumed his stroking. 'He is a long way away.'

Then he folded me to him again, and I made myself relax. The knowledge that Rollo was thinking of me was such a comfort; as was, I realized, the fact that Hrype had referred to him by name rather than *your Norman*, which was what he usually called him.

For a variety of reasons which I did not stop to define, I started to feel a bit better.

Hrype must have sensed it, for he let me go and we stood facing each other.

He'd been out of the village, and I had no idea how much he knew. 'I know who and what the red-haired giant is,' I began, 'and also what he's searching for, and there's another branch of the same family – headed by a wonderful old man called the Silver Dragon, although his real name's Thorfinn – and they say it's imperative that Skuli – he's the redhead – doesn't get this thing, because he's going to use it to guide him on a mission that's very dangerous – he's got to get through some rapids on this huge river in the great land to the south where his own grandfather perished – and lots of good men who loyally follow him will die, including two who are little more than boys and whose poor, widowed mother will miss them dreadfully if anything happens to them, and—'

'Steady, Lassair,' Hrype said, grinning. Then – and this took the breath out of me so effectively that I couldn't speak for a moment: 'I know.'

'*What* do you know?' I cried furiously, choking on the words in my fierce anger. 'How *can* you?' *And how much*, I wanted to demand, only it was still hard to speak, *of what I've so painfully learned over the past few weeks, were you already aware of?*

Hrype had let me go now, and taken a step away from me. Perhaps he'd thought I might hit him. It was, believe me, a distinct possibility.

'We – er, I . . .'

The correction was swiftly made, but I had heard what he said first. '*We?*' I asked icily. Aware as I was of the identity of Hrype's most intellectual and trusted confidant, the person with whom he habitually discusses things of a deeply cerebral nature, I had a good idea who it was that made up the other element of *we*.

'Gurdyman and I worked out quite a lot,' he confessed. Gurdyman. Yes, I was right. 'There were – er – facts of which I had been made aware, unknown to anyone else,'

Hrype went on, and I was sure I detected a very untypical note of hesitation – doubt, almost – in his voice. 'But I knew these facts because of a confidence; a secret I had once been told, which I knew I must not reveal until and unless I had no choice.'

'What . . .?' I began. I got no further than the one word before he stopped me.

'It is no use whatsoever asking me to tell you, Lassair, because I'm not going to,' he said very firmly. 'However, I came to believe that I was not the only person who was guarding a secret. Somebody had to be keeping another one; one which was as relevant to and as closely involved with this matter as my own.'

I was totally bemused. What on earth was he talking about? Without a doubt he wasn't going to reveal this other person's secret either, nor even his identity.

I was right: he didn't.

'Can't you tell me *anything*?' I asked in a small voice.

He smiled briefly. 'No,' he replied. But then, as if relenting, 'Not yet.'

Without another word, we set off in the direction of Aelf Fen. There was still far to go; we would be lucky to be back before dawn. Recalling my earlier fears about Skuli being there with his band, waiting for me, I was reassured to have Hrype beside me. Even so, we would be only two against Skuli and however many men he had, but there was a lot more to Hrype than met the eye.

I had still come up with no way out of my terrible dilemma. However, now I had Hrype's bright intelligence to help me. If anyone could think of how my brother, my nephew and I could be saved, short of presenting Skuli with something I didn't have and wasn't likely to find, it was Hrype.

We were within a mile of Aelf Fen. The faintest, pinkish light was appearing in the eastern sky. Had it not been for the fact that we'd been walking most of the night, I would have been very cold, for the temperature had dropped considerably as dawn approached.

My optimistic hopes of Hrype having solved my problem

for me by the time we got home had proved to be unfounded. Apart from an occasional comment to verify that we were going the right way, we hadn't exchanged a word. I could only pray that his silence implied he had been deep in thought, and that the solution I yearned for so desperately was about to be revealed.

We entered a short stretch of the track where it ran beneath a low bank up to the right, topped with some stunted hazels and contorted bramble bushes. To the left, the ground dropped away, growing increasingly damp and muddy until earth merged with water and the marsh began.

It was, with hindsight, the ideal place for anyone wishing to apprehend us to lie in wait.

I thought at first that I had somehow drifted into a sort of waking sleep, for the vision that I saw on the track in front of us was exactly how I had seen it in my imagination.

He stood staring at me, his pale eyes all but colourless in the thin light. There was madness in those eyes: I could both see it and sense it. He seemed to take up the entire width of the track, barring the way like a heavy gate. His fists were clenched, his chest was thrown out, his hair and beard stood out like an amber halo. And, even as I watched, four, five, six of his men strode out of their hiding places and went to form a semicircle around their leader.

Beside me, Hrype muttered an oath, spinning round even as he did so to look behind us. From somewhere beneath his dark robe, a knife had appeared. With his free hand he grabbed hold of me, pulling me close to him. 'We must . . .' he hissed.

But he did not finish whatever he had been about to say. His grasp on me slackened and his hand fell away. The point of his knife, which had been aimed so steadily at our foes, wavered and dropped.

And Hrype fell to the ground, a pool of blood staining the sandy soil beneath him.

With a wail of distress, I was on my knees beside him, my hands already searching for his wound. He must have been hit with a thrown or a propelled weapon – a knife, a spear, an arrow – for none of our enemies had been close enough to reach him with a blade held in the hand. I must . . .

Hands were on me, firm and strong on my shoulders, pulling me to my feet.

Away from Hrype.

The two men who had grabbed me marched me up the track until I was face to face with Skuli. I struggled hard, for I was desperate to get back to Hrype. He was losing a lot of blood, and unless I found where it was coming from and stemmed the flow, he might die. He *would* die. And my aunt loved him so much.

Skuli nodded at my captors, and they tightened their grip. Then Skuli came closer, staring down at me with an expression of such desperate ferocity that I shrank back.

The light was stronger now. I could see his face clearly, and it was obvious he had very recently been fighting. One eye was bruised and swollen, with a cut in the eyebrow that was still oozing blood. He had also taken a blow to his nose, for it too was swollen and there was dried blood crusting his left nostril and soaked into his moustache and beard. The front of his tunic was stained with blood, as was one thick thigh. I looked quickly at his men, on either side of him. Several of them, too, were wounded.

But I did not think those stains on Skuli's clothes had been made by *his* blood.

With a sick certainty, I understood where he had been.

They must have put up a fight, my family. They wouldn't have stood by while little Leir and the baby Ailsi were hurt; that I knew as well as I knew my own name.

Hurt. What a poor, inadequate word for what Skuli had vowed to do to them.

I stood quite still, forcing myself to stare right into those mad eyes. I was too late; my resolution to end my own life to save that of my brother and my nephew could no longer avail either of them. Somewhere deep inside me a great wail of agony was growing; a river of grief, for Leir, for Ailsi, for Hrype, bleeding out his life on the track behind me.

I said, quite surprised by how calm I sounded, 'I haven't got it, Skuli.'

His face darkened, as if the flesh had filled with his own black blood. 'But you have discovered where it is,' he said firmly. Perhaps he thought that if he spoke with enough conviction, it would make the statement true.

I shook my head. 'I haven't.'

His brows drew together. His face was thunderous now. 'You have been absent from your village all day,' he said, his voice icy. 'Where else have you been, other than to fulfil your mission?'

I hesitated. Ought I to tell him? I could see no reason not to; there was nobody else left to be hurt by my failure, so I might as well share it with him. There was always the faint hope that his fury might set off the sort of apoplectic seizure that kills a man stone dead. With his loyal band of men all around, Skuli's death wouldn't help me, but at least there would be one less murderous devil in the world.

'I went to find the little healer,' I said softly. 'I found out where she lived, and I walked all the way. But she wasn't a healer, she was a shepherd. And she was dead,' I added with vindictive emphasis. 'If she ever knew about your shining stone, Skuli – and I doubt very much that she did – then I got there too late to ask her.'

He was shaking his head slowly from side to side, as if in denial of my words. 'No,' he said, '*no*. She must have hidden it somewhere . . .' Wildly he turned to look at his men, ranged around him. 'We'll go to this place you found, find her house, take it apart until we find the hiding place, and—'

'*She never had it*,' I said loudly, speaking over his rising panic. 'Aren't you listening, Skuli? The only small clue I had regarding the stone's whereabouts has proved useless.' I felt my face stretch in a smile. 'You will *never* get your filthy hands on it.'

As I watched, I saw something break in him. He opened his mouth, but no words emerged. He raised his great head, eyes staring up into the sky. He muttered something – it sounded as if he was apologizing – but I could not make out the words.

A tear spilled out of his eye, running down his face to lose itself in his beard.

Then, abruptly, he returned from whatever dark place his thoughts had taken him to. He nodded at the two men holding me, and they forced me to my knees.

Then Skuli drew a large knife from its sheath on his belt. He held it up to the growing light, and its edge glistened. I could tell, all too clearly, that it was very, very sharp.

With a strangely detached part of my mind, I wondered where Thorfinn and Einar were, and the crew of Einar's ship. They had promised to watch over me, but now, in the time of greatest danger, they were nowhere to be seen. I was on my own.

I concentrated on sending out my love. To my sisters and my brothers; to my beloved Edild; to Hrype. To my mother; to my father. As his face appeared before me, I whispered, 'I am sorry, Father.'

If he was by some miracle still alive, he would grieve for me the most deeply. I imagined his big, strong arms around me; I imagined reaching up to kiss his dear face.

I sent all the rest of my love to Rollo. *I'm scared*, I admitted, saving the confession for him. *I'm terrified. I'm going to die, and I shall never see you again. I'm very afraid it's going to hurt, and I don't know what's going to be waiting on the other side.*

I saw my Granny. Quite clearly, standing just behind Skuli on the track. She smiled at me.

With her dear face a clear, final image, I closed my eyes and waited for death.

In the village, a small group of bloodstained, stunned men watched the sun come up. As soon as they could, they were going to hurry along to the church. Nights like the one just past did not come very often, and they felt an urgent need to kneel before their God.

They had been ready. As night fell, their leader had gathered together his eldest son and some of the toughest of his friends, warning them what would happen. 'None of you must feel compelled to stay,' he had said. 'You have families of your own, and do not need to suffer wounding or death to defend mine.'

Everyone had stayed.

The attack had come with horrible suddenness. The big, bearded men seemed surprised to have met such opposition.

They fought back hard, but they had been beaten off. Besides, once they had seen that only grown men (and one large, furious woman armed with a heavy iron pot) had been in the house, they had turned and fled.

Now all was quiet. Now the ragged band of defenders waited for whatever the new day would bring.

SIXTEEN

'And I can't see how our future together will be, if, indeed, we can ever be together, for she has her studies, both in her village and in a nearby town, and I am fully engaged in work for an exacting but generous paymaster, and so—'

Rollo broke off in mid-sentence, seized by cold fear so paralysing that it was only with an effort that he could breathe. Lassair. Oh, *no* . . . He could see fragmented images. A road, faintly lit by the rising sun. A blur of shapes, which were moving with swift, violent gestures. The glint of light on drawn swords.

It was early morning, and his mother had arrived with breakfast on a tray, wanting to hear more about the strange woman with whom her son had apparently fallen in love. He had thought he'd told her all there was to tell the previous evening, when they had talked together long into the night. Yet she had returned for more, and he had been trying to answer her question as to what he and Lassair planned to do next, when the terrible moment of fear had hit.

He sat now, straight-backed, every muscle tense as if he was about to plunge into action. He had felt something similar on his way home the previous day, yet it had been nowhere near as powerful as this.

He knew, without stopping to ask himself how he could be so sure, that Lassair was about to die.

And there was nothing he could do about it.

Barely aware of himself, he gave a moan of pain. Instantly Giuliana was beside him, a cool hand on his wrist, looking up into his face with anxious dark eyes. 'What is it, my son?'

He met her gaze. Of all people, she was perhaps the one most likely to believe what was happening to him. Whether or not she was truly a *strega*, she was certainly open-minded enough not to dismiss it out of hand.

'Lassair's in great danger – mortal danger,' he whispered. 'I think . . .' He could not bring himself to put it into words.

Beside him Giuliana waited, holding his hand. He felt the aftershocks of the terror work their way through him, and, glancing at his mother's face, he thought she felt them too. Then, abruptly, everything went still.

Calm, of a sort, descended.

After what seemed a very long time, Giuliana said, 'What are you sensing now, Rollo?'

'Nothing.' His voice broke on the word.

His mother squeezed his hand. 'Perhaps the moment of peril has passed?' she suggested.

He thought it was a faint hope. He said, his voice barely a whisper, 'Or else it is all over and she is—'

But his mother put a hand over his mouth before he spoke the word. 'No,' she said firmly. 'Do not even admit the possibility.'

He felt a moment of anger. 'It is better to know if she—'

'*No.*' Giuliana spoke more forcefully now. 'My son, you are many miles from this young woman whom you love, and it will be a very long time before you know what has been happening back in her country. You must convince yourself that all is well, and not allow yourself even to consider otherwise.'

He met her eyes for a long moment. 'I want to go now,' he whispered. Pain ripped through him; sudden, acute. '*Aaagh*, I feel as if I'm being torn apart.'

Compassion filled her eyes. 'Can you not return?' she asked.

'I could,' he said, 'but my task here is not really complete. I was planning to go on east, and seek audience with Emperor Alexius.'

She nodded. 'Yes, that would be the logical thing to do,' she agreed. 'His land is at the frontier between the Christian and Muslim worlds, and, besieged as he is, will be better able to provide the answers that your King William seeks to know.'

Rollo would have said he was beyond surprise at his mother's uncanny ability to be aware of things that she had not actually been told, but he discovered he wasn't. How did she do it? He had no more idea now than when he'd been a mystified and awestruck child, more than a little frightened by his mother's magic powers.

She was watching him steadily. 'What do you feel now?'

He closed his eyes, concentrating on Lassair. 'I . . . it's not clear.'

She sighed, and ran a hand over her face. Then, once more looking at him, she said, 'Have you anything of hers?'

He glanced down at his hand. The woven leather bracelet she had given him had not left his wrist since he began to be so very anxious about her. 'Yes,' he said softly.

Giuliana looked at the bracelet. 'It is beautiful,' she observed. 'Did she make it?'

'Yes.'

Silently she held out her hand. He drew his own away; he did not want to take off the bracelet. Not now . . .

His mother made an exasperated noise. 'If you want me to help you, son, I need to hold an object that holds her essence.'

'If I want you to help me?' he repeated stupidly. Had she suggested it? Had he missed that?

She was holding out her hand. Mutely he removed the bracelet and placed it in her palm. Her long fingers folded around it and she closed her eyes.

The cool, sunlit room was utterly silent as Giuliana put herself into the required trance.

I knelt before Skuli, waiting for the sword cut that would end my life.

Nothing happened.

I did not dare open my eyes, for I was clinging on to my courage with my fingertips, and if I saw the sword raised above me, I knew my terror would overcome me and I would somehow disgrace myself.

I waited for death.

Then, breaking the terrible silence like a great sheet of ice cracking under stress, I heard a clash of arms, swiftly followed by a shout: a great war cry. There were whoops and yells, and the harsh, metallic sound of metal on metal.

I opened my eyes, but my fear had affected me so deeply that what I saw made no sense. There seemed to be men everywhere; big, burly men, most of them long-haired and bearded, many wearing leather protective gear, all of them bearing swords. They were fighting – desperately, fiercely.

And *very* close to where I knelt.

Faint, my head spinning and vertigo rising like nausea in my throat, I threw myself sideways and scrambled to the side of the track. I managed to crawl up the bank that rose up to the right, and forced a way in beneath the scrubby, stunted trees that made up the hedge. Then I turned to watch.

Already recovering at least a portion of my senses, I realized, not without surprise, that I recognized some of the newcomers. I'd seen that stubble-headed giant with the tattoos on his arms before; I was quite sure of it.

I put my slowness down to the fact that I'd just had a very close embrace with death. The men were Einar's crew; of course they were. Even as understanding dawned, there was Einar himself, pounding down the track, yelling at the top of his voice, his sword in his hand already dripping blood from some recently accomplished, victorious encounter.

Skuli was engaged with one of Einar's men, and the man was getting the worst of it. Einar shouted at him and, although I didn't understand all the words, the meaning was clear: *get away from him, he's mine!*

The crewman stepped back – a swift expression of relief crossed his bloody face – and Einar stepped into his place.

Part of me wanted to watch, but I'd never seen close fighting before and soon I realized, sickened, that watching wasn't such a good idea after all. I turned away from the savage ferocity of Einar and Skuli's battle, only to be met with the same sight everywhere I looked.

Then, horrified that it hadn't occurred to me before, I remembered Hrype. Where was he? Frantically I stared down the track to where he had fallen, but he was no longer there. His blood still stained the ground, although the smooth pool it had formed was already scuffed and smeared.

He could not still be alive. Could he? He must have been carried to the side of the track, for I was certain he could not have made his own way.

I edged along the top of the bank, searching for him. He

must be on this side, I reasoned, for on the other side the ground was soggy and sloped quite steeply down into the water. It was no place to take a wounded man.

But all right for a dead body, came the thought.

No!

I hurried on.

I could see something on the bank just ahead of me: a long shape, lying on its side on the bank and wrapped in a cloak.

I leapt forward, already fumbling with the buckles of my satchel. I knelt down beside him, my hand going straight to his neck to feel for the life's beat that pulses there, beneath the angle of the jaw. At first I felt nothing. Then my trembling fingers felt a very faint movement.

He was alive.

Gently I turned him over so that I could see his face. His eyes were closed and there was a big bump on his forehead. It was likely, I decided, that he had struck a rock on the track as he fell.

But where was the wound that had felled him, and caused him to bleed so profusely? Even as my mind formed the question, my hands were going down inside his tunic, feeling for the wetness of blood.

There. I had it: a deep cut on the back of his left shoulder, perhaps two hands' breadths down. Gently I probed the wound, very afraid that I would find a broken-off arrow shaft, and the arrow head deeply embedded in Hrype's flesh. But there was no such thing. The wound had, I guessed, been made by a thrown knife, which had since fallen out.

Whoever had thrown it had been aiming for the heart. Such a throw – from behind, at someone quite unaware of impending attack – was cowardly in the extreme. The sort of act typical of someone who had chosen to follow a man prepared to hurt and maim babies and children in order to achieve his goal.

I turned my mind from such angry, agonizing thoughts. I was a healer with a wounded man on my hands, and it was up to me to stop the bleeding and try to save Hrype's life. Turning him so that the damaged shoulder was uppermost, I tore aside his garments and, reaching into my satchel for a pad of soft, wadded fabric, pushed the sides of the cut together with one hand and pressed down on the pad with the other. I would wait, then look, then repeat the pressure until the blood flow eased enough for me to stitch the wound.

As my concentration focused, the sounds of furious fighting seemed to fade. The cut wasn't as bad as I had initially feared. Quite soon I was able to put in a neat row of stitches, which I then soused with lavender oil against the dangerous red inflammation that often follows such wounds. I wrapped Hrype up in his cloak, rubbing his cold hands with my own.

I sat back on my heels, watching my patient.

It was only then that I realized everything had gone rather quiet.

I spun round, staring down on to the track. It was empty of fighting men, but I could see three bodies lying a little way along, beneath the overhanging boughs of a hazel tree. Further on were four more.

Seven dead? Could it really be so?

I felt sick.

Just as I was wondering whether there was anything I ought to have done for them – could still do – I became aware of a shadow over me. I looked up. Einar was standing on the bank beside me.

'I just saw the bodies,' I said in a horrified whisper.

'Yes,' he said calmly. 'Six of his; one of mine.' He paused, and a look of pain crossed his face. 'Snorri,' he added, half to himself, for the name meant nothing to me. 'He was growing old, and his reactions were not as fast as they once were.'

'I am sorry,' I said gravely.

'It is not your fault, Lassair.' He sighed. 'None of this is your fault. It is we, indeed, who should apologize to you, for you have unwittingly become embroiled in a feud between the two branches of my family, and this should not have happened.'

How right he was, I reflected. And what worse things was I going to face, once I got back to my village? But that thought was too awful to allow, and my mind sheered away. I would deal with it when I had to.

He stared down at Hrype. 'How is he?' he asked, his question dragging my mind back to the patient who was my immediate concern.

'He'll live,' I replied. 'He must be borne back to the village as quickly as possible. I don't want him to get cold.'

Einar nodded. 'Soon,' he said.

I had the sense that he was preoccupied, his mind busy somewhere other than our conversation. 'Are there any other wounded whom I can help?' I asked.

'A few minor cuts and bruises,' he said nonchalantly. 'Nothing that can't wait.'

I felt a chill run through me. 'Wait for what?'

He held out a hand, inviting me to get up. I put my hand in his, stepping down from the bank to stand beside him.

'There is a task for you to perform,' he said, his voice deep and grave. 'Come with me.'

He led me to a place just beside the track where several of his crew stood in a tight circle. They were obviously guarding something, or someone. As Einar and I approached, the circle opened to reveal Skuli, his hands bound behind him, kneeling on the ground.

There was a deep cut – probably a sword slash – in the top of his upper arm; the right one. His sword arm. It was bleeding, and the blood had soaked into the wool of his tunic.

I thought that Einar wanted me to tend the wound, but that was odd because I'd just asked if anyone else needed help and he said no.

Einar was still holding my hand. Now he put something in it: the hilt of a long, heavy knife with a sharp-edged blade.

His men stood in a silent circle, watching, waiting.

Then Einar said, 'This man Skuli, who now kneels before you, was on the very point of taking your life when we arrived to stop him. By the ancient laws, his life is now yours to claim.' With a strong hand, he closed my fingers round the hilt of his knife.

I stared down into Skuli's eyes.

He faced me as, not very long ago, I had faced him. I hadn't been able to keep my eyes open, but he was braver. The light blue eyes bored into mine and I saw no fear; no undermining touch of cowardice.

But I saw something else: I saw the clear taint of madness. Whatever drove him, it rode him hard and unyieldingly. It had already forced him to do dreadful deeds, and I feared it would continue to do so until he managed to achieve whatever he felt he must do to force it into submission.

What was it? What evil had wormed its way inside him, twisting him, turning his mind, forcing him on, ever on, to whatever fate awaited him? I did not know. I had learned of his grandfather's failures – both in being deemed unfit to receive the shining stone and in not having managed to conquer the fearsome rapids – and I wondered fleetingly if that deep shame for an ancestor's shortcomings was the cause.

But surely it wasn't sufficient to do *this* to a man.

Not without difficulty, I turned away from the mania in Skuli's eyes and stood facing Einar.

'I cannot kill this man,' I said firmly.

Einar grabbed the knife from me and raised it high in the air. Seeing, almost too late, what he was going to do, I jumped up and caught hold of his sword arm.

'I meant I don't want him to die!' I panted. 'I wasn't saying I couldn't do it, or that I wanted you to kill him for me!'

There was a sudden hush. I wondered if, by acting in that way, I had offended against some fundamental law of fighting men. Well, if I had then so be it.

Einar was staring at me. Then, very slowly, he put his knife back in its sheath. He gave me a curt bow, then abruptly turned on his heel and strode away.

I knelt down beside Skuli, undid my satchel again and tore aside his clothing. Then I cut the thong binding his wrists and set about dealing with the wound in his arm.

I felt quite safe. Yes, he was still the madman who had almost killed me. But he was wounded now, and, besides, he was unarmed and two of Einar's biggest fighters stood either side of him.

Presently he said, 'I would have killed you. Yet not only did you spare my life, but you are now mending my cut. Why do you act like this?'

'I'm a healer,' I said curtly. 'I save lives rather than taking them. And sewing people up is my speciality.'

There was quite a long silence while I finished putting in the stitches, broken only by an occasional stifled curse from my patient. I had the impression he was thinking.

I was right. When I'd bound up the arm and helped him rearrange his under shirt and tunic, he looked up at me. 'You have given life when you had the power and the right to take it,' he proclaimed solemnly. 'By so doing, you have laid an obligation upon me.'

'I haven't!' I protested. 'There's no need for you to—'

But he stopped me. 'It is the law,' he said simply. '*Our* law. One day, at some future time, I shall have someone at my mercy as I was at yours, and I shall spare his life. Only in this way will my debt be repaid.'

'But . . .' I began.

Skuli had closed his eyes and turned his face away.

I felt hands on my shoulders, pulling me up. I stood, turned, and found myself face to face with Thorfinn.

He took my hand and, gently but firmly, led me a little way down the track, so that we were out of earshot of the group still milling around in the aftermath of the fight.

Then, stopping, he turned to look down into my eyes. I tried to read the expression in his. I wasn't sure I could.

'Did I do well?' I asked. 'Was it the right thing, to spare Skuli's life?'

Thorfinn sighed. 'You did as your heart dictated,' he replied. 'No man would say that was wrong, child, when the heart in question is as honest and loving as yours.'

The words surprised me. Honest: yes, I suppose I was usually fairly honest. As for loving . . . Well, I loved my family, I loved Rollo, and quite a few other people had crept into my affections. Sibert, for example, and Gurdyman, and maybe even the chilly and distant Hrype. Nevertheless, *loving* wasn't a word I associated with myself. Long ago, Edild had cast my natal chart, and she had informed me that the stars at my birth told of someone who would always remain aloof and distant. *You are essentially a private person*, she had said. I would never forget her words. *Your friends and your lovers will sense that they are never truly close to you.*

I turned my mind away from that bitter memory and back

to the question of Skuli. 'What will happen to him now?' I asked. 'Will you take him back to your own land?'

Thorfinn shook his head. 'I am not a man of the law, and I have no jurisdiction over him,' he said.

'Then . . .' I found I could barely accept what I thought he was telling me. 'Then you're just going to let him go? But he's killed two of my kin!' My sister's late mother-in-law was not, strictly speaking, kin to me, but this was no time for such fine distinctions. 'He said he would do terrible things to—' *No*. I must not let myself think of that, for it would drive me mad with horror. 'He attacked people, broke into their houses, broke their possessions! He caused real fear hereabouts, all the time he was searching for this precious stone!'

'I know, child.' Thorfinn sighed. 'But what would you have me do? You have seen the wildness in Skuli's eyes; you have judged for yourself, I dare say, his state of mind. He is desperate, Lassair, and if I try to deprive him of his freedom and take him back home, I will be risking the lives of Einar's crew, for Skuli would without doubt continue to make escape attempts until he succeeded, whatever the cost in men's lives. Einar and his crew are good men, and I would not wish such peril on them.'

'So you're letting him go,' I repeated.

'I suppose I am,' Thorfinn agreed.

'But what about the shining stone? He hasn't got it, so won't he continue to be a danger all the while he's still looking for it?'

Thorfinn looked away, his eyes staring out over the water. 'I have persuaded him that it is lost,' he said distantly.

'You . . . Is that the truth?' I thought I already knew the answer.

Slowly Thorfinn shook his head.

'Yet Skuli believed you?'

He shrugged.

Perhaps Skuli had given up, I thought hopefully. He had, after all, hunted in all the places he could think of. I had been his last hope, and I too had failed to deliver to him what he so desperately sought. His ultimate inability to find the shining stone, combined with Thorfinn's misleading lie, could just be enough to persuade him.

I could not quite manage to convince myself.

We stood there in silence, Thorfinn and I. Then I thought of something: I remembered the weeping woman on the quay, as we had set off from Thorfinn's land. 'But what about that woman's two sons, who sail with Skuli?' I demanded. I forced myself to remember what Olaf had said. 'Your sister-in-law, who pleaded with you to bring her sons home? You said you'd do what you could – I heard you!'

Thorfinn smiled. 'I have kept my word,' he said. 'The two lads are safe in the care of a couple of Einar's more steady crewmen. They have been made to see the error of their ways, and will henceforth be sailing with us.'

I felt a surge of relief. I'm not sure why; I hadn't really known the sister-in-law – Gytha was her name, I now recalled – although my heart had gone out to her when I had observed her weeping so sorrowfully.

Perhaps it was just that Thorfinn had done what he had undertaken to do. He was, I reflected, a fine man.

He would be leaving soon. As we stood there, I recognized how much I was going to miss him. Without stopping to consider the wisdom of the act, I stepped right up to him and wrapped my arms round him in a tight hug. After a heartbeat, he hugged me back. Again, I had that fleeting sense of familiarity. He smelt of the sea, the salt spray, the heavy wool and the thick fur trimming of his garments. Was that what it was?

He murmured something, his lips against my hair.

'What did you say?' I disentangled myself and looked up at him.

He was smiling. 'I said you had a loving heart,' he remarked. 'Never doubt it, child.'

Then, with a nod, he turned away from me and strode back down the track.

SEVENTEEN

I did not know whether I would see Thorfinn or Einar and his crew again. They had disappeared into the growing light of early morning with surprising speed, hard on the heels of Skuli and his remaining followers. It was almost as if they were in pursuit, although I knew they were not. Skuli would head for his longboat, I thought, and, as soon as he could, would be setting off on his journey.

Without the stone.

Again, the question of what drove him so hard surfaced in my mind. He must be—

A low groan came from the spot beneath the hedge where I had tended Hrype. Hrype! Oh, I'd forgotten all about him!

I gathered up my skirts and raced up the track to where I had left him. He was sitting up, one hand on his forehead. His eyes, bruised-looking and full of pain, looked up at me.

I knelt beside him, gently preventing him from trying to get on to his feet. 'You hit your head, Hrype,' I said. 'Someone threw a knife at you, from behind, and it caught you in your shoulder. Here,' I put my hand to the wound, barely touching it.

Even so, he winced. 'Sore,' he managed.

'Yes, I'm sure it is,' I agreed. 'It wasn't too deep, but it was bleeding quite a lot and I've stitched it. I put on some lavender oil, too, against the red heat.' I hesitated. I wanted to feel inside Hrype's tunic and under shirt to see if there was any warmth developing around the wound, but I held back. Tending his bare flesh was one thing when he was unconscious; quite another now that he was awake and aware, with those silvery eyes boring into me.

He is your patient. I seemed to hear my aunt's firm, brooking-no-nonsense voice inside my head. *Put aside your foolish qualms and get on with it.*

'I need to check the wound,' I announced briskly.

With a small quirk of his lips, as if he knew exactly why I was reluctant, Hrype obligingly turned his back, presenting his shoulder. I slid my hand under his clothing, quickly establishing that the stitches were holding, the bleeding had stopped and the wound felt no warmer than the surrounding skin. I withdrew my hand. 'Thank you, all is well,' I said primly.

This time, it was more than a quirk; it was a definite smile.

I knew I must get him back to the village. He had lost a lot of blood; he needed a change of clothing; he would quickly become cold if we stayed out in the open, and that could be dangerous.

Besides, *I* needed to get back to the village. I could barely allow myself to think about my family; the agony was too much to bear. I was trying with all my might to remain hopeful, but it was a battle I was losing.

I stood up, looking down at Hrype. 'Can you walk, if I support you?' I asked. 'Or shall I go to the village to fetch help?'

He grasped my hands and stood up. He tried one step, then another. 'I can walk,' he said. I saw him gritting his teeth, and understood that the effort was causing pain already.

'I can be there and back quite quickly,' I said, 'and—'

'I said I can walk, Lassair,' he snapped. 'Come along. Get me to your aunt's, and she can inspect your handiwork.'

It was a little under a mile to Aelf Fen, but never had such a short distance seemed so long. As we stumbled along, with me taking more and more of his not inconsiderable weight, I realized why he had held out against my going for help.

Hrype wanted to go to Edild's house, and not only because she was the village healer: his injury would give them some precious time together. If men from the village carried him home, they would automatically take him to the house he shared with his brother's widow and the young man who everyone believed to be his nephew.

I understood. I struggled on, and bit back the complaints. I was sorely tempted to abandon him and race for home, throw myself into my parents' house and find out the worst. I managed to resist the temptation. Just.

Eventually we reached the village. It was still very early, and few people were about. Even so, I did not want curious eyes to see us, so I took the path up behind the settlement, over the higher ground and around the ancient oak tree, approaching Edild's little house from the rear. At long last, I could look forward to relinquishing my patient into her care and turning for home.

I'd been going to leave Hrype and Edild alone anyway, after a quick conversation with my aunt to tell her of the night's events and how it was that Hrype came to be injured. As it turned out, however, I didn't get further than 'We encountered the red-haired giant and his men and someone threw a knife at Hrype' before Edild stopped me with a look and, saying that she would see to him now, took him inside and firmly closed the door.

I ran all the way home, my heart thumping right up in my throat as I imagined what I was going to find. I could still see those marks on Skuli and his men that spoke so clearly of hard fighting. I could still see the blood that soaked Skuli's garments.

I felt sick with dread.

I heard the buzz of excited chatter as I approached.

Excited chatter . . .

No weeping? No grieving and tearing of hair?

I pushed open the door and fell into the house.

My father had a cut over one eyebrow, and the knuckles of both hands were grazed and oozing blood. Haward had a black eye, and was nursing his right arm with his left hand. Sibert – *Sibert?* – had a split lip, still bleeding because he didn't seem to be able to stop grinning.

The house seemed very full. There were other boys and men there – our neighbours, our friends.

I saw my mother, sitting on a bench trying to hold on to Leir, who was struggling and yelling that he didn't want to be there with her; he wanted to be outside with Squeak, watching out to make sure the bad men didn't come back.

Leir, it was perfectly clear, was quite unharmed. Swiftly I surveyed the rest of the crowd . . . and there was Zarina, with her infant son in her arms. Amazingly, given the noise level, Ailsi was fast asleep.

My father had taken hold of me and was hugging me, very tightly. 'You're all safe?' I asked him quietly. 'Nobody's been killed?'

'We're all safe, dearest child,' my father whispered back. 'And what of you? Are you unharmed?'

'Yes, yes,' I said impatiently. I didn't want to talk about myself; I wanted to know what had happened. 'You fought them off? Skuli and his men?'

'Skuli! Is that his name? The redhead?' I nodded. 'Yes, we fought them off.' There was a definite touch of pride in his voice.

'But . . .' *But they are hardened fighters and you're a bunch of villagers*, I wanted to say.

He chuckled. 'We were ready for them, Lassair. They were overheard, assembling on the edge of the village.' He nodded towards Sibert. 'Your friend there came to warn us, and Haward and I rounded up as many villagers as we could. When they came creeping up to the house, they got the sort of welcome they weren't expecting.' He smiled grimly. 'We might not have fine swords at our disposal, but it's amazing what can be done with a heavy iron cooking pan.'

'You hit someone with a pan?' I, too, found that I was smiling.

'Not me. I used the log-splitter.' He looked up, over the heads of the crowd, and I saw a tender expression cross his face. Turning to see who was the recipient, I met the eyes of my mother.

'*Mother?*' I whispered.

'Your mother,' he confirmed. 'She swung that pan as if it was a battle axe. You should have seen her, Lassair!'

I wished I had done. I stared up at my father, then turned to look at the others who had fought shoulder to shoulder with him, lastly gazing at my mother. I realized suddenly how naive Skuli had been, to think he could threaten the youngest members of my family with such terrible violence without anyone raising a finger to defend them. My father, my mother, my brothers, my friends and my neighbours had clearly fought like cornered bears.

No wonder Skuli and his band had looked so battered.
My heart filled with joy, and I laughed aloud.

I gave Edild and Hrype till evening to be alone, then I really
had to go and see them. I wanted to check on Hrype, for one
thing. Although he was now in my aunt's more than capable
hands, it was I who had treated him initially, and a good healer
always follows up on her patients.

In addition, there were still so many questions to which I
didn't have the answers. I didn't hold out any great hopes that
Edild or Hrype would be able to satisfy my curiosity, but at
least I could talk the whole business through with them. Hrype
was the nearest thing to a wise man we had in the village; he
knew far more about the big world beyond the fens than most
people. As I slipped out of my family home and hurried along
the track to Edild's little house, I prayed that Hrype would be
awake and sufficiently alert to talk to me.

Edild looked up from stoking the fire as I let myself quietly
inside. She acknowledged my presence with a lift of an
eyebrow, as if it was no surprise that I could no longer stay
away. Hrype was lying beside the fire on a pile of sheepskins
and soft blankets, propped up against pillows. He was still
pale, but greeted me with a smile.

'Edild probably won't tell you herself, in case you get
complacent,' he said, 'but she was quite impressed with your
handiwork on my shoulder.'

I sat down beside him. 'How are you feeling? Any pain?'

'Not much,' he said. 'Manageable.'

I looked up and met Edild's eyes. Could she not give him
something to make him more comfortable? I opened my mouth
to suggest it, but she spoke before I could.

'Don't you think I haven't tried?' she said crushingly. 'He's
so *stubborn*.' She sent him a look in which frustration and
love were present in equal parts. 'And he maintains that my
pain-easing remedies make him dozy and stupid.'

Neither of those were words that I would ever have used
to describe Hrype. I met my aunt's eyes, and she gave me a
reluctant smile.

'Why don't you make us all a good, hot, restoring drink,'

Hrype suggested, looking up at her, 'and then Lassair can tell us what it is she's come here to talk about.'

Edild gave a sniff, then turned to put out mugs and select suitable herbs from her shelves of pots and packages. Her hand hovered over the mandragora, but Hrype was watching.

Presently we were all settled together round the fire, hot drinks in hand – chamomile and verbena, sweetened with honey – and Hrype and Edild turned expectantly to me.

'Skuli and his men tried to attack my parents' home last night,' I began, 'and—'

'Yes, we know,' Hrype interrupted. 'Sibert came to tell us.'

'Oh.' I was temporarily silenced. Then I rallied. 'He was threatening to hurt the little ones, Leir and Ailsi,' I plunged on, 'to force me to tell him where this magical shining stone is hidden, but it would all have been for nothing, because I don't know.' I paused, the dreadful memories of last night returning in force. 'I thought he was going to kill me,' I whispered. 'Out there on the track, when Hrype was wounded and Skuli's men surrounded us, he made me kneel and I watched him draw his knife to cut my throat.' A shudder went through me. 'I *told* him I couldn't find his stone!' I burst out. 'I was on my way back from the only place I'd thought of where it might be, but I was wrong. I really have no idea. And why?' I went on, all but shouting now. 'What's it all for? All these threats, to the little ones, to me? Maiming, killing? What *is* this stone, that Skuli was prepared to do such terrible things in order to possess it?'

The echo of my hot, angry words died away, and there was silence in the little room. I was staring into the fire, but then an almost imperceptible movement caught my eye: Edild, shaking her head at Hrype's look of enquiry.

'What?' I stared from one to the other. '*What?*'

Hrype's eyes were still fixed on my aunt. 'Tell her,' he said softly. Again, she shook her head. 'Edild, it's time,' he said more firmly. 'After all Lassair has been through, don't you think she deserves to know what lies at the heart of all this?'

Edild was staring intently at me, her eyes boring right into me. Slowly she shook her head. 'It was not to be until she was older,' she muttered. 'She cannot surely have sufficient strength yet, and I would not put this upon her before she is fit to bear it.'

What was she talking about? What *was* this secret that I might or might not be strong enough to be told? I opened my mouth, about to protest that, whatever it was, what I'd just endured had toughened me up as if I'd fought a war, but Edild and Hrype had eyes only for each other. I might not have even been in the room.

'Edild, how will you know when she *is* fit?' Hrype was softly asking. 'What specific test must she pass, and has she not already shown she is equal to far more than we have any right to expect her to be?'

I could hardly believe what I was hearing. I had impressed Hrype! He had just said as much! Before the surge of joy that this knowledge gave me could stop my ears to anything else, I put it aside and made myself concentrate.

'But what if I judge wrong? What if—?' As if suddenly recalling my presence, Edild stopped. She turned to look at me, on her face an expression I had never seen before.

It was . . . could it be . . . respect?

No. It couldn't. My aunt was my teacher, cool-headed, efficient, demanding of me all that I could give and grudging in her praise. Of course it wasn't respect.

With a grunt of pain, Hrype reached for her hand. 'Edild, it is time,' he said, all but inaudibly. 'You know it is.'

Briefly Edild closed her eyes, her face full of anguish. Then she squeezed Hrype's hand, gave him a swift smile and, disengaging herself, got to her feet.

She looked down at Hrype, and I thought that some unspoken question passed from her to him. He shook his head. Then, turning to me, she said, 'Wrap up warmly in your shawl, Lassair. Despite the season, it is growing chilly outside.'

She picked up a lantern, then gathered up her own shawl, tied it briskly around her and headed for the door. I went outside after her, and followed her down the path away from the house.

I had no idea where we could be going. In the distance, the glow of fire and lamp light came from several of the village dwellings, but Edild's house is on the edge of the settlement, and we did not pass close by any of our neighbours. We were not heading for the village: when we reached the track, Edild turned left, towards the church and, further away, Lord Gilbert's manor of Lakehall.

Were we going to see *him*? Whatever could this matter have to do with the lord of our manor? Had he . . .?

Even before we reached the church, abruptly Edild left the track, turning to the right, out across the open fen and the water beyond.

The darkness seemed to settle around us. I told myself I wasn't afraid, but I could not quite believe it.

I stumbled along, keeping the dark, upright figure of my aunt in view. I did not want to lose sight of her. I was beset by the unreasonable fear that, if I did, she would judge that made me unfit for whatever secret she was about to tell me.

We drew close to the water. I could hear gentle little waves plopping softly on the marsh edge. I reckoned I knew where we were heading.

It was quite a lot warmer than when I had last made the crossing, but nevertheless the water struck icy-chill as we waded over to the island. I clambered up the bank after my aunt, trying to wring out the hem of my skirt where I had let it drag in the water.

Edild stopped, so suddenly that I bumped into her. She took out her flint, and, striking a spark, lit the wick inside her lantern. Then she strode off across the island.

I thought at first that we were going to the grave of one of the mighty ancestors. Perhaps the secret was connected with Vigge, who died defending King Edmund of the East Angles from the Vikings. Perhaps a sword with magical powers lay buried with him, which Edild was going to give to Hrype in case Skuli came back, so that he could face Skuli on equal terms. I pictured Skuli and his giants, alongside them Hrype's slender strength. It would have to be a wonder weapon indeed, for him to stand any chance.

Or maybe our goal was the grave of Ceadda, Keeper of Swans. His very name was magic to my kin, and it was said that he possessed extraordinary powers.

But Edild had not gone as far as the humps that marked the old graves of the distant ancestors. Already she had stopped and now, as I watched her, she was dropping down on to the grass. She put down the lantern and knelt beside the most recent grave: my Granny Cordeilla's.

I shook my head, not even beginning to understand. I knew what was in the grave, beside my grandmother's tiny body in its shroud. I knew, because I'd seen her there. We had sent her on to the afterlife with the possessions she had treasured in life. The fine bone comb; some loom weights; the tiny earthenware cup with a flower painted on it. Small, everyday objects, not one of them of any value except to the woman who had handled them and loved them. Not one of them any good against the foe who had so ruthlessly threatened our family.

Edild beckoned to me, and I hurried to help her shift the large, heavy slab that covered the grave. A generous layer of earth now covered it, and I heard the sound of grass stems and roots tearing.

The open grave yawned beneath us.

Edild knelt for a moment, lips moving in prayer. I guessed she would add an apology to Granny Cordeilla for the disturbance. I didn't want to look down; I had a fair idea what would be in the grave, and, as far as I was concerned, it was just the bodily remains; what was left of the flesh and bone that had housed Granny in her life. The real Granny Cordeilla – the big, generous heart, the love, the humour, the spirit – had long fled the earth. Not that I didn't still feel her close – I did, I do, and very often I even get a brief glimpse of her.

I sensed movement. I turned my head, and saw that Edild was lying flat on the ground, reaching with one hand down into the grave.

I waited.

A quick smile of satisfaction crossed her anxious face. She straightened up, then turned back to the grave and murmured more incantations. Once again, she nodded to me, and together we replaced the slab.

She straightened up, and for a long moment stood with bowed head and closed eyes. I had no idea what was happening, but we had just been in Granny's presence, and the sense of her was strong. I too closed my eyes and, in the privacy of my own head, spoke to her.

I felt Edild's touch on my arm. Opening my eyes, I saw her incline her head, and she stepped a few paces away from Granny's grave. I followed her.

She turned to me, and I saw her draw in a breath and square her shoulders, as if in preparation for some difficult task that would take all her strength. She held the lantern up high, in her left hand, and I saw that in the palm of her other hand lay an object, perhaps the size of her two closed fists, maybe a little smaller, wrapped in a length of worn sacking.

'*That* wasn't in Granny's grave!' I said. A stupid remark, quite evidently wrong since Granny's grave was precisely the place from where Edild had just extracted whatever it was.

'Not when you last saw inside; no, it wasn't,' Edild agreed. Then, watching me intently, she said, 'Lassair, do you recall the sequence of events, that morning you came back after Cordeilla's funeral rites?'

I did. It would be virtually impossible to forget, since I'd found the slab askew and, widening the gap, discovered there was another body down there beside Granny*. I'd raced back to fetch Edild, and we managed to get the other body out of the grave. Then Edild had sent me to the village for help, leaving her alone beside the grave.

Had the slab been back in place when I returned? I thought it had, although I couldn't now be sure.

And had Edild used the time of my absence to slip whatever it was she now held into the grave? Where it was hidden in a secret place known only to her?

I stared into her eyes. Slowly she nodded. 'Yes, I did. I put it in there with her that morning, while you were running to the village.'

'But . . . but how did you know you'd get that opportunity?' I demanded.

'I didn't – of course I didn't,' she said impatiently. 'I was going to hide it later that day, probably at dusk when

* See *Music of the Distant Stars*

I was unlikely to be seen. In the meantime, I kept it in a
leather bag, attached to my belt under my over gown. And
it's quite heavy,' she added, glancing at the sacking-wrapped
object.

'Why did you have to hide it so carefully?' I asked.

She looked straight into my eyes. 'Because at all costs you
weren't to find it.'

'*Me?*' It came out as a squeak.

'I had been left clear instructions. *This is for Lassair, when
she is old enough and wise enough to know how to use it, and
to treat it with the respect and the awe it demands.* In the
meantime, I was to hide it so well that nobody would be able
to find it.'

'So you put it in with Granny,' I whispered. In a flash like
a sudden shaft of light, something occurred to me. 'That was
why you were so worried, that day when I told you I'd been
out to the island to check that Granny's grave hadn't been
disturbed!' I cried, my voice rising with excitement. 'When I
found those signs that someone had been digging the recent
graves in the churchyard, remember? You went so white I
thought you were going to faint, and I thought it was because
you were worried for my safety! You weren't – you were
suddenly terrified I'd report that someone had robbed Granny's
grave, and it was that – that *thing* you're clutching – that you
were so worried about!'

'Hush,' Edild said warningly. 'Yes. I was afraid you'd given
away the hiding place,' she admitted. 'I'm sorry, Lassair. Of
course I was concerned for you too, but I confess that, in the
first moment, you weren't the most important aspect.'

I grunted a grudging acceptance of the apology.

Then I recalled what she'd just said: *This is for Lassair,
when she is old enough and wise enough.*

I stared at her. 'Am I old and wise enough, Edild?'

I fervently hoped so. I'd been through so much over the
past few weeks, enduring abduction, fear, pain, homesickness,
sorrow, and, worst of all, the very recent memory of Skuli's
terrible threat hanging over me unless I did the impossible
and found his shining stone for him.

I felt I deserved some reward, and, you never knew, this

mystery object might turn into something I might find useful
From what Edild had said, it sounded as if it had power . . .

A trickle of excitement ran up my spine, swiftly followed
by another, much stronger one.

I was in the presence of some unknown, potent force.

Edild met my eyes. 'It is time,' she whispered.

Slowly she extended her right hand, and I held out both of
mine. Slowly, reverently, she put the sacking-wrapped object
into my hands, gently closing my fingers over it. 'And so it
comes to pass,' she intoned, 'as it was foretold, that this is
transferred from he who gave it away, into the hands of she
who, it was believed, would one day be the right one to receive
it.'

To my utter amazement, she gave me a low bow. Then she
stepped back.

Beyond the village behind us, the moon was just rising
above the horizon. It was almost full, and its light shone
brightly in the indigo, star-studded sky. There was no more
need of lantern light: the spirits had provided all the illumina-
tion necessary. In the first brilliance of the night, I unwrapped
the sacking and gazed at what I held.

It was a heavy glass ball, dense, black, and it might have
been made to fit my hands. My fingers met around its circum
ference, their tips forming a neat, supportive, interlinked
pattern, almost like a cage of bone, sinew and flesh. My flesh.

I knew just exactly how it liked to be held: I swear I did.
It was as if I had performed the action many, many times.

I stared down into its dark depths and noticed a sudden
flash of green. Then, almost instantaneously, the moon's rays
caught a different area of the perfectly smooth surface, and a
dazzling gold light shone out at me.

I had barely finished admiring its wonderful beauty when,
as if it had been waiting, its power burst out and hit me square
in the chest.

Edild helped me to sit, then, my knees still trembling, to stand.
My backside was sore; I had not let go of the stone, and as a
consequence I had gone straight down, not breaking my fall
with my hands.

'It's safe,' I said quickly to Edild. 'I held it firmly.'

Her mouth twisted. 'It looks after itself,' she murmured.

I felt a stab of alarm. To take my mind off it, I examined the shining stone again. I sensed its power, just there beneath its black, gleaming surface, but it was veiled. For now.

Presently I looked up at Edild. 'Why me?'

Edild understood. 'Because Granny said so. You were the one. You were the natural inheritor, she said.'

'But *why* was I? Why not you? Or one of my siblings? And how did she know?'

'She understood what the stone was,' Edild replied. 'Also, she guessed – no, she *knew* – what you would become. You weren't ready then, when she died, so she told me to hide it and give it to you when the time came.'

'And that time is now? Really and truly?' It was a thrilling thought.

Edild smiled grimly. 'I would have said not, but events have overtaken us.' She studied me, frowning. 'You are ready, Lassair.' She muttered something else which sounded like, 'You'll have to be.'

My mind was galloping, busy with *how* and *why*. How did Granny come to have the stone? She must have known Thorfinn's little healer, whoever she was, but why had the woman given the precious thing to Granny?

Edild reached down a hand and helped me up. 'How did the stone . . .?' I began, but she shook her head.

'I know what you're going to ask,' she said, 'but it's no use, because I do not know.' She sighed. 'My task was simply to conceal it and give it to you when the time came. That I have done.'

She spun round, away from me, and I could not see her face. I did not need to, for I had heard the hurt in her voice. My Granny Cordeilla – Edild's own mother – had entrusted her with an important task, yes. But she had not seen fit to explain everything to her daughter; to reveal to her the full story.

Which, of course, meant that I wasn't going to know it either.

Frustration seethed in me. As if the stone picked up my

mood (surely not!) I felt a sudden heat in it. In my mind I heard Thorfinn's deep voice; *If a man believes himself up to the challenge, the stone will bring him face to face with himself.*

Was that what had just happened? Had the stone picked up my hot irritation and flashed it back at me?

It was a frightening thought.

Edild was walking away, back towards the water and, beyond it, the further shore. We would have to make that cold crossing once more. With a sigh, I wrapped the shining stone in its sacking and went after her.

We were on our way back to the village. We had not gone far when I saw someone standing quite still, waiting for us.

Straight away I saw, with huge relief, that the figure was not big or burly enough to be Skuli. My heartbeat slowed down.

Then I realized who it was.

Edild, perhaps with the eyes of love, had recognized him before I did, and was already running up to him, catching hold of his hands, muttering that he should not be out here in the cold when he had lately been so sorely injured. Gently but firmly he took her anxious hands away, and I heard him say, 'Do not worry, sweet. I will take no harm.'

'Come home!' Edild urged. Her face was taut with worry.

But Hrype shook his head, 'Not yet, Edild.' He glanced at me, then back at Edild. 'Go on back,' he said to her gently. 'Build up the fire, prepare a restorative. We will not be long.'

'You propose to stay out here? But . . .'

He put his hands on her shoulders, turned her so that she faced the village and gave her a small push. 'Go, Edild,' he repeated. 'I must speak to Lassair.'

She resisted for a long moment. Then she seemed to slump. Shaking her head, she began to walk away, her pace quickening so that soon she was almost running.

I stared after her. I felt very, very sorry for her.

But then, with renewed alarm, I heard again what Hrype had just said. What could he have to say to me, and why could Edild not stay to hear it?

Hrype and I stood out there on the marsh in the moonlight, and, hardly daring to breathe, I waited for him to speak.

'There was a secret, in the keeping of a dying woman,' he said, right in my ear. Without my noticing, he had silently come to stand right beside me. 'The secret had two distinct elements, which were passed to two different people, neither permitted to know the element entrusted to the other. I did not know until this night where Edild had hidden the stone, and, even now, I am only guessing.' He paused, and I saw that his eyes were fixed on the sacking-wrapped object in my hands. 'The other part of the secret – the reason for the stone's destiny – was placed solely in my care.'

'So that you – you could pass it on to *me*?' It was so unlikely, so preposterous, that I felt embarrassed even suggesting it.

But Hrype was nodding. 'Exactly so. The time for secrecy is over, for the safety of many is at stake.' He seemed to be gathering his thoughts, and then, of all unlikely things, said, 'Where, Lassair, do you think you and your aunt get your healing gift?'

'I . . . I have no idea.' It was obvious that I'd inherited it from Edild, but as to where *she* had acquired it, I'd never thought to ask. I suppose, if I had done, I'd merely have assumed she'd discovered it was something she could just do, rather like me and my ability to dowse.

'It is handed down from your grandmother,' Hrype said.

My mother's mother. Then I hadn't been far off the mark when I had believed that Ama – my grandmother's sister – had been the little healer who had tended Thorfinn. 'I never knew her,' I whispered. 'She died before I was born.'

Hrype let out a sound of exasperation. 'What's happened to your wits, Lassair?' he demanded crossly. 'You've just been presented with an object of power that was hidden in your paternal grandmother's grave, yet here you are talking about your *mother*'s mother.'

Granny *Cordeilla*? 'But Granny Cordeilla was a bard!' I said, stupefied.

'Yes, she was,' he said, a little less testily now. 'But she was a healer first, and a very fine one, by all accounts, with strong little hands and an instinct for seeking out and dissolving the dark thoughts that can trouble a man deeply, yet which give little outward sign.'

'I never knew her heal anybody!' I protested, still unable to believe what I was hearing.

'No, I'm sure you didn't.' I had the impression that, not without effort, he had mastered his annoyance at my slowness. 'When Cordeilla saw the talent emerge in Edild, you see, she stepped back. She gave way to her beloved daughter, letting Edild develop at her own pace and in her own way. Cordeilla didn't want to overshadow her. She guided her, but let her discover her skills and her talent for herself.'

Granny Cordeilla had been a healer. Slowly I shook my head in amazement. And – oh, dear Lord! – she'd had the stone, which meant she was *Thorfinn*'s healer. She was the punchy little woman who had saved his life and taken on the guardianship of his magic shining stone when it proved too much for him.

'Do you . . .?' My mouth was dry, and it was hard to speak. I tried again. 'Do you know any more about her?' I asked.

Hrype smiled. 'I do,' he said. 'I know rather a lot. Would you like to hear it?'

Did he think I'd say *no*? I nodded. 'Oh, yes, please.'

EIGHTEEN

'She was vibrant with life and full of sparkling magic, the young woman you only knew in old age,' Hrype began. 'They tried to control her, her kinsfolk and the village elders, for, loving her as they did, despite her waywardness and her utter refusal to accept restraint or advice, they feared she would stand out like the one tall stem of corn and, like it, be cut down. Then, as now,' he added, shooting me a glance, 'it did not do to be too different. When she was fifteen, Cordeilla married a calm, steady man, quite a few years older than her, and in a short time she produced two little sons in exactly his image, with not a spark of magic in either of them.'

'My uncles Ordic and Alwyn,' I interrupted. Yes, it was fair to say they had no magic. I wondered if I should tell Hrype that this part of the tale was already familiar to me, but held back in case it stopped his flow.

As soon as he picked up the narrative, I was glad I hadn't, for the things that he now revealed to me I had neither known nor even suspected.

'The years passed slowly for Cordeilla, for, although her husband was a good man, the truth was that he bored her. She loved her little sons – of that I have no doubt – but the daily round of washing, cleaning, cooking, and the unremitting toil that was her lot wore her down. Her days were no tougher than those of any other woman,' he added, perhaps sensing the protest forming in my mind, 'but Cordeilla's particular form of suffering was that she no longer had time for the free, wide-ranging thinking that had entranced her in her youth. Her days were just too full and, when she tumbled into bed at night, she was far too tired to do anything but fall instantly asleep.'

Would it be like that if I married and had children, I wondered? Would the daily grind effectively close iron doors in my mind, shutting out the wonder of the world and its endless possibilities? *It depends upon who you marry, a very* familiar voice said inside my head.

I smiled. I'd hoped Granny was with me just then. It was good – oh, better than good – to know I was right.

'Then Cordeilla conceived again,' Hrype went on, 'and, hopeful this time for a child in her own image, her mercurial spirits rose and she was full of joy. When she miscarried, it seemed to her, for a time, that her world was covered with darkness, and she could find no light.'

Oh, Granny! I whispered silently to her.

Past and gone now, child, she replied briskly. It was not easy to detect the tremor in her voice, but it was there.

Some pains never really go away . . .

'Her husband feared for her sanity,' Hrype's soft voice continued, 'and, greatly missing her smile like the noonday sun that had once brightened the monotony and the hardship of his days, he too suffered. Unable to come up with a way to draw her out of her misery, he consulted the elders of the village. One of them, pointing out that Cordeilla came from a line of healers and wise women, said, why not let Cordeilla try to discover whether she shared the gift? To cut the story short, she reached out with both hands for this life-saving rope that was thrown to her, and, hurling herself into the study and practices taught to her, she found a reason to go on living.'

'Was she good?' I asked.

Hrype smiled at me. 'The best,' he replied.

As I watched, his smile faded. I'd been hoping he'd tell me that this discovery of her skills returned Cordeilla to her true self, but I sensed it did not happen like that. 'The healing wasn't enough, was it?' I said in a small voice.

'No,' Hrype confirmed. 'She mourned still for the lost child, and, in the hope that a new baby would ease her pain, she longed to conceive again. But her husband – no doubt acting as he had been advised, and wanting only for Cordeilla to get better – did not think the time was right for another pregnancy. In his clumsy way, he tried to make her forget the miscarriage, telling her that such things happened; that it was God's will, and mere humans should not question the decisions of the Almighty. His remarks, far from consoling his wife, pushed her further back into her darkness. Her constant, ill-humoured mood drove her husband away, so that he spent as little time at home with her as he could. There were rumours that he sought comfort elsewhere, and, indeed, if they were true, who can blame him? If Cordeilla suspected or knew, she kept it to herself. Perhaps, understanding his distress and what had caused it, she felt he deserved some comfort. But it did not help: on the outside, she was a dutiful mother, wife and healer. On the inside, grieving, estranged from her husband, she was dying.'

I wondered what it had been about that particular pregnancy, that Cordeilla should grieve its loss so inconsolably. Miscarriages were, after all, a regular occurrence, and while I would not have presumed to minimize the pain they caused, I had observed with my own eyes how most women seemed to overcome their sorrow.

When another baby comes along, said Granny in my head. Ah. Yes . . .

There was a short silence, and I felt Hrype was preparing for the next part of his tale. Taking a breath, he spoke. 'All this time, a bright new star was poised to come blasting across Cordeilla's sky, in the shape of a giant of a man by the name of Thorfinn Ofnirsson.'

In my mind's eye I saw Thorfinn as I knew him. Without any apparent effort from me, slowly the image changed. The shock of silver hair that I had observed turned pale blond, here and there streaked white by sun and salt; the creases and wrinkles of age smoothed away. In this earlier Thorfinn, his brows were bound with a plait of leather, beneath which two thick plaits swung either side of his laughing face. Tall, broad and upright, he was in his prime.

'Thorfinn was a mariner,' Hrype was saying, 'one of the finest of his generation, based in Iceland and with close kin on the Faroe Islands. He was the descendant of other sailors and explorers, one of whom made an extraordinary voyage, first sailing north-west from his home to Greenland, then south-west to Helluland, Markland, Vinland, and on, always on, further than any of his kinsman had dared to go or even dreamed of going.'

The land behind the sun, I thought, remembering the words of Thorfinn and his daughter. I knew this story already, for it was Thorkel's tale. But Hrype, it seemed, knew where the place with the mystical-sounding name was to be found. Where was it? To the west, it appeared. I went over his description in my head, but the words made little sense. I would have to ask Gurdyman. He seemed to know how the lands of the earth were disposed.

I knew what Hrype was going to say next. I waited, keeping silent while he told me again what I already knew. Once more, I listened to the tale of what had happened to Thorkel and his treasure; how and why it had eventually come to Thorfinn. I heard again – and, as before, it pained me – what Thorfinn's inheritance had led to: his slow, steady disintegration, from the instant when he received a black stone with unimaginable power, once acquired from a dark-skinned stranger with feathers in his hair, right up to the moment when he lay, battered, bruised, broken, beside my grandmother's hearth.

'And in the end,' Hrype concluded, 'his heart full of despair, Thorfinn understood that he and his shining stone must part. Although it tore out a part of him, he gave it to Cordeilla, and told her to hide it away, out of the earth's light, until the right hands should come to claim it.'

Skuli believed his were the right hands, I thought, more than half entranced by the power of the story. Furiously resentful of the fact that it had passed down through the female side rather than via his father to himself, he had done his utmost to find it and claim it. He had failed.

And now, the shining stone had been bestowed somewhere quite different . . .

Suddenly feeling it heavy in my palms, I whispered, 'It has come into *my* hands.'

Panicking now, I met Hrype's eyes. 'I am surely not the rightful recipient!' I cried, almost sobbing from fear. 'You must have been mistaken, Hrype, or else Granny was confused and . . . and . . .'

I was never confused! Granny protested firmly inside my head. *I knew exactly what I was doing, Lassair child. It is yours.*

I wondered if Hrype could hear her too.

I stared at him. 'Why?' I said, the word more a breath than audible speech.

For a moment, his face twisted in compassion. Then, appearing to wipe the emotion away, he said, 'Put yourself, if you can, into Cordeilla's shoes. Into Thorfinn's. There you had two people, both suffering, whom circumstance had drawn into close proximity. Both were in need of comfort and compassion. Because of what they were to each other – patient and healer – there had been, of necessity, intimacy between them. Both were young; both were vibrant and attractive.'

He paused, as if leaving it to me to speak the words. 'They fell in love,' I said. I knew it was so; it was the inevitable end to their tale.

'They fell in love,' Hrype confirmed. 'For the brief weeks of one midsummer, they were lovers. Then Thorfinn, healed both in body and in mind, sailed away. Cordeilla never saw him again.'

'Did he not come back to her?' Tears were rolling down my face. 'Not even once?'

'He did not dare,' Hrype said heavily, 'for he feared that the temptation to take back his shining stone would prove too great. He truly believed that he could only go on living if he no longer possessed it. Perhaps,' he added softly, 'it is more accurate to say, if *it* no longer possessed *him.*'

This talk of the stone's uncanny power was deeply disturbing. Again, I seemed to feel the heaviness of it in my hands. I longed to put it down, but something stopped me. It – *it* – would not let me. It was as if, I thought wildly, it had to be assured that I was strong enough to deal with it.

I was not at all sure I was.

'Cordeilla grieved for him,' Hrype went on, picking up the story, 'but she had a husband, two small sons and a home to care for, and she had no choice but to gather up her courage and move on. She loved her little boys, and her husband was not a bad man. It was not his fault that he lacked the imagination and the wild flair she needed in a mate. She told herself firmly that she must not waste her life mourning for something she could not have, and she made up her mind to make the best of what she did have.'

I smiled. That sounded like Granny Cordeilla. She had always been a practical, courageous and resolute woman.

I became aware that the pause between one sentence and the next had lengthened somewhat. Alarmed suddenly, although I did not know why, I brought my attention right back to Hrype.

Acknowledging the fact, he nodded. 'And then,' he said, 'Cordeilla discovered she was pregnant.'

I think I knew the truth, instantly, even while my mind was weaving about trying to evade it.

Fighting what I'm sure I had already accepted, I thought, *Cordeilla's husband changed his mind, and the result was this new conception.*

Next: *She knew the child wasn't her husband's, and she quietly aborted it.*

Then: *The child was born but did not survive.*

I forced myself to look at Hrype. 'Did the child live to adulthood?'

'He did.'

After that, there was nowhere else to go. No comforting explanation behind which to hide.

My grandmother's third-born child was my father.

'Nobody knew,' Hrype said presently, as if that made a difference. 'Cordeilla and Thorfinn had been very discreet. In addition, she had shared her husband's bed during the summer, so there was no reason for him to think the baby was not his. When the child was born, Cordeilla explained its dissimilarity to her husband by telling everyone it looked like her brothers. Which, indeed, it did.'

Slowly I nodded. I hope Hrype saw; I couldn't have spoken just then, but I didn't want him to think that shock had closed my ears and I was no longer listening.

'The years rolled by,' he resumed, 'and, a couple of years on, Cordeilla conceived again, giving birth to twin daughters. The elder, as you know, is a true child of her mother, with Cordeilla's quick intelligence, wits, magical ability and, of course, her healer's touch. Her appearance, fortuitously, supported Cordeilla's claim that her third son's colouring and large frame came from her side of the family, for, although she did not have the large stature, Edild did inherit reddish-fair hair and light green eyes, just like her uncles. The second twin, poor Alvela, was small and dark, like her father and the eldest pair of brothers.'

Hrype paused, looking at me closely as if to gauge my reaction to this astounding news. Deliberately I kept my expression neutral. If he suspected a fragment of what I was feeling, he would probably stop. I could barely endure to learn more, but it would be even worse if I didn't hear the end.

After some time, he said quietly, 'Cordeilla loved all five of her children, but Edild and Wymond were the ones she kept closest to her heart. And it was Wymond, of course, with whom she chose to live when she could no longer manage alone.'

She clove to Edild because she was so like herself, I thought, both in character and abilities, and she had the healer's gift.

And to Wymond – my father – because he was Thorfinn's son.

If Thorfinn was his father, that made him my grandfather.

It was no wonder I'd grown so quickly to love him.

I was still clutching the shining stone. My grandfather's stone, left in the care of my grandmother to be passed on to someone who, in the fullness of time, would be the right recipient.

That someone was me, and the awareness of my responsibility was only just beginning to dawn on me. To say I was apprehensive nowhere near described the storm of emotions I was suffering, chief among which was terror.

I wanted to put the stone down.

I didn't think I could.

Do it, a voice seemed to say.

I gathered all my courage, drew a deep breath and, slowly, carefully, reverently, laid the sacking-wrapped stone on the damp earth.

Instantly I felt so light-headed that I could have sworn my feet left the ground.

I was vaguely aware of Hrype, looking over his shoulder in the direction of the village

He turned back to face me. 'Are you all right?'

I nodded.

He reached out and briefly touched my arm, giving it a quick squeeze. His hand was warm, and very comforting. The he said, 'I'm going to leave you here.'

I was too distraught to ask why. Perhaps he thought I needed some time alone to adjust to all that I had just learned. To adjust, too, to being the new keeper of my family's great treasure . . .

He was walking away. Something occurred to me: something vital. 'Hrype!' I called out.

He spun round. 'Yes?'

'Does my father know?'

Slowly he shook his head. 'No, Lassair. The only person here to whom Cordeilla revealed her secret was me.'

I had not the least idea whether to be glad or sorry.

I stood there alone, and slowly time passed. I had the sense that I was waiting for something.

Some*one*.

A mist had fallen, obscuring the moonlight. Presently, a tall, broad figure loomed up out of the darkness.

Thorfinn said, 'So now you know.'

I nodded. 'Yes,' I whispered. Then, the tangle of my thoughts straightened itself out a little and I said, '*You* knew too?' He had to; why else had all this happened?

'I did,' he admitted. 'Not until many years after the child, your father, was born. She sent word, you see. Ships sailed by my kinsmen regularly visited the fens, as indeed they still do, and it was not hard for her to find someone kindly and discreet who knew where to find me and could take a message. Once she knew I would not come back to claim her and my son, she felt it was the right thing to do.'

'Why would you not come back?' I was weeping again.

'I was married, with a growing family of my own. She knew that – knew, too, that I could not abandon them.'

'You could have just visited!' I cried. 'Didn't you want to

see your son? Couldn't you have spared just a few days – a few hours, even – to see what he was like?'

Thorfinn sighed. 'It would have been too painful for both Cordeilla and for me,' he said heavily. 'But, as to not wishing to see him, I have regretted every single day of my life that I was not able to.'

I knew he spoke the truth; the naked emotion in his voice came from his heart.

He could not see his son, my father, even now; the resemblance between them would be clear, for those with eyes to see it. In a flash I recalled those moments back in Iceland when I had experienced a sense of familiarity about Thorfinn. I understood now why they had happened: in some subtle way, in some deep place inside my head far from conscious thought, Thorfinn reminded me of my father.

He might not be able to see his son, but there was something I *could* offer. Looking at him with a smile, I said, 'Do you mind getting a bit wet?'

I stood back and let him go on to her alone. It was a moment of intense privacy, and I didn't think he'd want anyone with him.

From a distance of a few paces, I watched as, at long last, my grandfather knelt on the ground and, head bowed, joined his spirit once again with that of the woman he had loved and lost.

Back on the mainland once more, I thought I should quickly get Thorfinn back to warmth and comfort. He was well wrapped, but he was wet to the thighs, and I didn't think it could be good for him. Somewhere, there must be a bed waiting for him; Einar and his crewmen could not be far away.

But my grandfather had other ideas.

Ignoring my protests, he took a firm hold of my arm and led me away from the village, down to a slight rise on the southern edge of the bulge that is Aelf Fen. We drew to a halt, and he pointed out over the restless water.

I followed the line of his outstretched arm. I saw a sleek longship: a dramatic, dark shape against the silvery, moonlit water. She was moving away, slowly and carefully, her swift power reined in, for her crew would be all too aware that they rowed in shallow, unknown and possibly treacherous marshland waters.

Even moving at walking pace, it was clear what she was. A true Norse longship, with shields along the gunwales and a fierce serpent figurehead, she was truly magnificent.

She was all but indistinguishable from the ship of my vision. '*Malice-striker*,' I whispered.

Thorfinn gave a grunt. There was pain in the sound. 'No, but Skuli's ship is very like my own craft, as she was in her prime,' he said gruffly.

'I've seen your ship,' I reminded him softly. I had seen both the living ship, with the inner sight of vision, and also what remained of Thorfinn's *Malice-striker*, on a faraway shore in Iceland.

It was here, though, in the fens – almost on this very spot – that I had seen the dream ship. There was magic about tonight, too, as there had been then, and such a thing seemed not only possible but entirely probable.

Thorfinn turned to me, about to speak, but I did not let him. 'I don't mean the skeleton ship on the shore in your homeland,' I said softly. 'I meant my dream vision.'

And, at last, I told him what I had seen,

He listened, accepting my quiet words, as I had known he would, with a nod. 'I sailed here, long ago,' he murmured. 'As you now know.' The shadow of a grin creased his face. 'You probably caught a whisper of the shade of that earlier time, for, as with all things, it is still here to see for those who look with the right eyes.'

I looked out over the water again, aware that Thorfinn, beside me, was doing the same. Skuli's ship was gaining speed. He was going, away from me, out of my life. Without the stone for which he had risked so much and caused such a sum of trouble, grief and pain.

'Where is he going?' I asked in a hushed voice. 'Is he heading for those fearsome rapids, where his grandfather –' who must have been Thorfinn's uncle, I thought suddenly, my mind reeling; his mother's brother – 'met his death?'

For some time, Thorfinn did not answer. After a while, and it sounded more as if he were intoning a chant than speaking, he said, 'They will sail out into the North Sea, then into the great river network that forges its way through the vast continent over there to the south and the east; the route that leads from the Varyani to the Greeks.'

I did not know what he meant. 'From the Gulf of Finland up the River Neva, through Lake Ladoga, the River Volkhov,' he sang, 'on, on, passing out of the northern forests and emerging on to the steppes; by portage to the Dneiper, and on to the great power centre of Kiev, where men of all shapes and hues come to buy and sell. But that is not the end of the voyage, for it goes still on, on, across the Black Sea until at last, if the gods smile on them, they will reach their journey's end.'

I did not ask where that was. I did not want to break the spell, and, anyway, I believed I already knew.

But my grandfather told me anyway.

'Skuli and his crew are going to Miklagard.'

NINETEEN

t was wonderful to spend a couple of days in Aelf Fen with my family, just happy to be together, unharmed and safe, as we all put the drama of the past few days and weeks behind us. As people do when they have emerged on the sunny side of bad events, we kept repeating things that had happened, even though most of us knew every last detail by then. It is the way, I believe, that we assimilate traumatic happenings and put them firmly behind us.

My own favourite bit was the description of my mother and her pan. I just wish I'd been there to see it.

I tried, as much as I could, to remain in the shadows and just watch and listen to everyone else having fun. I just wasn't in the mood for merrymaking. For one thing, I was having to keep several things secret. My parents and my brothers didn't know about how I'd been abducted by Einar and spirited off to Iceland. Nobody had told them. They thought I'd been in Cambridge with Gurdyman the whole time, and I saw no reason to alter that. If I now revealed the truth, I'd have to explain, and I really didn't want to do that.

Besides, I was now occasionally experiencing the disturbing feeling that something else was going to happen.

No matter how hard I tried to tell myself it was nothing more than the after-effect of all the excitement, I could not quite make myself believe it.

In addition, I had to keep from my beloved father the fact that Thorfinn and his son were very closely related to him: about as close as you can be, in Thorfinn's case. If I told them about Iceland, I'd have to explain why Thorfinn had been so eager to meet me, and to have me mix with my kinsfolk and experience a small taste of what their life was like on that extraordinary island so far away to the north.

I did wonder if my father suspected the truth. The story I told was that the Norsemen knew the shining stone had been

left in the keeping of a woman called Cordeilla who lived at
Aelf Fen, and had sought me out to help them find it because
they knew I was Cordeilla's granddaughter. The family
appeared to believe it, but once or twice I looked up to find
my father watching me with an expression on his face that
suggested he knew I was holding something back, and that by
doing so I had hurt him.

I found that all but unendurable.

The trouble was, it wasn't my secret to tell. His mother,
whom he had both loved and respected, had slept with another
man, and my father was the result. If Cordeilla had chosen
not to tell him, I did not think it was up to me to reveal the
truth.

The reasoning was sound. It didn't make it any easier.

The other factor in my not being terribly enthusiastic about
the celebrations was that I was missing Thorfinn. I had watched
Malice-striker sail away, and the big, broad-shouldered figure
that I knew to be Thorfinn remained standing in the stern until,
blinded by tears, I could no longer make him out.

The only person in the village who knew what Thorfinn
and I really were to each other, and why it was so hard to see
him go, was Hrype. For a variety of reasons, I didn't feel I
could go and cry on his shoulder.

Therefore it was with considerable relief that, on the morning
of the third day, I announced I was going back to Cambridge.
It might have been my imagination, but I thought my father's
farewell hug was tighter than usual. As I hugged him back, I
whispered to him that I loved him.

I *do* hope he knew it was true.

Gurdyman greeted me with a smile and a hot meal. As soon
as I set eyes on him, I felt a huge stab of guilt: just how long,
I wondered, had he been worrying about me?

He didn't look like a man who'd been tearing his hair and
pacing the midnight hours away, though, and I berated myself
for exaggerating my self-importance. He'd probably been so
preoccupied with his work and his experiments that he hadn't
even missed me.

Sitting in the courtyard, gobbling down the (excellent) food,

I felt his gaze on me and dropped my head, embarrassed, hoping he didn't perceive the turbulence of my thoughts.

He did. I felt a cool hand on my shoulder, and he said softly, 'Hrype sent word when you returned to the village. I gather there have been further dramas, but your presence back here with me suggests they are now over.'

I looked up at him. 'They are,' I said.

He nodded. 'Finish your meal,' he said calmly, 'then you shall tell me all about it.'

It was he, in fact, who began the narration. He said, as I was gathering myself to begin, 'A moment, Lassair.'

Something in his tone alerted me. I looked at him closely, and saw an odd expression on his face. If it didn't seem so unlikely, I'd have said he felt guilty.

'I know something of what has been happening,' he said, staring down at his hands folded in his lap. 'Rather a lot, in fact; Hrype has told me much.' Now he met my eyes, and his emotion was all too clear. He *was* guilty, and he was also in some anguish. 'I – we – owe you an apology, Lassair. Hrype and I knew about your treasure, and, although we had no idea precisely what it was, we knew it was of value to a mariner such as Skuli. Hrype learned of his existence, and we knew – or, I should say, we guessed – that it was he who had come searching for it.'

They *knew*? In my amazement, I could only manage one word: 'How?'

'Concerning Skuli,' Gurdyman said, 'Hrype, as I dare say you know, has mysterious contacts in many places, not a few of which are on the coast. I imagine that gossip concerning a man such as Skuli would spread among the Norse mariners and those with whom they trade, and Hrype is very good at uncovering what he wants to know. Concerning matters closer to your own kin –' now his tone became grave – 'your grandmother Cordeilla confided the secret of your father's parentage to Hrype as she was dying, as now you will be aware. Hrype knew, too, that some precious object had been left in her care by her lover, and he guessed that it had been entrusted to Edild, although he never discussed it with her. Our guilt,' he went on, 'Hrype's and mine, is because, had we explained to

Edild that danger threatened, in the shape of a very forceful and slightly deranged giant determined at any cost to get his hands on the treasure, then it is highly likely she would have shared her part of the secret with Hrype. Had that been so, you would not have been abducted and put in such danger.'

I felt deep pity for him. It was quite clear his guilt was eating into him. I could see two objections to what he had just said, and, pausing briefly to arrange my thoughts, I voiced them.

'There is no need for guilt,' I said, trying to keep my voice calm. 'For one thing, there's no reason why Hrype and my aunt pooling their information would have stopped any of what happened subsequently. Unless you're suggesting that Hrype should simply have given Skuli the stone, then he'd still have gone on the rampage while he searched for it. We could, I suppose, have warned the households he ransacked and the people he killed and hurt, although we'd have had to know exactly where he was going to look.'

I drew a breath, then said, 'The second thing is personal to me.' I hesitated. Was this really the moment for levity, when two women were dead and the toll of death and maiming might very well have been a lot worse? *Oh*, I thought, *why not?* 'Dear Gurdyman,' I said softly, 'I have, as I dare say you know, been to Iceland and back. Believe me, I would not have missed that for the world.'

His eyes rounded. 'You *enjoyed* it?' he said, his incredulity making his voice almost a squeak. 'All the way across those furious, icy seas in an open boat, and an uncertain welcome when you got there?'

'But I thought you . . .' I'd been about to say that I thought he'd told me he had travelled extensively in his youth, so surely he would understand. Something in his face, however, warned me not to. Perhaps the contrast between the free-roving spirit he had been when young, and the old man living his life within his own four walls as he was now, was something of which he preferred not to be reminded.

'I loved being on board *Malice-striker*,' I assured him instead, 'once I'd got over the seasickness. And my welcome in Iceland could not have been warmer.'

'Well, they are, after all, your kinsfolk,' Gurdyman muttered. He risked a small smile, then a larger one. 'You really are not angry with us? With Hrype and me, who should have entrusted you with what we suspected?'

'No,' I said very firmly. 'Not in the least.'

Now he was beaming. 'In that case –' he leaned forward and poured chilled white wine into our cups – 'tell me the whole story.'

He must have been bursting with impatience to see the shining stone, probably from the moment I walked into the twisty-turny house, but he restrained himself. It was only when I had finished my tale that he said in a whisper, 'May I be allowed to see this magical object?'

I went to fetch it from where I had stowed it, with my satchel, up in my attic room. I laid it on the table in the court-yard, and slowly, reverently – half, I admit, reluctantly – unwrapped the sacking.

As the sun's rays fell upon it, the shining stone shot out a great flash of gold. Gurdyman made an odd sound – a sort of gasp – and instinctively drew back. Then, his eyes wide with wonder, he leaned forward and very gently touched the smooth, glassy surface with the very tips of his fingers.

I waited. I could see he was deep in thought – lost in it, indeed – and I did not want to interrupt.

Finally, after what seemed a very long time, he said softly, 'Cover it now, Lassair, if you would.'

I did as he asked.

He sat looking at the sacking, so intently that it was as if his eyes were trying to penetrate through to the stone. Then he drew a shaky breath and said, 'Remind me where this came from.'

I closed my eyes, the better to remember how Freydis had described that strange land where Thorkel acquired the stone. It helps, I find, that I'm training to be a bard, for my memory seems to be developing the facility to recall bits of other people's narratives. Especially the dramatic parts.

'Thorkel sailed to the land behind the sun,' I said, eyes still shut, 'driven by a prophecy that he would cross the endless seas and come to a land of liquid gold. He described this land to his crewmen, telling them it was a place of brilliant light and colour, where they worshipped strange spirits under a sun so hot that men's skins turned brown, and where the fierce, hungry gods had to be appeased with the blood of the people.' I opened my eyes. 'I don't know where that land is,' I admitted. 'Nobody in Iceland actually said, although Hrype said it was in the west.'

And, I could have added, I had been hoping and praying ever since hearing the story that somebody else would elucidate; somebody, in fact, who was now sitting across the table from me.

As if he knew exactly what I was thinking, Gurdyman smiled. Then he reached over to his work table and picked up a large rolled parchment. Even as he untied the ribbon that held it in its roll, I knew what it was.

I waited while he spread it out.

It was the map I had seen before, but now it was twice as big, for another whole section had been stuck to its left-hand side. I leaned forward, trying to take it all in at once.

Gurdyman was pointing at a dot about halfway across the new section, high up towards the parchment's upper edge. 'This represents Iceland, where you have lately voyaged,' he said. I nodded encouragingly, eager to hear more. 'Here –' his finger moved left and up a little – 'is Greenland, although men say it is covered in ice and snow, and there is little green to be seen. Here is Helluland –' he had moved left again – 'and here Markland, and, below it, Vinland.' Now he moved down and a little to the right.

The names that Hrype mentioned, I thought, remembering. I stared at where Gurdyman was pointing. The wavy line that I knew represented the edge of the land ambled on down the page, moving generally left, but there were no details and no more carefully written words.

Feeling my spirits sink in disappointment, I looked up at him and said, 'Is that it? Is that all?'

'*All?*' I heard him echo, with an ironic laugh. 'Lassair, if you only knew the toil, the head-scratching, the quill-biting and the pain it has taken to work it out this far!'

'I'm sorry,' I said instantly, 'I didn't mean to diminish your achievement. It's just that . . .' I stopped. *Just that I was hoping to see exactly where Thorkel went ashore and returned to his ship a changed man* sounded hopelessly optimistic and rather naive, so I kept it to myself.

I think Gurdyman understood, anyway, for he patted my arm in an absent-minded but kindly way, then said, 'The lands where your ancestor sailed may be a mystery to us, but I do know what your stone is, or, at least, I believe I do.'

'You know what it is?' It was more than I could have hoped for.

'Would you like me to tell you?' Now there was a definite glint of mischief in his eyes.

What a silly question. Since I could hardly say that, I simply replied, 'Oh, yes please!'

I wondered if he would need to look at or hold the stone again, but it seemed not. 'This is also known as a shining mirror,' he began, indicating the stone in its wrappings. *Yes*, I thought excitedly. *Freydis referred to it in those words.* 'It is properly called obsidian; that is the name bestowed upon it by the lifelong student of natural history who observed at first hand its method of formation. But I am wandering from the point.' He frowned in thought, then went on: 'You will never guess, Lassair, where and how it originates, and so I shall tell you.'

He turned to his work table, rummaging among the parchments until he found the piece of vellum he used for the rough notes and jottings he habitually makes while a line of thought is coming to fruition. He smoothed it out, then dipped his quill in the ink horn and swiftly drew a little picture.

I stared at it as it formed beneath his skilful hand. It was cone-shaped, and the cone had steep, regular sides. Its base flattened out either side into smooth lines, and I realized he had drawn a hill, or perhaps a mountain. The top of the mountain had a cut-off appearance. Once he was satisfied with the outline, he dipped the quill again and a sudden explosion of straight and wavy lines appeared, as if the insides of the earth were pouring out of the mountain's summit.

'This, Lassair, is a volcano,' he said, still drawing. 'It is named for Vulcan, who was the Roman god of the forge and its fire. Volcanoes form where the molten rock within the earth has no more room to expand, and comes blasting out of the weakest point in the cone.'

'*Molten* rock?' I repeated. Surely not . . .

'Yes indeed. Melted,' he said firmly, clearly picking up my incredulity. 'Rock heated to so high a temperature that it becomes liquid.'

'*Liquid?*' I was finding this very hard to accept. Surely he was wrong?

'When this substance encounters water,' he went on, sensibly ignoring my interruption, 'when, for instance, it flows into a lake, a river or the sea, it cools very quickly – and what do you think happens?' He turned to me enquiringly.

'Er . . .'

His little sigh was all but inaudible. 'It is only molten because it is very, very hot,' he said patiently. 'As soon as it cools, it—'

'It turns back into rock!' I cried triumphantly, suddenly seeing what he was explaining.

'It does indeed!' He beamed. 'But its nature is forever changed from what it was, for the cooling process is too fast for it to resume its former nature.' His eyes strayed to the sacking-wrapped object, and I guessed he was visualizing the shining stone. 'It is as if, through the medium of fire and water, rock has been turned to glass . . .' His eyes seemed to slide out of focus, and I sensed he was lost in some private reverie.

An aspect, indeed, of what he had just said was reminding me of something he'd once taught me; something very, very important. I forced myself to concentrate, and out of the depths of my mind I heard a whisper: *alchemy*.

I left Gurdyman to his meditation as long as I could bear. When he showed no sign of returning his attention to me, and to the here and now, eventually I said softly, 'Gurdyman?'

He turned to me, his expression hazy, as if he was still absorbed in whatever he had been contemplating so deeply. 'Lassair!' It seemed to come as a surprise that I was there.

I should have left him to his thoughts, but my anxiety was too great to let me. 'Is the shining stone dangerous?' I hissed in an urgent whisper. I was very afraid: the stone had come into being via an arcane, magical process that I didn't even dare think about; it had the power to summon spirits; it forced you to face up to your true self; it had almost driven Thorfinn out of his mind, and Skuli had been prepared to kill in order to get his hands on it.

And I had just asked Gurdyman if it was *dangerous*!

With a visible effort, he came back to me. 'It is an object of very great power,' he said, 'but you already know that, Lassair.' He studied me keenly. 'Its power is neutral: it is neither good nor bad. It will do what it does, and it is up to whoever holds it to channel the power.' He paused, perhaps sensing that I did not fully understand. Then he said, 'Imagine, if you can, a magnificent horse; a stallion. He is swift, strong, eager, and his strength far outweighs that of any man who would try to ride him. One man tries, but he is overconfident and tries to master the stallion with harsh bit, spurs and whip. A second man tries, but he has taken the trouble to become an expert rider; moreover, before he even attempts to mount the fierce stallion, he spends a long time getting to know the animal. Once he feels that he has sufficient respect for the stallion's nature, he mounts him, and the two remain bonded for life.'

'So – so you're saying I must study the stone before I begin to use it?' Oh, but using it was the furthest thing from my mind! 'Gurdyman, I don't want to use it!' I wailed. 'I'm terri- fied of what it might do!'

'You must use it.' His eyes were staring right into mine, as if he was seeing inside my head. I made a pathetic little sound, practically a whimper. His expression softened. 'I will help you,' he said kindly. 'I will teach you all that I know, and we shall hope that will be enough.'

My eyes slid away and once more I stared at the stone beneath its sacking wrappings. *We shall hope that will be enough* really didn't sound very reassuring.

'For now,' he added, very quietly, 'why not put it away, safely, up in your room?'

It was the most welcome suggestion he'd made for some time.

As if he were very aware that we had touched on the edge of dangerous waters, Gurdyman made sure that our preoccupations for the rest of the day were of the most prosaic nature. He pointed out that the house had become very untidy and not a little dirty in my absence, and together we set about putting that right. He sorted out the great drift of parchments, books, odds and ends of food and drink, half-completed experiments and *things set aside to think about later*, as he expressed it, while I tucked up my skirts, rolled up my sleeves and washed every dusty, sticky surface until the whole house shone with cleanliness. It smelt nice, too, for Gurdyman had given me a little bottle of fragrant oil, and I had put a few drops in the final bucketful of rinsing water.

Tired out, I put away the broom, mop and pail and, rolling down my sleeves, went out to the courtyard to join Gurdyman in the last of the day's sunlight. He was sitting in his chair, the big parchment spread out across his knees.

I went to crouch beside him. I studied the wiggling line stretching away to the lower right of the great map. Then I looked at the vast stretch of sea that opened up to the left. Then something occurred to me: stretching out my hand, I measured the distance between the mark that was the fens and the blob in the middle of the sea that was Iceland.

Thus far I have travelled, I thought. Then, holding my thumb and middle finger the same stretch apart, I measured how much further it was to go right down to the middle sea, where Skuli was bound. How much further to go, as Thorkel had done, on from Iceland to Greenland, and then to explore the eastern shores of that vast and unknown land mass beyond, which even Gurdyman, in all his wisdom and knowledge, could only guess at.

I whispered, 'Can the world really be so big?'

He smiled. 'Bigger, far bigger, than this.' His hand brushed over his careful work.

I shivered. 'That's very frightening.'

'Frightening?' He considered it. 'Perhaps.' His smile broadened.

'What is it?' I asked. 'What are you thinking, and why is it amusing you?'

He reached out and, just for a moment, took my hand. 'You're the descendant of Norse mariners, child.'

He seemed to think that was sufficient explanation. It wasn't. 'What of it?'

He laughed softly. 'It's in your blood.'

'*What* is?' I was worrying now.

The laughter had gone, and he was no longer smiling. Looking right into my eyes, he said, 'The hunger for travelling. The urge to go and see for yourself.'

I shivered again, a great shudder that went right through me. I might have recently discovered my true ancestry, but I wasn't going to let it change me. I was the daughter of an eel catcher and a woman who came from a long line of shepherds. I was a fenland woman, and that was that.

I wasn't going to be travelling *anywhere*.

POSTSCRIPT

R ollo stood on deck, watching the land of his birth disappear into the hazy light of early morning. The ship had sailed at dawn; the bustle and hurry of departure were now just a memory. Above him, the big sail filled with the westerly wind, so that the sleek craft sped over the deep, profoundly blue water.

Rollo was thinking about his kinsman, Roger Guiscard. He pictured the handsome face; heard in his head Bosso's smooth, civilized tones that masked the reality of the man's tough, ruthless nature.

Roger had a personal motto: *The right hand of God raised me up; the right hand of God gave me courage.*

With a wry smile, Rollo wondered if the Almighty had bestowed a little of that courage on him, too. He was going to need it.

Rollo had sent word home to King William. Via an elaborate chain of discreet men and women, many of whom Rollo had himself recruited, he had dispatched a carefully coded message, telling William what he had found out concerning the rumours of an expedition to rescue the Holy Land from the Muslims. In what Rollo sincerely hoped was in a still deeper and more impenetrable level of code, he had added a brief, succinct report on the Norman kingdom of the South, and its ruler's current opinions and preoccupations.

Count Roger, Rollo reflected as the distance between the ship and Sicily steadily increased, could not have so much as had a suspicion of the report's existence, let alone set eyes on or, God forbid, interpreted it. Not that Rollo had done anything but give his king a fair and accurate account; the sin, in Count Roger's eyes, would be in Rollo's sending the report at all. If the Count had discovered the treason – for it was certain that it would be in those terms he would view it – then Rollo would not be where he now was. He'd probably be . . .

Bearing in mind Count Roger's views on the suitable treatment of those who had, in his view, betrayed him, Rollo did not permit himself to dwell on that.

He had waited, staying with his mother in Sicily, for King William's response. From time to time, he had imagined the message speeding on its way to him. He was proud of his men and women. He had chosen them carefully, looking out always for people who stood a little apart; who observed with intelligence but were not overhasty to give an opinion. His approach usually followed the same pattern. He would find an opportunity to speak privately to the potential recruit, and, within quite a short time, would have an idea whether or not the person had what he was looking for. Sometimes he got it wrong. Far more often, his initial instincts were right.

The work he required of his recruits usually amounted to no more than the passing on of written and sometimes verbal messages to the next person in the chain. For this they were well-paid, and the reward guaranteed continued efficiency. Very occasionally, he would seek out someone who happened to live in a place where certain information could be found, and, again, the reward was not inconsiderable. Rollo believed he had a solid network of discreet, reliable spies, for want of a better word. It was at times reassuring to remember the achievement.

The king's reply had reached him a week ago. With it, Rollo's faint hope of being able to return swiftly to England dissolved like smoke and blew away.

King William wasted only a few words in recognition of what Rollo had told him so far, and *thank you* were not among them. Kings did not habitually thank their subjects for services rendered. Then he had gone on to give Rollo his further orders. Now, in response to them, Rollo was setting out in a very different direction from the one which, were his heart to lead the way, he would have pursued.

He gazed down into the blue water, creasing out in a great white-tipped 'V' from the ship's stern. England. If his life

were his own, he'd have gone north to England. His heart
suddenly heavy with longing, he wished there were some way
he could send word to Lassair.

His mother had succeeded in setting his mind at rest; that
was something for which he could be very thankful. Her
trance-induced vision, as she sat with closed eyes clutching
the bracelet Lassair had given to her son, had revealed a picture
of danger dissipating. Rollo had known there was danger: he
had sensed the treat to Lassair within his own body. Or perhaps
it was his soul . . . he did not know. There was no way of
discovering what the nature of the danger had been; he was
resigned to that. The crucial thing was that it had passed.

In addition to what Giuliana had revealed to him, his own
gut feelings told him Lassair was safe.

For now.

That, he reflected wryly, was something else it was better
not to dwell on.

There was a long way to go before he could once more turn
for England. The ship was sailing east: heading for Byzantium.
Rollo's mission now was to discover how matters lay with
Emperor Alexius Comnenus.

Balancing his weight evenly on both feet, and resting his
folded arms comfortably on the ship's stern rail, Rollo went
over all that he knew and had recently found out.

In the dozen or so years that he had worn his crown, Alexius
had made his great capital a centre for Christian freedom and
learning. It had been no mean feat, Rollo reflected, bearing in
mind the constant threat that Alexius faced from the Seljuk
Turks. Recent converts to Islam, and with the single-minded
zeal of the new recruit, these Turks were steadily, stealthily
conquering all the lands around them, including Jerusalem,
doing everything in their power to win over the inhabitants to
Islam as they did so.

Their capital was a mere hundred miles from Alexius's
beautiful, sophisticated city. Bearing in mind the success they
had experienced so far, Rollo doubted whether Alexius slept
easily in his bed at night. Did he lie awake, picturing the
invasion that must surely come? He would be aware, no doubt,

of the difficulties of pilgrims attempting to visit the Holy Places. Would he, man of the world that he was said to be, condemn the Turks for their intransigence? Would he think them foolish, for refusing to countenance a constant stream of visitors who could have been exploited for much-needed income? Would he be furiously indignant at the very idea of the fierce nomadic Turks who now held the sites treating Christian pilgrims so cruelly?

The rumour-mongers and the gossips – those who liked to predict what the great and the good would do next – were already muttering that Alexius would surely appeal to Rome. He would ask the pope for some sort of armed force to assist him, both in protecting his own lands and also with the aim of driving the Turks from Eastern Christendom. It was, people muttered, in the pope's interests to comply with the request, given the wild stories about good Christians cruelly and ruthlessly being converted from their faith by a knife at the throat.

Rollo speculated about what might be the result of such an appeal. He could not make himself believe in a picture of ordered ranks of well-drilled soldiery, sent by the pope to come to the aid of his embattled brother-in-faith in the east. Religion, after all, was a matter for the heart, not the head, and, once the heart got involved, good sense and rational thought tended to fly away.

Rollo drifted into reverie.

Fuelled by his apprehension, he saw in his mind's eye a vision of the future. He saw not a tight, professional army, but a vast rabble of ordinary folk, hurrying over all the endless miles to Jerusalem, the fervour of faith lighting their eyes and numbing the pain in their half-starved, stumbling bodies.

Who would lead them?

Rollo's inner vision roamed on, on, over the masses of suffering people who only went on, doggedly moving forward, because their faith would not let them stop.

After a while – and it seemed to take a long time, for there were men, women and even children in their thousands upon thousands – he visualized the head of the enormous, makeshift army. There, on magnificent horses richly caparisoned, rode a group of powerful, ruthlessly ambitious lords and kings of the West. They too were alight with fever. But their goal was something more than that of their humble followers: their besotted, fanatically determined eyes saw, shining with eternal light, brilliant and gorgeous under the eastern sun, a Christian empire of the East.

Was King William right? Rollo wondered. When, as it seemed it inevitably would, the time came, would Duke Robert of Normandy be there in the vanguard, as gorgeously and extravagantly decked out as the rest and every last soldier, boot, arrow, water bottle and stirrup financed by his brother William and the use of Normandy as security?

Rollo didn't know. He did, however, have a strong presentiment that the king's prediction would come true. *I need to find out more*, he thought, his mind seeming to fly over endless vistas of sun-baked sand under a deep blue sky. *I have to go there, on towards the land where that vast wedge of humanity will make for, and see for myself . . .*

With a start, Rollo pulled himself out of the vision and back to the present.

He was shaken by what his imagination had just shown him. *It may not come to that*, he told himself.

But he was very afraid that it would.

Distracting his mind, he turned his thoughts to Alexius's capital.

It was, he had been told, a big, bubbling stew pot of a city, where men and women from all over the world came to trade, to fight, to study, and to learn a little of one another's ways. Peoples of different faiths lived there, apparently in harmony, each accepting that others had the right to view God in the way that their own priests told them they should.

It was a place where adventurers went seeking their fortune. A place to which soldiers were drawn, in the hope that their talents would be hired by some lord spoiling for a fight. Vikings had gone there; later, following the Norman Conquest and the sea change in the nature of life in Britain, many of the defeated Anglo-Saxons had also fled south, offering their services to a new master and mixing their Norse and Saxon blood with the hot blood of the south.

In a sudden clear memory, Rollo recalled that Lassair had

once told him of her great-uncles, the younger brothers of her beloved grandmother. Three had fought at Hastings, she'd said; two died there on the field, and one, the youngest, disappeared and was never heard of again.

Reflecting on it now, Rollo would have put money on that one having quietly slipped away and gone to join the Varangian Guard.

Maybe the old man was still alive, he mused. It was less than thirty years since the Conquest, and the man would have been in his prime back then. Lassair's Granny Cordeilla had only died a couple of years ago, after all, and the brother who had fled England – Harald, as far as Rollo remembered, the name seeming to float effortlessly up to the surface of his mind – would have been several years younger.

I might even come across the old man, Rollo thought. *I might be sitting in a tavern one sunny morning, next to a scarred old giant of a man with many a story to tell, and never know that he is the great-uncle of the woman I love.*

He sighed, turning away from the ship's rail and the last sight of the land of his birth. He did not know how far he would venture eastwards: to Byzantium, certainly; maybe even as far as the Holy Land. Wherever he finished up, he would be a long, long way from England.

Part of him still pined to turn round and set off northwards. Without actually knowing when it had happened, it seemed that Lassair had quietly taken up a place in his heart. He missed her; he longed to be with her.

'But I cannot return yet,' he said softly to himself.

For one thing, he had a duty to the king. William was an exacting but generous employer; serving him as he did, Rollo was steadily becoming a wealthy man, for he had little time or opportunity to spend what he earned. Besides, he could scarcely envisage announcing to King William that he'd had enough of being his spy and wanted to quit, in order to settle down and become a . . . a what? A farmer? A fenland fisherman? Rollo smiled.

In a moment of total honesty, he forced himself to recognize that there was another reason why he did not follow his heart and turn for England.

I am good at what I do, he thought. *And, human nature being what it is, we tend to like doing the things we are good at.*

He wasn't going to return to Lassair just yet because the thought of what lay ahead was more of a draw than what lay behind.

The admission did not make him feel especially proud of himself. *I am sorry, Lassair*, he thought.

He hoped that, when finally he returned, she would be waiting for him.

But first, before he saw England's shores again, he was going to Constantinople.